Acclaim for Kathleen Fuller

"*Treasuring Emma* is a heartwarming story
filled with real-life situations and well-developed characters.
I rooted for Emma and Adam until the very last page.
Fans of Amish fiction and those seeking an endearing romance
will enjoy this love story. Highly recommended."
—Beth Wiseman, bestselling author of
The Daughters of the Promise series

"*Treasuring Emma* is a charming, emotionally layered story of the
value of friendship in love and discovering the truth of the heart.
A true treasure of a read!"
—Kelly Long, bestselling author of *Lilly's Wedding Quilt*

"A fresh and captivating voice in the Amish genre,
Kathleen Fuller weaves a richly patterned story
[in *A Man of His Word*] that explores not only the depths of the
Amish faith but also the most intimate struggles of the heart."
—Tamera Alexander, bestselling author of *The Inheritance,
Beyond This Moment* and *From a Distance*

"*A Man of His Word* by Kathleen Fuller
is a heartwarming story of how faith and commitment
can overcome betrayal. Highly recommended!"
—Colleen Coble, bestselling author of
The Lightkeeper's Ball

"Terrific! I was totally engaged in the characters
and the families in this lovely story. With Gabriel as the hero,
the title is certainly well chosen. His faith, along with Moriah's,
represents a steady, underlying conviction and peacefulness
despite the very real struggles they face within the pages.
[*A Man of His Word*] is a story...I didn't want to leave."
—Maureen Lang, author of *My Sister Dilly*

"Kathleen Fuller has done it again. [*An Honest Love* is a]
wonderful tale of love, friendship, and loss that kept me up late
just to see how it would end."
—Jenny B. Jones, author of *Save the Date*

Treasuring Emma

KATHLEEN FULLER

Treasuring Emma

A
MIDDLEFIELD
FAMILY
Novel

Love Inspired

Recycling programs
for this product may
not exist in your area.

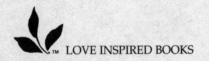

LOVE INSPIRED BOOKS

ISBN-13: 978-0-373-78708-1

TREASURING EMMA

First published by Thomas Nelson, Inc. 2011

www.LoveInspiredBooks.com

Printed in U.S.A.

To Eleanora Daly—thank you for everything.

Glossary

ab im kopp—addled in the head

aenti—aunt

appeditlich—delicious

bann—excommunicatin from the Amish church

boppli—baby

bu, buwe—boy, boys

daed—dad, father

danki—thank you

Dietsch—Pennsylvania Dutch, the language spoken by the Amish

dummkopf—dummy

Dutch Blitz—Amish card game

familye—family

fraa—wife, woman

freind—friend

geh—go

grosskinskind—great-grandchild

grossmammi, grossmudder—grandmother

grossvadder—grandfather

gude mariye—good morning

gut daag—good day

gut nacht—good night

haus—house

hungerich—hungry

kapp—prayer covering worn by women

kinn—child

kinner—children

kumme—come

leib—love

maedel—girl

mammi, mamm—mom, mother

mann—man

mariye-esse—breakfast

mei—my

meidung—shunning

menner—men

mudder—mother

onkel—uncle

Ordnung—the unwritten Amish rule of life

rumspringa—the period between ages sixteen and twenty-four, loosely translated as "running around time." For Amish young adults, *rumspringa* ends when they join the church.

schee—pretty, handsome

schwester—sister

seltsam—strange, unnatural

sohn—son

vadder—father

verboten—forbidden

willkum—welcome

ya—yes

yung—young

Chapter One

"Emma, I'm so sorry."

Emma Shetler lifted her gaze to meet Moriah Miller's eyes. Moriah had been a good friend to her over the past year, and Emma had never noticed until now how blue her eyes were. Blue like the summer sky, and at this moment, full of compassion.

Emma tried to swallow down the thorn of grief that blocked her throat. "I appreciate you and your *familye* coming by this afternoon."

"Your *mammi* was a very special *fraa*." Moriah laid a hand on Emma's shoulder. The warmth of the gentle touch seeped through the thin fabric of Emma's black dress.

The color of mourning. Of death.

Despite Moriah's comfort, that's what Emma felt inside. Dead.

She glanced around the living room. As expected, most members of the church district were here to pay their respects and show their support. Dark dresses and white *kapps* for the women, black pants and hats for the men—all of them in mourning clothes. They milled around the living room. Conversation and movement blurred into a meaningless cacophony of sound and motion.

Emma tapped her toe against the polished wood floor of the old farmhouse, her nerves strung tight as a barbed wire fence. She should have been in the kitchen, preparing and serving the traditional meal. But her sister, Clara, had taken over the cooking and banished her to the living room. This was supposed to make her feel better—stuck here, doing nothing?

She spied her grandmother Leona across the room. Clara must have chased her out of the kitchen too. Several women between the ages of fifty and seventy created a circle of support around *Grossmammi*. Emma smiled to herself as she noticed the women's ample hips drooping over the seats of creaking wooden folding chairs. They spoke in low tones, nodding and shaking their heads. The thin ribbons of their white prayer *kapps* swayed against the stiff white aprons covering their dresses. Emma had no doubt they were offering comforting passages of Scripture and words of encouragement to their old friend.

During the seventy-five years God had granted

her, Leona Shetler had loved her family deeply. But that love came with a cost. Three years ago her son—Emma's father, James—had passed away. Now she had to deal with the death of a daughter-in-law she loved as her own.

Emma felt the grief stab at her. First her father, then her mother. It didn't seem fair. She wished she could muster even a small measure of the grace and peace her grandmother demonstrated. But instead she simply felt bereft, abandoned, and confused.

"Emma?"

She turned her attention back to Moriah. "Sorry. Did you say something?"

"I asked if you needed anything else."

"Oh, *ya*. I did hear you say that." The words clanged around in her head, empty noise. "*Nee*, I'm fine."

"All right." Moriah lifted an eyebrow. Her concern echoed that of her sisters, Elisabeth and Ruth, along with everyone else who had passed by Emma's chair. The same question over and over: *How are you holding up?*

How did they think she was holding up? She had nursed her mother through a painful, deadly cancer. She buried her today.

Emma fought to contain her emotions: Anger. Resentment. Guilt. The community's heartfelt concern didn't deserve such rudeness. But nothing anyone said could penetrate the emotional wall that was growing around her, inch by excruciating inch.

Throughout the rest of the afternoon, people paused to talk. Relived special moments they'd shared with Emma's mother and father. Assured Emma of God's will, His plan. Phrase after empty phrase about God's comfort and mercy.

She nodded and smiled and tried to look peaceful, while her foot went on tapping incessantly against the floor she'd scrubbed on her hands and knees. Why wouldn't they just leave her alone? That's what she wanted.

No, that wasn't the truth. There was one person she longed to have by her side. Only one. His words, spoken in a soft, deep voice that never failed to affect her, had the best chance of soothing her broken heart.

But he wouldn't come. He had walked out of her life two years ago, and she had no hope he would walk back into it now.

Emma stood and stretched and walked around, but kept herself apart from the rest of the visitors. Moriah and Gabriel Miller were the first to leave, followed by a steady stream of other guests. Clara stood by the front door and thanked each person for coming. The perfect hostess.

When the last guest disappeared, Clara turned to Emma. "Where's *Grossmammi*?"

Emma looked at her grandmother's empty chair and shrugged. "She probably went upstairs to her room."

"I'm sure she's exhausted. It's been a long day. For all of us."

Peter King, Clara's husband, came inside wearing his hat and a navy blue jacket. A burst of cool October air wafted in behind him. The screen door shut, and he looked at Clara. "Buggy's ready. We should get back to the *kinner*."

Clara's lips pressed into a quick frown. "There are a few more things I need to do in the kitchen."

"I can finish up here, Clara," Emma said. "I haven't done anything all day."

"It won't take me long. Just five, maybe ten minutes."

"Clara."

That one word commanded the attention of both Clara and Emma.

"We need to *geh* home. Now."

Clara didn't protest; the pinch above the bridge of her nose was response enough. "I'll get my shawl." She disappeared from the living room.

Peter turned to Emma. "Are you okay?"

Would she have to hear that question for the rest of her life? "I'm fine."

"You'd tell me and Clara if you weren't, *ya*?"

Emma nodded, but she didn't mean it, and neither did he. His questions arose more out of duty

than familial concern. She never had confided
in her sister or brother-in-law, and the death of
their father and their mother's ensuing illness
had made the sisters' relationship tenuous at
best. Now that *Mammi* was gone, Emma doubted
she'd see much of Clara and her family, except
for church service every other Sunday.

Peter stepped forward. "I wanted to ask you
something."

The low tone of his voice surprised her.
"What?"

"I'd like you and Leona to consider moving
in with us." His voice was nearly a whisper now.
"As soon as possible."

His question shocked her. She started to shake
her head. "There's not enough room—"

"I can add on. It wouldn't take me more than
a couple of days."

She thought about their tiny house. Her neph-
ews, Junior and Melvin, shared a room, and as
far as she knew baby Magdalena's crib was still
in Clara and Peter's bedroom. "You and Clara
have your own *familye* to take care of."

"You and Leona are part of that *familye*,
Emma. I've figured everything out. You and
Grossmammi can share Junior and Melvin's
room. They can sleep on the couch until the addition is finished. It's not a problem."

"What's not a problem?" Clara appeared, her

black bonnet tied in place, the bow perfectly formed under her pointy chin. A large safety pin fastened the corner of her black shawl to her shoulder.

He let out a deep breath. "I've asked Emma and Leona to move in with us."

"Without telling me?" She spoke the question softly. Politely. But the edge was there.

"I don't need your permission."

"We could have at least talked about it." She turned to Emma. "Do you and *Grossmammi* want to leave this *haus*?"

Emma wasn't fooled. Her sister knew how much the place meant to her and their grandmother—the old farmhouse, with its five acres of farmland, sturdy barn, and wood shop. *Grossmammi* would never leave, nor would Emma. Besides, Clara didn't really want them to move in with her.

"We'll be fine here."

"But what about the work it takes to run this place?" Peter asked. "I know Norman Otto has been a big help, but you can't always count on him to be there for you."

"God will provide." The words came out of Emma's mouth automatically, without any feeling or conviction behind them.

"Like He provided a cure for *Mammi's* cancer?" Clara said. She scowled and crossed her thin arms over her chest, then glanced away. "Sorry."

Emma knew she should reach out to Clara. Hug her, or at least give an encouraging touch on the shoulder, as so many of their family and friends had done for her throughout the past few days since *Mammi's* death. Yet her body wouldn't move. "You should get back home. I'm sure the *kinner* miss you."

"Maybe you shouldn't be alone." Peter looked at Clara. "*Mei fraa* can stay the night, at least. It wouldn't be a *gut* idea for you and Leona to be all by yourself tonight."

Clara looked at her husband, her dark eyes narrowing. *"Ya,"* she said, with about as much enthusiasm as a cat volunteering for a soapy bath. "I can stay."

"It's the least she could do," Peter added.

Emma glanced at Clara. The least she could have done was to help with her own mother's care during the long and painful process of dying. The least she could have done was to be a sister when Emma most needed one. But none of that happened. Emma had been taking care of things by herself for a long time, and she didn't much need or want Clara's help now.

"That's not necessary. *Grossmammi* is probably asleep already." For added effect, Emma yawned. "I'm tired too."

"It looks like you don't need me, then." Clara straightened her shoulders and uncrossed her arms.

"But she'll be by in the morning," Peter said.

"*Ya.* I'll be by in the morning."

Emma shrugged. She could disagree, but what was the point? Peter would make sure Clara would be here. It was the Amish way, and Peter was nothing if not thoroughly Amish. He opened the door, and the three of them stepped onto the front porch. Layers of grayish-blue hues stretched endlessly across the dusky sky. Peter hurried down the steps to the buggy, pausing to motion for Clara to follow.

Clara turned to Emma. She could barely make out her sister's sharp features; only her stiff white *kapp* contrasted against the shadowy evening.

"I know Peter offered to let you stay with us," Clara said, "but let me talk to him about it first. It's not that you and *Grossmammi* aren't welcome, of course."

Emma knew perfectly well that her sister didn't want them living under the same roof, but she kept silent.

"There are other things to consider," Clara continued in a rush, "and we haven't had a chance to discuss them. You know Peter. He can be impulsive. But he means well." She paused. "He always means well."

Peter hesitated before climbing into the buggy. "Clara."

Clara hurried toward the buggy. Emma waited until they disappeared down Bundysburg Road before she sat down in her father's old hickory rocker in the corner of the warped front porch.

The back of the rocker touched the peeling white siding on the house. Flakes of old paint dotted the backrest of the chair.

Emma ran her fingers over the worn wood of the smooth, curved armrest. She glanced at her mother's matching chair beside her. So many evenings her parents would sit in these chairs, talking as they rocked back and forth. Or sometimes they said nothing at all, simply gazing at one another now and then, or touching fingertips as the rockers moved back and forth. It was the closest they ever came to expressing outward affection.

Bright headlights appeared. She looked up. A car moved slowly down Bundysburg Road. The hum of the engine faded in the distance, replaced with the shrill chirping of crickets and deep throaty moans of bullfrogs.

Shelby the cat jumped into her lap and added her purring to the night music. Emma rubbed the cat behind her ears. Yet even the presence of one of her beloved pets couldn't keep the emptiness at bay.

For the past eighteen months her sole focus

had been to care for her mother. The animals—
two cats and three dogs, plus the chestnut mare,
Dill—had received less attention than normal.
Now *Mammi* was gone, and what kind of future
did Emma have? Living with her sister for the
rest of her life?

Exhaustion rolled over her in a wave, and
her stomach churned. Marriage was an option.
Maybe. But she was twenty-four years old, an
old maid by some Amish standards. Besides that,
she wasn't even sure if she wanted to marry. Not
after what happened with Adam.

She closed her eyes and tried to push him out
of her thoughts. Still, the split second of attention she gave to him made her heart twist. Two
years since he left Middlefield. How long would
she continue to love him?

"Emma?"

The timbre of the deep male voice sent a shiver
through her. Shelby leapt from her lap.

"Adam?"

As soon as she said his name, her cheeks
heated with embarrassment. How foolish could
she be? The man who stood at the foot of the
porch, holding a rusted, old-fashioned gas lantern, was not Adam Otto.

"I'm sorry," Norman Otto said. "I didn't mean
to startle you. I thought you heard me coming."

Emma stood from the chair and went to the

edge of the porch. "I guess I was deep in my own thoughts."

To her relief, he offered no comment about what those thoughts might be. "I see Clara and Peter left."

"Ya."

Norman glanced at the ground, then looked up at her. "Just watered your horse and put down some straw in her stall. The dog bowls still had food in them, so I didn't add any more. The three of them were curled up on a pile of hay in the corner when I left. Also filled the cat bowls. One of them put a dead mouse at my feet."

For the first time in what seemed like weeks, Emma mustered a half smile. "That would be Tommy. He likes to give presents."

Norman nodded but didn't say anything more. A man of few words, that was Adam's father. He'd been their neighbor for years, and she'd never heard him string together more than a sentence or two.

Norman's help with the animals and chores, however, wasn't merely a neighborly gesture. As a deacon of the church, the responsibility fell on him to take care of the poor and widows in their district. He'd been helping the Shetlers since her father died.

"Emma." Norman's voice cracked. He let out

a sharp cough. "No matter what you need, let me know. I'll take care of it for you."

"Danki," she said. But there was only one thing she needed. One person. And both of them knew Norman couldn't do anything about that.

"I best be getting home now. Carol said to let you know that she'll be over in the morning with breakfast."

"She doesn't have to do that."

"You know she wants to." He paused. "Your *mammi…*" He cleared his throat again and straightened his yellow straw hat. "We'll all miss her." He turned and headed for his house, the light from his lantern flickering with each step.

Emma's eyes burned. Memories broke through her fragile defenses again—this time not only of her parents but of times she and Adam spent together as kids. She remembered how they played on the front porch, games like Dutch Blitz or checkers. The times they chased fireflies in the front yard and put them in a glass jar, its lid filled with holes he'd poked using an awl. The night she'd noticed him as more than a friend. The dreams she'd had of marrying him.

She could still remember details, like how his honey-colored eyes were a shade lighter than his straight, dark blond hair. The way the dimples in his cheeks deepened when he flashed his lopsided smile. The natural huskiness of his voice, so like his father's.

The emptiness gnawed at her. She sat down in the rocker and pressed her palm against her forehead. She should be grieving her mother, not thinking about the man who broke her heart. Her eyes grew hot, yet she couldn't bring herself to cry.

Hadn't she wept rivers of tears when her father died? When Adam left? As she watched life slowly drain from her mother over the past few months?

Now she couldn't generate so much as a single tear. She didn't have anything left. Nothing at all. Her life, at one time full of excitement and hope, had shattered into a broken, empty shell.

And she didn't know if she'd ever feel whole again.

Chapter Two

"Adam?"

Adam Otto shifted away from the woman sitting next to him. He leaned forward on the lumpy red sofa, his shoulder-length hair shielding the sides of his face. He stared at the hundred-dollar tennis shoes on his feet. Whatever possessed him to spend that kind of money on sneakers?

Ashley moved closer to him. She pushed a hank of his hair behind his ear. "Adam. Look at me."

He didn't move. If he did, he'd give in to her, like he had the last two times.

Nothing about his life was right. Especially his relationship with Ashley.

He heard her huff and get up off the couch. Heard her bare feet padding against the mud-colored carpet in his cheap one-bedroom apartment. The squeak of the fridge hinges. The pop of a beer bottle cap.

"Here." She sat down next to him, her jean-clad thigh pressing against his. "You need to chill."

He took the amber bottle from her grasp and set it on the floor a few inches from his shoes.

"You don't want it?"

Finally he looked at her. "No."

She lifted her lip in a half smile. "You've been acting weird lately." Her slender fingers threaded through his hair. She touched his chin with her other hand, rubbing her fingertips against the whiskers before snaking her arm around his neck. But when she moved to press her mouth to his, he backed away.

Her smile widened. "Oh. I get it. You want a little show."

The flowery scent of her perfume tickled his nose. He held back a sneeze.

She unzipped her tight hooded sweatshirt and removed it, tossing it next to her on the couch. When she lifted the hem of her T-shirt, he jumped up.

"Don't do that."

She paused, gazing at him through her thick black lashes. "Why? You never wanted me to stop before."

He gritted his teeth against the battle waging

within him. It had been a mistake to sleep with her. He knew that the first time. It hadn't taken much for her to convince him to do it a second time. Even now he fought his body's reaction. "I mean it."

"I don't get it. You're acting like such a prude."

"I'm not a prude."

Then again, maybe he was. Adam had grown up in a strict Amish family, stricter than most. For the sake of his sanity, he'd had to escape. And the road to freedom had led to Warren, Michigan.

No more dumb-looking clothes and endless rules. He had a pickup truck. A cell phone. At work he clocked in using a computerized swipe card. He watched mindless reality television. Next thing on his list, when he could afford it, was a laptop computer.

Granted, his apartment was a dump and his job wasn't exactly thrilling, but it was better than shoveling dung out of the barn and sitting through three hours of boring church sermons.

Or was it?

He'd been so deep in his thoughts he hadn't noticed Ashley standing there watching him. Her thin, arched eyebrows lifted. "Adam. What's wrong? You're not acting like yourself."

He hadn't acted like himself for a long time. He turned away from her, kicked the bottle with the toe of his shoe, and watched as beer soaked into the carpet. Great. His landlord would love that.

"I'm fine."

Her features relaxed. She pressed her hand against his chest. "Good. Then we can get back to what we were doing."

They'd only known each other a couple of months. Had she always been this thickheaded? Maybe she had, but he'd been too distracted by her looks, and then her actions, to notice. "Ashley, I meant what I said. We can't sleep together anymore. Ever."

She batted her eyelashes and gave him a coy smile. "We weren't exactly sleeping."

"You know what I mean."

"No, I don't." She tossed a lock of streaky blond hair over her shoulder. "Making love is supposed to bring us closer, not pull us apart."

"Ashley, I don't love you."

Her mouth dropped open. Then she shut it and smiled again. "Of course you don't. I don't love you either. But that doesn't mean we won't ever love each other. And in the meantime, we should enjoy the side benefits of our friendship."

He closed his eyes. He didn't want to hurt her, but he couldn't imagine spending the rest of his life with this girl. He could barely stand to be in the same room with her. So what were they doing together?

"This isn't working out, Ashley."

"Is this about Mike?"

"Who?"

"Mike, at work. It was just that one time, you know. No big deal. He's just a friend, Adam. So are Tanner and Steve. You don't have to be jealous." She narrowed her eyes. "You do believe me, don't you?"

He had no idea if she was telling the truth or not, but he didn't really care. Her eyes, the same shade as lush summer grass, were blank. "It doesn't matter."

"It does to me. I want us to be together."

"Why?"

His question brought her up short. "What do you mean, why?"

"Why should we keep dating? What kind of future will we have?"

"Future? We're only twenty-three."

"I'm twenty-four."

"Whatever." She frowned at him. "It's still young. Too young to be worrying about the future."

"Or about marriage?"

"Who needs marriage?" Ashley shook her head. "Adam, I know you grew up Amish and they have all these old-fashioned ideas. But you're living in the real world now."

The real world. How real was a world where

people fell together on a whim, and then fell apart again? A world where, he realized with a rush of humiliation, he'd have to go to some anonymous clinic and be tested for STDs because he'd slept with a girl who'd slept with some other guy who'd slept with who knows how many more? A world where people paid more for sneakers than it would take to feed a small village of hungry children for months?

Shame washed over him. Had he left all his values behind when he left his Amish upbringing? Had he abandoned his soul as well?

She moved closer to him, ran a hand over his faded red T-shirt. "You're bumming me out with all this serious talk. Why can't we relax and have some fun?"

He removed her hand from his chest. "I think you should go."

"I don't believe this." She moved away from him. "What else is going on?" She crossed her arms over her chest. "Are you cheating on me?"

He held out his hands. "Why would you even think that?"

"Because of this conversation. We've been so good together, Adam. Then suddenly you don't want to have anything to do with me." Her voice faltered. "It's like I'm not good enough for you anymore."

Adam shook his head. "I've never thought that, Ashley. I'm not better than anyone else."

"Then why are you breaking up with me?"

How could he explain it to her, when he barely understood it himself? Two years ago he couldn't wait to be where he was right now. Free from rules, his parents. Free from the ministers who dictated every aspect of his life. From the bishop who warned him to avoid the "devil's play-ground," the outside world that had intrigued and fascinated him for so long.

He just wanted a little space. A little peace.

Then he found Ashley. Beautiful. A little wild. So different from the Amish girls he'd grown up with.

He'd found his freedom. But the peace never came. He didn't belong in the Amish world. Yet it was becoming clear he didn't belong in this one either.

"So this is how it ends?" Ashley's arms fell to her sides. "You tell me to leave and it's over?"

"Ashley." He felt like such a jerk. "I never meant to—"

"Hurt me?" She snatched her sweatshirt off the couch. "I can't tell you how many times I've heard that before."

He wanted to comfort her, but he had to be honest. "It's not you, it's—"

"Me?" When she shot a look at him, he

nodded. "You know what? I've heard that before too." She swiped a finger under her eye. "I seem to have a gift for dating scumbags. Don't worry, I won't bother you anymore." The front door slammed behind her.

Adam flinched. "That could have gone better," he said to the empty apartment. But what else could he have done? She wanted something from him he couldn't give.

He picked up the beer bottle and dumped the remaining contents down the drain. Two months ago he would have considered such waste a sacrilege. Now he wished he hadn't spent money on the six-pack.

He plopped down on the couch and flipped on the TV, trying to forget about Ashley. After cycling through shopping, sports, movies, and endless news channels with the remote, he snapped it off and went outside to check the mail.

Stepping into the fresh air calmed him. He breathed in deeply, not the aromas of fresh-cut hay, burning leaves, or manure, but car exhaust, with undertones of dryer sheets from the laundry building near his apartment. Still, it was better than the stale atmosphere of his apartment.

Barefoot, Adam crossed the parking lot to the array of mailboxes. He barely noticed the gravel digging into the soles of his feet. He'd grown up shoeless for most of his life, except for winter, or when he went to school and church.

He stuck his key into the lock of number 114 and twisted it. Probably bills, some junk mail. Maybe a letter from home. His mother often wrote, but never his father or anyone else from Middlefield. Why would they? He had rejected them and their way of life when he left.

He pulled out the mail and was about to close the door when he noticed a small envelope tucked in the back. The right corner curled up. He pulled it out and read the address. The letter wasn't from his mother. It was from Leona Shetler.

Why would she write to him? He slammed the mailbox door shut, jerked out the key, and ran back to the apartment. He dumped the rest of the mail on the kitchen counter and ripped open the envelope, almost shredding part of it as he yanked it from the tight pocket.

Dear Adam,

I'm sure you are surprised to hear from me. Shame on me for not keeping in touch. I hope you are well. I have prayed for you from the moment you left. Just wanted you to know that.

There are two things I need to tell you. The first is that Emma's mother died last week. She got cancer shortly after you went

*to Michigan, and the Lord ended her suf-
fering. She put up a good fight. Emma is
taking the news real badly.*

Adam stopped reading. Emma Shetler. She'd
intruded into his thoughts off and on over the
past two years. They had been childhood play-
mates, and in many ways she had been his best
friend. But she ruined everything the night before
he left. She had tried to convince him to stay, telling him anything she thought he wanted to hear.
Even that she cared about him as more than a
friend. He'd laughed it off, partially out of embarrassment, partly out of disbelief. They were
friends. That's all they ever would be.

He rubbed his hand over his face, his mustache
and beard tickling his palm. Poor Emma. She'd
lost her father, now her mother. He frowned as
he continued reading.

*The second thing you need to know con-
cerns your mother. I'm worried about her.
She hasn't been herself for the past couple
of months. She's been sad, and acts like
her mind is somewhere else. I don't know
for sure, as she isn't interested in talking
much beyond pleasantries like the weather
and how many tomatoes she's canned. But
there's something deeper going on. I don't*

*know if it has to do with you, but I suspect
it might.*

*I'm asking you to think about coming
back to Middlefield. For a visit, at least.
Your father has been as kind as ever to
us, especially since Mary's funeral. Don't
let the shunning stop you from loving the
woman who gave you birth.*

*I don't want to make you feel guilty, but
if you do and it makes you come home, then
I won't be sorry about that.*
Sincerely,
Leona Shetler

He sat down on the couch, read the letter
again, and then folded the paper. What could be
wrong with his mother? Was she sick? Had she
hurt herself somehow? If his mother was ill, why
hadn't his father contacted him?

Adam knew the answer to that. His father
would never break the *bann*. Even though some
Amish in their district didn't hold to strict shunning, his father did. He followed all the rules of
the Amish to the letter, and expected his wife
and son to do the same. Variance wasn't toler-
ated. Neither was doubt or questioning.

There was only one way to find out what was
going on. He'd have to return to Middlefield.

Suddenly he wished he hadn't tossed that

beer down the sink. But alcohol wouldn't give him the courage to face his family. He'd have to muster that himself. Or ask God to help him, as his father would say.

God will never turn His back on you.

Those were his mother's last words to him before he left Middlefield. But Adam and God hadn't been on good terms for a long while. And his mother hadn't lived Adam's life. She hadn't doubted or questioned. She'd always been committed to the Lord, her faith, her family.

Adam had fled from all those things, straight into the "devil's playground." Had he even thought about God since leaving home? Only when he needed something, like a job or a car. Then he'd tossed out a flippant prayer for help. Lately he hadn't even bothered to do that.

Was it possible to find his way back?

Should he even try?

Chapter Three

"Why did you ask Emma to stay with us?"

Peter stared straight ahead, holding the reins lightly in his hand. The horse's hooves clopped against the asphalt road. Although it was still early evening, there were few cars out. "It was the right thing to do. Besides, I didn't just ask Emma. I want Leona to stay with us too."

Clara clenched her fist. "You should have said something to me first."

"But we already talked about this. You said more than once the past few months that you were worried how Emma and Leona were going to take care of the *haus*. If they stay with us, they don't have to."

Clara hesitated. She needed to choose her words carefully. Peter hadn't consulted with her, but she hadn't made her thoughts known either. "Maybe we could move in with them." Clara turned and looked out the buggy window at the shadowy outlines of Amish houses.

"Why would we do that?"

"It's more practical. Their *haus* is larger than our cramped one."

"I thought you loved our house." He shifted in the seat but kept his gaze straight ahead. "At least that's what you said when I built it."

Five years and three children ago. "We need to be realistic, Peter. Our *haus* is full. We don't have room for anyone else."

"It wouldn't take long to add a room in the back."

"How would we do that? We don't have any extra money for building supplies. Do you expect *mei grossmudder* to pay for the addition?"

"Of course not."

"Then how can you build it?"

"Why are you always worried about money?" His tone turned sharp.

"Someone has to."

"Worrying about it doesn't help."

Clara knew what he would say next. *God will provide.* The same thing Emma said. But Peter was out of work, and she had yet to see any sign of God's generosity. "What about *mei grossvadder's haus*? Is it supposed to stand empty until it falls down from rot?"

He shifted again. "I hadn't thought that far."

Clara didn't respond. She didn't have the strength to argue with her husband tonight. He turned into the driveway and pulled the buggy up to the front of the house. She climbed out and left him to put the buggy in the barn and settle the horse down for the night.

Before she reached the kitchen, Clara knew that Julia had been baking again. There was no mistaking the sweet, fruity scent of fresh cherry pie. She entered the kitchen to see her neighbor standing in front of the sink.

Julia shut off the tap and turned around. "Your *kinner* were perfect tonight." She wiped her hands on a kitchen towel and laid it on the counter. "The *buwe* even helped me bake. I won't tell Peter, though."

Clara didn't care whether Peter knew. She was more concerned with Julia using the pie filling she'd canned a few weeks ago. She had been saving the ingredients to make cherry strudel to take to church. Now she would have to come up with something else. Julia might have meant well, but it wasn't in Clara's budget to buy more dessert ingredients.

"I hope you don't mind," Julia said, gesturing to the pie on the counter. "We made two of them. The *kinner* and I ate the other one."

Clara looked at Julia's rotund figure. She could guess who had eaten the majority of the first pie.

But at least she had something to take to church. She managed a brief smile. "I appreciate you watching the *kinner* while we were gone."

"Anytime you need me to watch them for you, I'm glad to do it. My own are grown, so I have time on my hands. At least until they start giving me grandchildren." She laughed, her wide face breaking into a thick-lipped grin. "Hopefully that will be soon."

Peter entered the room, scratching his beard. He said hello to Julia and inhaled deeply. His eyes danced with anticipation. "Smells like your famous cherry pie in here."

"Peter, you're too nice." Julia's chubby cheeks blushed. She looked to Clara again. "I didn't get a chance to tell you, but I'm sorry about your *mudder*. She was a sweet *fraa*."

Clara moved away from Julia. She wiped a spot of flour off the table with her fingers. "*Ya*, she was."

"You two must be tired." Julia reached for the bonnet hanging on a peg beside the back door. "The *kinner* are asleep upstairs."

"We should do the same." Peter walked over to the counter. "As soon as I have a piece of your *appeditlich* pie."

Clara cleared her throat. "Don't you think you've eaten enough today?"

Peter shot a glance at her, his expression stern. But she saw the questions in his eyes as well.

Julia grabbed her shawl and threw it over her shoulders. "Well, then. I'll be on my way." She dashed out the door.

Clara removed her bonnet and placed it on an empty peg. Peter didn't say anything, merely hung his black hat next to hers. He left the room, ignoring the pie.

Clara unpinned her shawl and placed it next to her bonnet. She spent the next few minutes wrapping the pie in foil, crimping the edges to make a tight seal. She hid the pie in the back of the pantry. Maybe Peter wouldn't think to look there.

When she came into the bedroom, she saw Peter's sleeping form huddled under the quilt. She let out a small sigh of relief. With silent movements she undressed, left her *kapp* on the dresser, and slipped into her nightgown. She sat down on her side of the bed. The springs let out a soft creak. When Peter moved, she froze.

"I would appreciate it if you wouldn't embarrass me like that again."

"I'm sorry." She kept her back to him.

"We need to talk."

"I thought you were tired."

"How can I sleep when you're upset?" He sat up and moved behind her.

"I'm not upset. It's been a long day." The image of her mother's burial made tears burn in her eyes. She refused to let them fall. If Peter saw her crying, he would never leave her alone.

He touched her shoulder. It took everything she had not to shrug off his hand. "If you don't want your *schwester* and *grossmammi* to move in, then they don't have to. Emma didn't seem thrilled with the idea when I brought it up."

Clara had noticed. If Peter had bothered to tell her his plan, she could have told him it wouldn't work. Emma didn't want to live with Clara any more than Clara wanted her here.

"So they should stay in their own *haus*." Peter scooted closer to her, his breath low in her ear. "We should still think about adding a room here, though. Or two." He wrapped his arms around her waist. "In case God blesses us with more *kinner*."

Clara closed her eyes. She felt trapped enough with three. But Peter never stopped talking about having a large family. He never stopped trying to make it happen, even when Clara didn't want to. But she couldn't bring herself to give in to him. Not tonight.

He pressed a kiss to her shoulder. She cringed. To her surprise he pulled away. "*Gut nacht*, Clara."

Relieved, she slipped beneath the covers but still couldn't bring herself to look at him.

"I love you, Clara."

She forced the words out. "I love you too." But even to her own ears, they sounded false and hollow.

After Norman left, Emma sat outside for a few moments longer. She shivered in the evening chill. When she couldn't stand the cold any longer, she went inside. But not before glancing at Adam's house. Did he know *Mammi* had died? If he did, would he even care? She had no idea. Her childhood friend, the man she grew up with and fell in love with, was a stranger to her.

She climbed the stairs to the bedroom, careful not to disturb her grandmother in the room down the hall. Emma sat on the edge of the bed and pulled the bobby pins out of her hair. A few strands of hair came with them. She undid her bun but didn't bother to brush out the tangled mass.

For a while she tossed restlessly. She pulled the covers up to her chin. Kicked them off again. Punched at the pillow. Willed sleep to come.

Maybe a glass of milk would help her sleep. Or maybe she'd forget about sleep altogether. As she approached the kitchen, a faint light glowed from the doorway. She entered the room and saw her grandmother seated at the table. A candle flickered a few inches away. The old woman turned, her thin lips forming a half smile.

"Couldn't sleep either?"

Emma shook her head. Instead of going to the ice chest for milk, she sat down. "I thought you were already in bed."

"I was. Fell asleep, even." She sighed, placing one gnarled hand on the table. "But the Lord woke me up. Said I needed to pray. So that's what I'm doing."

"In the kitchen?"

"Well, I was a little hungry too."

Emma noticed the empty saucer to her grandmother's left. A fork rested on the small dish, which still held crumbs from whatever dessert *Grossmammi* had eaten. One thing they had plenty of right now was food. Family and friends from church had brought over enough casseroles, pickles, salads, breads, and desserts to keep them fed for the next week. She placed her hands on the table, tried to suppress a sigh.

Her grandmother reached for her hand. "You're troubled, *ya*? Maybe you should do some praying too."

Emma pressed her lips together but didn't say anything. How could she admit to her *grossmammi* that she hadn't prayed in days?

"Take comfort, *kinn*. Your *mammi* isn't suffering anymore."

"I am thankful for that."

"And you did the best you could for her. She died here, just as she wanted. You made that possible."

Her grandmother didn't need to know the real reason her mother wanted to die at home. About the doctor and hospital bills. The cost of her medication. Expenses they didn't have the money to cover.

"I know Clara would have helped out more, if she could. In the end I think your *mammi* made a wise choice. It wouldn't have been *gut* for the *yung kinner* to see their *grossmammi* so sick." The old woman released Emma's hand. "At least she got to spend a little time with them before the cancer took hold. They'll have *gut* memories of her."

"They will." Emma glanced down at the oak table her father had made the year after she was born. It had a few scratches but was still sturdy and beautiful. Her fingers caressed the smooth, glossy wood.

"Emma."

After a pause, she looked at her grandmother.

"Is something else bothering you?" *Grossmammi's* gray eyes blinked behind plain silver-rimmed glasses.

Emma didn't know where to start, so she said nothing. She would keep her worries about money and her thoughts about Adam to herself. "*Nee*. I'm fine. Just worn out from today."

Her grandmother pursed her lips together. Emma couldn't blame *Grossmammi* for doubting her. She didn't exactly sound convincing.

"All right then. I'm going back to bed." Her grandmother pushed back from the table and picked up the wooden cane leaning against the edge. As she shuffled past Emma, she paused and put her hand on her shoulder. "Remember, *kinn*. Whatever is bothering you, take it to the Lord. He'll bring you the comfort you need."

Emma heard her grandmother's slippers slide against the wood floor as she made her way up the stairs. How easy her grandmother made it sound. As if all Emma had to do was say a few prayers and everything would be all right again.

But she could pray for hours and her mother would still be dead. So would her father. And Adam would still be hundreds of miles away, if not thousands by now.

He had made his decision clear. She hadn't heard a word from him since he left. And she didn't care anymore.

Only that wasn't true. She cared.

Far too much, she cared.

Chapter Four

The next morning Emma was already dressed and outside before the sun rose. Her body ached with weariness. But chores didn't disappear because she couldn't sleep. There were animals to feed. Eggs to collect. Breakfast to make.

She held a kerosene lantern in one hand and a basket in the other. Her feet traveled the worn path through the grass to the barn. Tommy dashed in front of her, followed by Shelby. They both disappeared into the barn, awaiting their morning meal.

The scent of manure in the barn nearly overpowered her. Peter had cleaned it two weeks ago, but it was long past time to remove the manure again and replenish the straw. She didn't want to ask him for help again. Or appeal to Norman. She'd do it herself.

She heard her horse, Dill, whinny in her stall.

The chestnut mare snorted as Emma hung the lantern on a hook on the wall. Hazy light filled the barn, enough to see that Dill was limping when she made her way over to the feed trough.

A knot formed in Emma's stomach. Was it the leg or the foot? She knelt down beside the mare and lifted the horse's hoof, but couldn't see anything lodged there. She'd have to call for a vet. She couldn't allow Dill to become lame. She rose and patted the horse's flank. "We'll get your leg taken care of." Another bill.

The words echoed in her head: *God will provide.* Well, maybe if she just prayed harder, God would rain money from the sky. She felt a twist of guilt at the sarcastic thought.

Emma moved from the stall to the laying boxes on the other side of the barn. When she thrust her hand beneath one of the brown birds, all six chickens panicked and flew away. Emma filled the egg basket and tossed a couple of handfuls of chicken feed on the barn floor.

A few grains landed on Tommy's back; he didn't seem to notice. He crouched by his dish, meowing. Shelby sat by her bowl on the other side. Emma filled their food bowls with kibble.

Both cats pounced on the crunchy bits of food. Their purrs filled the barn as faint, rose-hued sunlight sifted through the slats.

The mutts, Rodney and Archie, must have

crept out of the barn in the night. They often went out exploring the woods behind the house. Molly was probably still under the porch, where she stayed most of the time. She filled all their food bowls, extinguished the lantern, and left the barn.

Dawn cast an ethereal light over the familiar landscape. As she turned to go to the house, Emma stopped to look at the large, dilapidated shed that had been her grandfather's workshop over forty years ago. After his retirement the building had been used for storage, and had been pretty much ignored since her father's death.

Emma thought it would make a perfect dog kennel, but it would take a lot of work and money to turn it into one. For years she had held a secret desire to establish an animal rescue center—a dream she'd never told anyone except Adam. He had shown little enthusiasm. But then again, he'd never owned any pets; his father had forbidden them. The only animals Norman Otto spent money on were the ones that would pay him back after a trip to the slaughterhouse.

Emma had always been attached to the animals. Most people here figured that when an animal died, it was simply part of the ebb and flow of life. But Emma mourned each one of them. She treated her dogs and cats and horse like family—even the chickens held a special

place in her affection. She would love to spend
her time rescuing neglected and abused animals.
But no one in Middlefield would understand it.

Her eyes drifted from the shed to the house
itself. The soft light of morning illuminated the
lines and planes of the house, outlining the gables
in gold and shadowing the porch in silver. She
could almost see it as it once had been—a sturdy,
beautiful farmhouse built for a large family, situated on five acres of prime property.

At one time her grandparents' house had been
in pristine condition, and Emma's parents had
made sure it stayed that way. But then her father
died, and her mother was diagnosed with cancer,
and Emma had all she could do to care for her
mother and grandmother and keep herself from
falling apart. The last three years had taken a
heavy toll on the house, the shop, even the land.

Emma longed to bring the place back, to re-
store everything to the way it used to be.

The house. The property.

Her life.

Clara and Peter ate their breakfast in silence,
speaking only to discipline the children, who
were full of their usual endless energy. She
picked up Magdalena from her high chair and
wiped the strawberry jelly off her pink cheeks.

"Junior, Melvin."

Both boys looked up at their father. *"Ya, Daed?"*

"Could you gather the eggs for me?"

Junior nodded and retrieved his hat from the peg by the door. He picked up the egg basket and looked back at his father. "Are you coming?"

"Nee. I'm taking your *mammi* to your *Aenti* Emma's today."

"Can't she walk there?"

"Ya, but I want to give her a ride. Now, enough questions." He tapped Junior on the brim of his hat. *"Geh,* do what I asked you to do."

The two young boys scrambled out of the house, fighting to see who could get to the chicken coop first. Their boyish screaming grated on Clara's nerves.

Peter wiped his mouth and beard with the napkin. "Will you be ready to leave in a few minutes?"

"Ya. After I wash the dishes, change the *boppli,* sweep the floors, find something to cook for supper tonight, and get properly dressed."

"So five minutes, then?"

Clara looked at him, not amused by the teasing grin on his face. His good-natured smile disappeared. "Anything I can do to help?"

Get a job.

"Nee. I'll get it all done. You should check on

the *buwe* and make sure they're not having a fight with the raw eggs."

He snatched his hat off the peg and went outside. The door slammed behind him. Clara didn't turn around.

Her ire grew as she finished her chores, and reached its limit when she looked at the sparse pantry. How could she make so few ingredients last all week? She wiped her forehead with the back of her hand, dislodging her *kapp*. For the past year she had tried to be supportive of her husband. She struggled to understand the economy—how no one was hiring construction workers right now. The building boom hadn't slowed down just in Middlefield, but all the way to Cleveland and beyond.

What she didn't understand was why Peter wouldn't do anything else. Why he wouldn't at least check the want ads in the paper. Or tell other people in the community that he needed work.

God will provide, he said. Sounded a lot like a holy handout to Clara. What her dim-witted husband didn't understand was that God helps those who help themselves, not the ones who sit around and wait for good fortune to happen.

Guilt assaulted her, but the feeling didn't last long. What did she have to feel guilty about? If she were a man, she'd be able to find work. Maybe even start her own business.

Start my own business…

Peter came back into the kitchen. "The buggy's ready. Junior and Melvin went down the street to play with the Keims' *buwe. Fraa* Keim said she didn't mind watching them while we're gone."

"I'll be ready right away."

She slipped a light purple dress over Magdalena's chubby body, a sudden idea churning in her mind. It could work. And someone had to think about the future—not only her family's, but her sister's and grandmother's.

If she didn't, no one else would.

"Let's *geh*." Magdalena in her arms, Clara hurried past Peter and walked out the door.

He followed behind. "Now you're eager to get going? Just a minute ago you weren't in that much of a hurry."

"The day's wasting." Clara clutched her daughter and climbed into the buggy. Peter joined her and they were on their way.

Within ten minutes, they pulled up in front of the farmhouse. Clara handed the baby to Peter. "Can you watch her for a while? I need to talk to Emma. Privately."

"About what?"

"Things."

Doubt entered his eyes. "What kind of things?"

"Just…things."

"I don't like the idea of keeping secrets from each other, Clara."

"Like you asking Emma to move in with us?"

His gaze narrowed. "That wasn't a secret. I was trying to help our *familye*." He tucked Magdalena into the crook of his arm. "Guess I'll visit Dave Fisher a few doors down."

But Clara didn't respond. She had already jumped out of the buggy and was heading to her grandparents' house. She kept her back turned until she heard Peter leave. Then she knocked on the door.

Emma answered it.

"I need to talk to you."

"*Gude mariye* to you too." Emma opened the door a little wider. "Do you want to come in, or do we have to stand on the porch?"

"I'll come in." Clara couldn't keep the impatience from her voice. The more she thought about her plan, the more it made sense. She had to convince Emma of that.

She followed her sister into the kitchen. Emma walked to the sink and turned on the water. The ends of the strands of her white *kapp* were twisted together and hung down her back. "I've got to finish the breakfast dishes."

"Can't you do that later? I want you to listen to what I have to say." She paused. "It's important."

"Fine." Emma walked over to the table and sat down. "But make it quick; I have a lot of work to do around here."

"I know you do." Clara sat across from her. She folded her hands and put them on the table, her thin fingers intertwining with each other. Emma placed one stubby hand on the table.

Clara leaned forward. "Now that the funeral is over, we need to talk about your future."

"Can't this wait? We just buried *Mammi* yesterday."

"Emma, I don't mean to sound unfeeling about *Mammi*, but we all knew this would happen. We should be grateful that God took her when He did so she didn't have to suffer long."

Emma clenched her fists on the tabletop. "She suffered enough. You weren't here, Clara. You didn't have to force her to eat, or sponge the sweat off her body, or listen to her cry out in the middle of night, her body filled with pain."

"I would have helped if I could. I had to take care of my *familye*."

"And since I don't have a *familye*, I had to take care of her."

"If you resented it so much, you should have said something."

"I didn't resent *Mammi*." Emma's shoulders slumped. Her voice was low, filled with grief. "I would never resent her."

Clara leaned forward. "Emma, what's past is past. We need to focus on the future."

"I already told Peter we don't want to move in

with you." As if she realized how harsh her words sounded, she added, "Your *haus* is too small. The *kinner* deserve room to run and play. Not two more adults to displace them."

"But you do understand he meant well. We're both concerned about you and *Grossmammi* living in this big *haus* all by yourself. She's having trouble getting around."

"She does fine."

"She can barely walk."

"She has arthritis. You make it sound like she has one foot in the grave." Emma popped up from the chair. "We've been surviving quite well without your help, and we will continue to do so."

"Emma, sit down." Clara lowered her voice. "Please. I didn't mean to upset you."

Emma glared at her sister for a moment. Finally she sat back down.

"Emma, I know you don't want to hear this. But it's important. You can't take care of this place."

"I've been taking care of it just fine."

"But you shouldn't have to. Not alone."

Emma frowned. "Are you talking about moving in with us?" A hint of challenge gave an edge to her voice.

"Why would we want to move?" It was more of an evasion than an outright lie, but close enough to make Clara uncomfortable with herself. "Peter is very happy with our *haus*."

"Are you?"

Clara paused. "It's adequate. But that's not what I wanted to talk about. I'm sure you have bills from *Mammi's* illness, *ya*?"

Emma looked away.

"Do you have any marriage prospects?"

Her eyes hardened. "You know I don't."

"Then you have to figure out a way to support yourself. And this *haus* and property. And *Grossmammi*—"

Emma held up her hand. "You made your point."

"You don't have to get curt with me." Clara buttoned up her jacket and touched the top of her *kapp*. "I'm speaking out of love for you and *Grossmammi*. Think about her for a minute. Do you really want her to live in a run-down *haus*? To barely have enough food to eat? Because that's what's going to happen if you don't take things seriously."

Emma rose from the chair and walked over to the sink. Her shoulders sagged. "What did you have in mind?"

"An idea that will solve all our problems."

Chapter Five

Adam Otto picked up a gray sweatshirt with the word *Michigan* across the front. He tossed it into his suitcase, along with two pairs of jeans, a toothbrush, and his razor, even though he hadn't used it in months. He zipped up the case. Would he be gone a couple of days? A week? He had no idea, but he'd asked for two weeks off from work.

He looked at the black suitcase, his mind still filled with doubt. Would his mother want to see him? He hoped so but couldn't be all that sure. His father's reaction was more predictable. He wouldn't be thrilled to see Adam, but he wouldn't kick him out of the house either.

The *Ordnung* stated that one must be willing to forgive.

The rules. His father would never break the rules.

A knock sounded on the door. He set his suitcase down next to the couch and opened the door. "Ashley?"

"Can I come in?"

Against his better judgment he let her.

"Shane told me you were leaving."

Their coworker at the restaurant. A kid who couldn't keep his mouth shut even through three layers of duct tape.

"It's not true, is it?" Her gaze went to the suitcase on the floor. "Then again, maybe it is."

"Ashley, why are you here?"

"Because I'm trying to keep you from making a big mistake."

"Visiting my mom is a mistake?"

"That's why you're leaving?"

He nodded.

She moved toward him. "Awesome. I thought you were leaving because of us."

"And I thought we straightened all this out. There isn't an *us*."

"That's where you're wrong." Her eyes shone with hope. "I thought a lot about what happened yesterday. If you don't want us to be serious, I can be down with that. We can chill out together as friends. Hang out. Have a few beers together. Watch *Jersey Shore*."

"I can't stand that show."

The hope turned to desperation. "Okay, football or basketball or whatever you're into." She adjusted her purse on her shoulder. "It doesn't matter. Just so we can be together."

"Ashley, you need a girl to hang out with. Not me."

She lifted her chin. "I have plenty of girl-friends to hang with."

"Then go find one of them. I have to go." He reached for his suitcase, but she blocked his way.

"Let me come with you. I've never seen anyone Amish before. I bet it will be cool, with all those dorky hats and old-timey carts."

She made them sound like a circus sideshow. "Buggies," he corrected. "This isn't a vacation, Ashley. I'm going to visit my mother. I don't know how long I'll be gone."

She didn't say anything for a minute or two. "I don't want to lose you, Adam. You're a nice guy. Nicer than anyone else I've dated. And even though you hurt my feelings the other day, I for-give you. I know you didn't mean to."

"You're right. I didn't, and I'm sorry."

"So give me a call when you get to Ohio. And when you come back to Michigan." She smiled, although there was a sadness to it. "We can start over. As friends. We'll keep it simple. I promise."

He nodded. When she left he picked up his suitcase, shut off the lights, and headed for the door.

He stopped at the threshold, dug into the pockets of his jeans, and came up with his cell phone. For a second or two he stared at it. Felt the weight in his hand. Then he tossed it on the couch and left.

Four hours later he drove his black pickup truck into his parents' driveway, his headlights piercing the darkness and flashing across the front of the house. He killed the lights and waited, expecting his father to come outside. But the house remained dark.

Adam checked his watch. Nine o'clock. His parents would be asleep already.

He got out of the truck and shut the door, then stood there while his senses adjusted. The trill of crickets mixed with the sound of the deep-throated bullfrogs that lived in the pond behind the house.

Darkness enveloped him. There were no streetlights on this end of their road. His tennis shoes crunched across the gravel driveway as he rounded the bed of the truck. He leaned against the other side and looked at the Shetlers' house. Like his parents' place, it was also completely dark.

Adam thought about Emma: her full, round face, so different from Ashley's thin, narrow one. He saw the shadow of an animal flit across her yard, followed by another. Cats, he thought.

Or maybe small dogs. Emma and her pets. That hadn't changed.

At the sound of a cat's meow, he turned and looked down to see a light-colored cat weaving around his ankles. He bent to pick up the animal. But when his fingers brushed its fur, the cat dashed off.

He walked back to his truck, retrieved his suitcase, and took a deep breath. He couldn't wait out here all night. On the other hand, maybe he could. It was certainly tempting to bunk in the barn until morning, instead of disturbing his parents. Especially his father.

But concern for his mother spurred him on.

Tentatively he knocked on the door and waited, gripping the handle of his suitcase. When no one answered he reached up to knock again, only to hear the sound of his mother's voice coming through the wood. "Who is it?"

Her soothing lilt instantly comforted him. "It's me, *Mamm*. Adam."

Before he finished saying his name, the door flung open. His mother pushed open the screen door and wrapped her arms around him. The suitcase fell to the front porch with a thud.

"Welcome home, *sohn*. *Willkum* home."

"Do you still like your eggs scrambled?"

Adam looked at his mother and nodded. He sat

down at the kitchen table. Yeast bread baked in the oven, bacon sizzled on the stove. His stomach growled. He missed home-cooked meals. He watched his mother as she prepared breakfast. She seemed the same to him, efficient and comfortable in the kitchen. Maybe Leona was imagining things, and this had been a wasted trip.

But seeing his mother again, being in the house he grew up in, gave him a sense of peace he hadn't expected.

The back door slammed. He heard movement in the mud-room, his father removing his boots. Adam gripped his knees, his palms damp against his blue jeans.

"Sorry it took me so long," his father said as he came into the kitchen. He looked at his wife standing in front of the stove. "Cows were being lazy today. Had to herd them into the pasture by my—"

His gaze went to Adam. He peered at him as if he couldn't see clearly. "Adam?"

Adam nodded but didn't move from the chair. His father also remained frozen in place. The enticing smells of breakfast faded as the men looked at each other.

After a moment, his father spoke. "Are you in trouble?"

"Nee." Figures that would be the first thing his father would assume. "I'm not in trouble."

His father crossed his arms over his chest. "Then why are you here?"

Adam glanced at his mother. Her back was to both of them. She was putting fluffy yellow eggs on an old white platter she'd had as long as Adam could remember. Should he mention Leona's letter? For some reason that seemed a bad idea. "I came for a...visit."

"Why?"

Adam's mother rushed to the table. "Time to eat!" She nearly dropped the platter, catching herself at the last minute. "I know you two must be *hungerich*."

His father didn't uncross his arms or move. He scrutinized Adam, his greenish-brown eyes raking him up and down.

Adam squirmed. He could only imagine what his father was thinking about his long hair, scruffy beard and mustache, jeans, and plaid flannel shirt. Yankee clothes. Forbidden in his house.

"You are in the *bann*. You cannot eat at the same table with us."

"Norman."

Both men looked at her. Unshed tears shone in her hazel eyes.

Without saying a word Adam's father walked past Adam and sat down at the table. "Let's eat. I have a busy day."

That was it? Adam turned to his father, but he had already bowed his head for the silent prayer. There was nothing else to do but join him.

After prayer, they all ate in silence. Adam looked from his father to his mother. Both were intent on eating. His father inhaled the food, while his mother ate more slowly, slicing a small mound of eggs with the edge of her fork.

Suddenly hunger overrode everything else. Adam dug into his meal, savoring the salty crispness of the bacon and the buttery smoothness of the eggs. He had just reached for a piece of hot bread when his father stood, wiped his graying beard with his napkin, and left the room.

Adam put down his fork. "He could have at least said something before he left."

His mother sighed. "Actually, that was better than I expected."

"It was?"

"Ya." She faced Adam. "You don't know how deeply you hurt your *daed* when you left. He's a deacon. Highly respected in the community. And to have his only *sohn* leave the church…" She shook her head. "It was difficult for him. If you hadn't been baptized, it would have been easier."

Adam didn't want to talk about his father. He wasn't here for him. "How are you doing?"

"Me?" She picked up her napkin from her lap and laid it over her half-eaten meal, keeping her gaze averted. "I'm fine." At last she looked up and smiled. "I'm very happy to see you. Even if you do look like a wild man."

He touched his shoulder-length hair. *"Ya."* He marveled at how quickly and easily he slipped back into the *Dietsch* he hadn't used in two years. "I suppose I need a haircut."

"I could give you one."

Adam saw the eagerness in her eyes. Different from when his father was in the room. "Sure. I wouldn't mind that." He crumpled his napkin in his fist and glanced down at his lap. "Why aren't you angry with me? *Daed* is."

His mother reached for his hand. She squeezed his fingers and released them. "You're my *sohn*. You're here. That's all that matters to me."

Chapter Six

❧

Dry leaves crunched beneath Emma's feet as she neared the house. Her morning chores were finished, but her mind still worked at full speed. Over and over while she'd taken care of the animals, collected the eggs, and checked on Dill's leg, she thought about Clara's proposal. When Emma balked at the idea, her sister had asked her to pray about it.

Emma didn't need to pray to say no. Clara had to be out of her mind to think she and *Grossmammi* would agree to such a thing. But Emma had to figure out her future before it disintegrated along with her increasingly dilapidated house.

She slipped off her shoes near the door and walked into the kitchen to find her grandmother standing in front of the pantry. "You're up early," Emma said. She set the basket of eggs on the counter.

"I'm always up early." *Grossmammi* placed a wrinkled finger on her lips as she scanned the pantry's contents. "I just usually don't come downstairs at this hour." She glanced over one hunched shoulder. "I'm making breakfast this morning."

"Oh *nee*." Emma stood beside her. The top of the old woman's *kapp* barely reached Emma's shoulder. "I'll do it."

Her grandmother gently shrugged her off. "Mind your elders." She took down the canister of all-purpose flour and tucked it in the crook of her arm. "It's been ages since I've made pumpkin pancakes. You love those, *ya*?"

"You know I do." Emma had tried more than once to duplicate the recipe. Each attempt had been a failure. They were never as light and fluffy, or had the perfect blend of cinnamon flavor her grandmother's had.

"Then you deserve some pumpkin pancakes." The old woman frowned, leaning against the white pantry door. "Where's the sugar?"

"Right here." Emma moved around a few glass jars of green beans, found the sugar canister, and shook it. "At least I thought we had some. Looks like we're out."

Her grandmother retrieved a can of pumpkin and shuffled to the table. She set down the ingredients and grabbed her cane.

"Where are you going?"

"Next door. I'm sure Carol has some sugar."

"The recipe only calls for a little," Emma said. "We can do without it."

"Won't taste the same." *Grossmammi* headed for the door.

Emma blocked her way. "Don't trouble yourself. We have plenty of eggs. I can make a nice omelet. If you want something sweet, we have leftover chocolate coffee cake."

Grossmammi held up her hand and set her chin in that determined tilt Emma knew so well. "It'll take half a minute to get the sugar."

It would take a lot longer than that. Because of her advanced arthritis, Emma's grandmother was dangerously unsteady on her feet. When she stood for any length of time or walked even short distances, her ankles would swell. Even with the cane, Emma worried about her falling.

But how could Emma refuse her? Cooking and baking were two of the things she could still do.

"What if I get the sugar?"

"*Gut* idea. I'll have the batter mixed up by the time you come back. We'll toss in the sugar and be ready to eat in no time." Her grandmother turned and slowly made her way back to the table, humming an old hymn.

Emma hurried across her backyard. She passed her overgrown garden and the tall, thick oak tree that divided the Shetler property from the Ottos'. The fallen leaves created a brown carpet at the foot of the tree's trunk. More than once when they were kids, she and Adam had climbed it, Adam always reaching the higher limbs before scampering down. The memory stabbed like a needle to the heart.

A truck sat parked in the Ottos' driveway. Maybe someone was there to see Norman about the cows. He often sold a few of his steers to a couple of local butchers.

She rapped her knuckles against the white frame of the back screen door. She was as familiar with Adam's house as she was her own, but unlike her back door with its caked and peeling paint, this door—indeed, the entire house—was bright and spotless. She waited for a moment before knocking again. Carol Otto poked her head outside. "Emma. *Gude mariye.* How are you doing?"

Emma hesitated. Carol looked different. She was smiling so broadly that her face glowed. Emma hadn't seen her look so happy in a long time. "I'm well, *Fraa* Otto. I don't want to trouble you, but could I borrow a cup of sugar?"

"Of course. Oh, wait. I used the last of it yesterday morning. But I have another bag in the basement." She opened the door wider. "Come on in and I'll fetch some for you. There's coffee on the stove, if you'd like. It's fresh perked."

Emma followed her through the mudroom. Carol took the stairs down to the basement, and Emma hesitated for a moment. She hadn't had coffee yet, and the rich aroma drifting from the kitchen tempted her. She stepped into the room, and the breath went out of her as if she'd been punched in the stomach.

Sitting at the table, a towel draped over his neck and half of his hair cut off, was Adam Otto.

"Melvin, I told you to stop climbing on the table." Clara grabbed her son from behind and plopped him into the chair. She shoved it toward the kitchen table.

"Ow, *Mammi*! That hurt."

"*Nee*, it did not. But if you continue to disobey me, I will spank you. That will hurt."

Melvin nodded and faced the table. Clara motioned for Junior to sit down. It was nearly seven o'clock. Peter had gone to get Magdalena ready for breakfast almost twenty minutes ago. The eggs were getting cold. She slammed a glass of water down in front of Junior.

"I want milk." He shoved the water away.

"You can have milk for supper." She went to the kitchen doorway. "Peter! Breakfast is ready."

A few minutes later Peter entered the room.

He pinched Magdalena's round, pink cheek, and she giggled.

"The eggs are cold." Clara sat down.

Peter looked at Clara. "Sorry. Magdalena is in a *gut* mood this morning. Aren't you, *lieb*?"

The baby grabbed a small tuft of Peter's hair and laughed.

"Can we just eat, Peter?"

He nodded and set the baby in her wooden high chair, then joined the rest of the family and bowed his head. After the silent prayer they began to eat.

Within a minute or two Junior had cleaned his plate. "Can I have more?"

"That's all there is." Clara stood. She picked up Junior's plate and carried it to the sink.

"But I'm still hungry."

"Clara, there has to be more," Peter said. "An egg and a piece of toast isn't enough for a growing *bu*."

She turned. "If we had more, I'd give it to him."

His face turned white. "Junior, will you and Melvin take Magdalena outside for a little while? You can play in the sandbox."

Junior shook his head. "*Mammi* doesn't like the sandbox. She says it leaves a mess in the *haus*."

"Junior, do as I say. And help your *bruder* and

schwester put on their jackets." Peter lifted Magdalena out of her high chair and handed her over.

Junior cradled the little girl against his shoulder. She was half his size, but he had been holding her since she was a tiny baby. He grabbed his little brother by the arm and ushered him out the door.

When the children left, Peter shoved back from the table. "What was that about, Clara?"

She turned and leaned her hands against the sink.

"I asked you a question."

She whirled around. "What do you think it was about? I'm trying to conserve our food, Peter. You're not working. There's no money coming in." She looked down. "It's not as if the *kinner* are starving."

"They will if you barely feed them!" He stomped to the pantry and opened the door, displaying the half-filled shelves. "We have food here. Enough to give our *sohn* another piece of bread, at least."

"And what happens when that runs out?"

"The Lord—"

"Has not provided!"

He moved to put his arms around her. "I know you're upset about your *mammi*—"

"This has nothing to do with her." She stepped back from him. "You haven't worked in weeks."

"I've been looking for jobs." His face reddened, his eyes narrowing. "They're hard to come by, especially here."

"Then maybe we should have stayed in Kentucky."

"We, Clara? Or me?" He let out a deep breath. "You weren't happy there. I knew you wanted to come home. I had hoped—prayed—that finding work here would be easier. And I'm sure something will be available soon. We can't lose faith."

"I'm not. But God helps those who help themselves." Even though Emma had resisted her plan, she knew Peter couldn't argue with it. She had to convince him so he could help her convince Emma. "I talked to *mei schwester* yesterday."

"How is she doing?"

"Fine." Clara waved her hand. "I have an idea about *mei grossvadder's haus*. I think we should—"

A knock sounded on the door. "Are you expecting anyone?" Peter asked.

Clara shook her head. They both went to the door, and Peter opened it to reveal a tall, slim man standing on the porch. A frayed, yellow straw hat covered his black hair. His dark blue eyes and square jaw resembled Peter's, but Clara had never seen him before.

"Mark?" Peter stepped forward and clapped the man on the shoulder. "What are you doing here?"

The man grinned, a boyish smile showing a chipped front tooth. "Can't I come visit my cousin every once in a while?"

"Of course you can." Peter laughed and motioned him inside. The door closed. "How long has it been? Ten years?"

"Eleven."

"How are *Aenti* Bertha and *Onkel* Andrew?"

"They're well. Wishing you would come back to Kentucky." He turned to Clara. "So this is the reason you left home and moved all the way to northern Ohio."

Despite herself, Clara blushed. She didn't remember Mark, but then she and Peter had lived in Kentucky only a short time, a couple of months after they married. Peter had never mentioned him.

"Come in and sit down." Peter gestured to the sofa against the wall in the living room. Clara hoped Mark wouldn't notice the lumps in the cushions, and then wondered why it would matter to her.

"Clara, can you bring us some coffee?" Peter sat in the old stuffed chair next to the couch. "Mark and I have a lot to catch up on."

She nodded. She and Peter would have to put off their conversation until later. But they would talk, and soon. None of them could wait much longer.

* * *

"Adam?"

He felt his face heat at the sight of Emma gaping at him. He had to look like an idiot. Cool air hit one side of his neck while his longer hair tickled the other side. He squirmed.

"What are you doing here?" she asked.

"Getting a haircut." He cringed. "Um, you want some coffee?" He tried to smile. This wasn't how he imagined seeing her again after all this time.

She stared at the percolator on the stove as if she had no idea what it was. "I'm waiting for… for…" She turned back to him, her eyes still round with surprise. "What are you doing here?"

"I came back. For a visit."

"When?"

"Last night. What are you waiting for again?"

Her cheeks turned rosy. Seeing her blush made him smile. He remembered how easily she embarrassed. She'd always been a little on the plump side, and he saw that hadn't changed. She was still cute, her round face free of makeup. Her skin looked soft, smooth.

"Sugar."

He noticed the cup in her hand. Her fingers had turned white from gripping it. They weren't used to being uncomfortable with one another. Then again, the last time they saw each other…

"How are you?" he asked.

"Fine."

"I heard about your *mammi*."

She looked up. "How?"

"Leona. She sent me a letter."

"*Grossmammi* wrote to you?" She tugged on the bottom of her sweater, pulling it over her hips. The last button remained unfastened. "Why?"

Before he could answer, his mother breezed into the kitchen carrying a ten-pound bag of sugar. "I'm sorry it took me so long. Norman rearranged the shelves the other day and put this in the wrong spot." She looked at Emma and smiled. "Isn't it wonderful that Adam's home?"

"For a visit," he said. He didn't want to give his mother false hope.

"*Ya*. Great." Emma's gaze went to Adam. "You look ridiculous."

Carol paused, her mouth dropping open. Adam quickly laughed off the insult, which eased the tension between his mother and Emma. But not between Emma and Adam. She had moved to the doorway of the kitchen, her body half in, half out of the room.

Carol retrieved a bowl from the cabinet and poured a generous amount of sugar. She handed the bowl to Emma.

"I don't need this much. A cup will do. Actually, a couple of tablespoons will do. *Grossmammi* is making pumpkin pancakes this morning."

Adam's mouth watered at the memory of Leona's pumpkin pancakes.

"We have plenty of sugar, more than we need." Carol held the bowl out to her.

Emma took it. *"Danki."* She left without another look at Adam.

His mother picked up the scissors and resumed her work on Adam's hair. After a few minutes of silence he said, "Emma's changed."

His mother paused with the scissors in midair. "We've all changed, Adam." A quick snip. "More than you know."

Chapter Seven

It was nearly noon. Clara steamed and stewed as she cleaned the kitchen, made beds, picked up after the *kinner*. At last Peter came back into the kitchen, and she had a chance to say what was on her mind.

"He can't stay here."

"Clara, keep your voice down. He's in the next room!" Peter rarely shouted, but Clara could tell he was about to. "Do you want him to hear us arguing?"

"Nee." She backed against the kitchen counter and lowered her tone. "Why did you tell him he could live here?"

"It's only temporary. He's passing through on his way to New York. We have some distant relatives there he's been writing to. Said he wanted to stay a little while before he goes to meet them."

"How long?"

"Has he been writing them?"

Clara's temper flared again. "How long will he stay?" She twisted the end of one of the frayed ribbons of her *kapp*.

"He didn't say." Peter crossed his arms and looked down at her. "But he will be welcome as long as he wants to. He's *familye*."

"And another mouth to feed."

Peter placed his hands on the back of a kitchen chair. "Is this how it's going to be, Clara? Arguing every minute of the day?"

His words silenced her. She didn't want to argue. But she didn't want to feel helpless either. Or hopeless. How could she be a dutiful wife when she couldn't stop questioning her husband's every decision?

"Mark will have Junior and Melvin's bedroom." Peter looked up, his eyes hard. "I'll move one of their beds into our room and put it sideways against the foot of our bed. The *buwe* can sleep head-to-toe."

His tone made it clear that there would be no further discussion, but Clara couldn't help herself. "And what about our privacy?"

Peter's gaze pierced her. "We're not doing anything but sleeping in there, remember? We don't need privacy."

Clara flinched.

He walked out of the room and returned a few

seconds later with Mark in tow. "I'm sure Mark is hungry." Peter glanced at his cousin but avoided Clara's gaze. "Will you make lunch while I check on the *kinner*?"

Clara turned and looked at Mark, tried to muster a polite smile.

"I hope I'm not causing a problem." Mark twirled his hat in his hands. "I can find another place to stay. A hotel. Bed-and-breakfast, even. There's always one—or fifty—in Amish country." He gave her that grin again, showing his chipped tooth.

She smiled a tiny bit. "Tourists do love them around here. But we won't hear of you staying somewhere else. You are welcome in our home." She went to the pantry and tried to focus on being a good hostess. "What would you like to eat? I have some bread and meat for sandwiches. Or some chicken noodle soup I canned a couple of weeks ago."

"Anything will be fine." Mark sat down at the table.

Clara could feel his gaze on her while she prepared the soup. The kids would want some. If Peter was hungry for something else, he could fix it himself. She kept the bitterness out of her tone when addressing Mark. "What brings you to Middlefield?"

"A taste for adventure." He chuckled, then

added, "At least as far as a bus line can take me. Airplanes are *verboten*, of course."

She smiled at him. He was charming, the way Peter had been during their early days of court-ing. "Would you like something to drink? I have iced tea."

"Sounds *gut*."

She fixed him a glass, handed it to him, and hurried back to the stove. His eyes and chin might resemble Peter's, but the similarities ended there. Mark was wiry, thin. Clean shaven, and thus unmarried. A scar on his chin, the chipped tooth. A good-looking man.

She stirred the soup. Steam rose from the broth, mingling with the heat on her skin. She shouldn't be thinking about Peter's cousin, not in that way. She sneaked another glance at him.

"I have to admit I was surprised when I heard you and Peter were married."

"Why?"

He leaned back in the chair, his arms crossed over his chest. Black suspenders over a light blue shirt. "Seemed out of character for him. Thought he would always marry a *maedel* from home. There were more than a few *maed* interested in him. But then he started getting your letters, and no one else mattered."

Clara added salt to the soup. Their courtship had been...well, unusual. One of her mother's friends had suggested Clara write to Peter, a nephew in Kentucky. Clara didn't think anything would come of it. But she'd fallen in love with the sweet man through his honest, funny letters. And when she met him for the first time—

Her heart constricted in her chest. She'd known immediately that he was the man she would marry. And she loved him enough to move to Kentucky, until homesickness overcame her. He'd agreed to go to Middlefield, to Iowa, to Canada if she wanted to. "Where you *geh*, Clara, I will follow," he had said. And he'd done just that.

What happened to their optimism? Their hope? Their love?

"Clara, are you all right?"

She looked up to see Mark standing next to her, frowning. She wiped her cheeks with the back of her hand. "Just a little hot. Too close to the stove."

"I thought maybe I'd upset you somehow." He looked at her, his eyes unblinking.

His intense gaze unnerved her. "What?"

"I can see why Peter chose you as his *fraa*." His tone was low. Soft. Sending a not unpleasant chill through her.

"*Mammi*, I'm *hungerich*!"

Clara jumped away from Mark, almost knocking the pot of soup off the stove. "Lunch will be ready in a minute." Her voice sounded an octave higher than normal. She brushed past Mark, making sure she didn't touch him.

Junior moved to sit down as Melvin, Peter, and the baby came inside.

"You know the rules, Junior," Peter said. "Wash your hands first. You too, Melvin."

"Who's that?" Melvin pointed at Mark.

Mark crouched in front of him. "I'm your *daed's* cousin. But you can call me *Onkel* Mark. I'm visiting for a while."

"Cool!" Junior said.

Peter shot him a sharp look. "Where did you hear that word?"

Junior shrugged. "Some of the kids down the street. They're Yankees. And they're real old. Shane's almost nine."

"That is old." Mark winked at Peter, and the boys left to wash up. Peter handed Magdalena to Clara and followed his sons to the bathroom.

"You have a *schee familye.*" Mark smiled. But he wasn't looking at the baby. His eyes were on Clara.

It was almost lunchtime, and Emma could still taste the pumpkin pancakes *Grossmammi* had made for breakfast. She had eaten more than she ought, just as she always did when stressed or unhappy. Now she felt slow and sluggish, and it was taking her forever to accomplish the smallest tasks.

She had set the plate of leftover pancakes on the back of the stove and was just finishing the breakfast dishes when she heard the tapping of *Grossmammi's* cane behind her. She tried to arrange her face in the semblance of a smile. "What would you like for lunch?"

"I'm not really hungry, since we had such a heavy breakfast."

"We can skip lunch, if you like, and have an early dinner." *And I'll eat the leftover pancakes later*, Emma thought.

The old woman rapped the end of her cane on the hard tile floor. "Let's finish the coffee, then." She sat down at the table. "What's wrong, *kinn*? Be honest with me."

Emma leaned against the counter, willing her pulse to slow down. She didn't know how to explain to her grandmother what she was feeling. Adam had come back. For a visit only.

That didn't make her feelings for him any different than when he left Middlefield. Physically he'd changed. He'd let his hair grow to his shoulders. His beard and mustache, facial hair forbidden for a single Amish man, showed he'd embraced the Yankee world fully. Yet one thing hadn't changed. His eyes. A golden hazel, the color of swirled honey. She remembered how easily they filled with emotion. Quick laughter. Frustration with his parents and the church. Sorrow on the day her father had died. She pressed her hand against her chest, forcing the sudden pain away.

"Emma?" *Grossmammi* repeated.

Emma turned to meet her grandmother's gaze. "Why didn't you tell me you wrote Adam?"

The old woman's eyes widened. She mouthed a few words but didn't emit a sound. "He came back, then," she finally said.

"*Ya.* He's back." Emma yanked open the kitchen drawer and jerked out a couple of coffee spoons. She slammed the drawer shut.

"Those drawers have lasted fifty years, Emma." Her grandmother frowned. "I expect them to last fifty more."

"Sorry, *Grossmammi.*" She set cups and the sugar bowl on the table and poured coffee for both of them.

"I thought you would be happy to see Adam."

"I…am."

"That didn't sound convincing."

Emma sat down across from her grandmother. "I'm wondering why he's here. He was in such a hurry to leave all of us behind."

"He's not the first *bu* to leave our faith. He won't be the last." She stirred her coffee and took a sip.

"You don't sound very concerned."

"That's where you're wrong." She looked at Emma over the rims of her glasses. "I, and many others, are concerned every time someone leaves us. We worry about them. Pray for them. And hope God leads them back."

Emma pondered her words. Was God leading Adam back? His mother was giving him an Amish haircut. But maybe he had agreed to that out of respect for his parents, not a desire to rejoin the faith. Hair grew back easily. Repentance and forgiveness came at a much steeper price.

Emma looked away and tried not to think about Adam. When she looked back, her grandmother was staring at her.

"What did you and Clara talk about yesterday? Neither of you seemed too happy when she left."

"I take it we're finished talking about Adam?"

"For now."

Emma was glad to hear it. "*Mei schwester* is worried about us. About how we'll keep everything running around here."

"And what did you tell her?"

"That we had it under control."

Grossmammi chuckled. "Emma, the only one who has anything under control is the Lord."

"I know that." Emma said the words automatically, but God wasn't on her mind right now. She had to prove her sister wrong. "Clara has no idea about our lives here. She's too busy with Peter and the *kinner*."

"As she should be."

"Then she shouldn't tell me what I'm supposed to do with *mei haus*." Emma motioned with her coffee cup. "I mean our *haus*."

"I knew what you meant." *Grossmammi* looked at her. "What did Clara say?"

Emma put her cup down. "She wants to change *Grossvadder's* workshop. She wants to sell all his tools. She wants to open—" Emma grimaced. "A yarn and fabric store."

"Would that be so terrible?"

"*Ya!* I don't know anything about running a store. Neither does Clara. I can't sew, and the only knitting I've done had more dropped stitches than normal ones." Emma's throat burned. "It's *Grossvadder's* shop. He used to take me in there when I was a *kinn* and show me his tools. I still have the piece of wood he let me use to practice pounding nails. He never minded when I watched him make furniture or fix those broken little machines people kept bringing to him. He never acted like I was a bother."

"*Nee*. He never did."

"We can't sell his tools. We can't fill his machine shop with pink fabric and purple yarn and needles and thimbles." She touched her fingertips to her mouth, shaking her head. "He wouldn't want that."

"So you say. But why does Clara want this?"

"Are you agreeing with her? I thought you'd want to preserve *Grossvadder's* legacy."

"Emma. I only asked a question." Her voice was calm. Soothing.

Emma took a breath. "Clara says the store will bring in money. Pay our bills." She didn't mention their mother's hospital bills. "Buy our food. Maybe hire someone to help us make some of the repairs on the *haus*. But the *haus* is fine. Sure, it might need some paint and a few shingles, and possibly a—"

"How is Dill?"

Emma went to the stove and brought back the plate of leftover pancakes. She picked up one, tore it in pieces, and ate it without registering the taste. "Fine."

"*Nee.* She's not. Norman told me before the funeral he thought she might be lame." *Grossmammi* touched Emma's arm. "How will we pay to get her the help she needs?"

Emma swallowed, her stomach churning. "We'll figure out another way. I'd never let anything happen to Dill."

Her grandmother didn't say anything for a moment. "Emma, if you had a choice, what would you want to do with the workshop?"

"I'd keep it the way it is."

"What if you could use it to sustain us? You might not like it, but Clara is right. There are bills to pay. Your mother and I were able to make ends meet by using the money your father had saved before he died. We also made jams and breads and sold them to tourists passing by."

Emma nodded. "I know."

"So what if you could turn the workshop into something profitable? Other than the fabric shop Clara wants?" Her grandmother stood, shuffled over to the sink, and rinsed out her cup. "I promise you, your *grossvadder* would want his shop to benefit you both. Think about it. Maybe together you and Clara can find a compromise."

Alone at the table, Emma ate another pancake and finished her coffee. Compromise? With her sister? That would never happen.

Clara would get her way. She always did.

Chapter Eight

"There. Now you look Amish. At least a bit more than when you got here." Adam's mother stepped back and admired her work.

Hair covered the towel wrapped around his shoulders. She folded the hair up in the towel, but some of the clippings remained on his shirt.

Adam met his mother's gaze, searching her face for a sign of trouble. If anything, she looked genuinely happy, and had since he arrived. He was more convinced than ever that Leona had been wrong. The thought comforted him. That and the filling breakfast he'd consumed.

He turned to go upstairs. "I'm going to wash the hair off."

"Adam?"

He faced his mother.

"I still have all your old clothes." She glanced

to one side before looking at him again. "They're in your closet, if you want them."

Adam nodded but remained noncommittal. When he reached his bedroom, he went straight to the closet. Three pairs of denim broadfall pants. Six short-sleeved shirts, hand stitched, three pale yellow and three light blue. A couple of jackets. A spotless long-sleeved white shirt, black trousers, vest, and suspenders—his church clothes. Everything just as he had left it.

He looked down at his Yankee clothes. Plaid shirt. Blue jeans. The hundred-dollar running shoes he wished he'd never bought. He fingered the thin cotton fabric of a blue shirt hanging in front of him. Paused, and closed the closet door.

Adam rummaged through his suitcase for clean clothes. He saw the razor, grabbed it, and went to the bathroom, shutting the door behind him.

He looked in the mirror, checking out the bowl-shaped haircut. He'd agreed to the haircut to make his mother happy, but it didn't bother him as much as he thought it might. He'd get it shortened up and cropped closer to his head when he got back to Michigan.

He ran a hand over his beard and mustache. He was tempted to use the razor, too, but he didn't want to get his mother's hopes up. He shook his head and started the shower.

Later he bounded downstairs wearing his Michigan sweatshirt over a white T-shirt. He found his mother in the kitchen, kneading a ball of white dough. When she saw him, her lips curved into a smile.

"*Daed* still out with the cows?"

Her smile dimmed. "I suppose so."

Adam debated whether to seek out his father. They would probably end up arguing. They always had, up until the moment he left home. "Maybe I'll *geh* next door. Check on Emma and Leona."

"That's a *gut* idea. I know Leona will be glad to see you." She shaped the dough into a smooth loaf and set it in a metal pan.

Adam thought his mother might encourage him to speak to his father instead. She was always the buffer between them. But she didn't mention him. She didn't mention Emma either. Strange. "Is there anything you need before I *geh*?"

She looked at him for a moment, her brows angled inward. Then she shook her head. "*Nee.* You *geh* on."

"All right." He didn't move. Now she was acting odd; maybe Leona had been right after all. Maybe something was wrong. "I'll be back in a few minutes." He had nearly left the room when she called after him.

"Adam?"

"Ya?"

She brushed flour off her hands. "How long are you planning to stay? Here, at home."

He hesitated before answering. "I'm not sure, *Mamm*. No definite plans right now."

It wasn't a very good answer, but one she'd just have to accept right now. He left before she could ask him anything else.

Outside, the scent of burning leaves floated on the air. The smell of fall. He breathed deeply and strode toward the Shetlers' house. At the big oak tree, he paused. A thick layer of leaves lay scattered on the ground and throughout the yard. He and Emma used to rake the leaves into piles when they were *kinner*. Jump into them. Burrow tunnels. Throw handfuls in the air. He would sneeze for days afterward, but it was worth it.

A breeze attacked two brown, crinkled leaves on the lowest branch. They clung for a second before being carried off on the whim of the wind. Adam kicked at a few more stray leaves as he walked toward the house.

On the porch, his gaze went to the two rockers in the corner. Memories of his friendship with Emma and her family filled his mind and brought a knot to his throat. He turned away and knocked on the front door, harder than he intended to. It seemed no one was home, even though the buggy was parked near the barn.

He knocked again. Finally the door opened.

"Adam." Leona smiled. She opened the door wide. "Come in, come in."

He followed her inside. Like his parents' home, the Shetlers' house hadn't changed much. A plain brown sofa, a small end table holding a gas lamp, two chairs, and Leona's hickory rocking chair. Plain but comfortable.

"We can visit in the kitchen." She moved slowly, and Adam measured his steps behind her. The kitchen, too, had stood still in time. A pitcher of lemonade sat on the round table.

"Thirsty?"

He wasn't, but he nodded anyway. *"Ya."*

Leona followed his gaze. "Do you want ice? We have some in the cooler in the basement."

"I don't want you to *geh* to any trouble."

"It's *nee* trouble, Adam."

"I'd rather have it without."

Leona's hands trembled as she filled his glass, then poured one for herself. She sat next to him. "I added extra sugar."

He took a sip, peering at her over the rim. "You were expecting me."

"Eventually. Emma said she saw you this morning."

"With half my hair chopped off."

"Ah." Leona chuckled. "Carol gave you a haircut, *ya*? I see she couldn't talk you into shaving that fur off your face."

"She didn't try." He folded his hands on the table and leaned forward. "I'm glad you wrote to tell me about *Mamm*, but I don't think there's anything wrong with her. At least nothing I could tell." The small niggling of doubt he'd experienced a minute ago was a figment of his imagination. Had to be.

"Oh, there is." Leona didn't pick up her lemonade. "Your coming back has helped her, I'm sure."

"I never said I came back."

"You've given her something to focus on."

He noticed that she ignored his denial. He watched her face intently. The house might not have changed in two years, but Leona had. The lines had increased around her eyes, her cheeks grown more narrow and sunken. "What do you mean?"

"It's not my place to say, Adam. Like I told you, Carol hasn't said much to me. That right there made me wonder. Now, don't take this wrong. I'm not here to beat you with a stick for leaving. Everyone has to do what God tells them to."

Adam cupped his hand around the glass. God didn't have anything to do with him leaving the

Amish, or coming back to Middlefield. But he had too much respect for Leona to say so.

"She wasn't the same after you left. And then Mary died."

Guilt bit into him. "I didn't know."

"How could you, when you weren't here?" Leona shrugged.

The guilt burrowed deeper. He crossed his arms over his chest. "What can I do?"

"Be here." She took his hand. "Be here for your *mamm*. At least for a few days."

"I don't want her to think I'm coming back for *gut*. I'll be hurting her all over again when I go back to Michigan."

"Are you happy there?"

Adam took a long drink of his lemonade. "I'm…content."

"I see." She didn't say anything else.

He guessed they were finished speaking about his mother. "Where's Emma?"

"She went to Nature's Nook. We needed a few things."

"Like sugar." He smiled a little bit. "But the buggy is here."

"She walked."

"Why?"

"Dill's got a problem with her leg." Leona took her first small sip of the lemonade.

"Did my *daed* look at her?"

"Briefly. But with the funeral and every-thing…" She set down the glass.

Finally he felt useful. "I can take a look at her for you."

Leona tilted her head. "I would appreciate that. You always had a way with horses. Like Emma and her animals."

Her comment pleased him. He'd missed the horses since leaving. "Maybe it's just a pebble in her shoe that's making her limp." He didn't mention that his father probably would have checked that first thing. But if that was the case, then why hadn't he tended to the horse? Or at least called the vet?

"I hope that's all."

Leona followed him as he headed for the front door. Before he walked out, she grabbed his hand. He looked down, seeing the dark blue veins stark against her translucent skin.

"*Willkum* home, Adam."

He frowned. How many times did he have to remind everyone he wasn't here to stay? But he didn't correct her. Instead he squeezed her hand and went off to the barn to check on the horse.

"I don't believe this!" Emma trudged back home, furious. How could she have forgotten her purse? Thinking about money, Clara, and Adam undoubtedly had something to do with it. Still, who went shopping without a wallet?

She'd trekked partway down Bundysburg Road when she realized her mistake. More time wasted while she backtracked to retrieve her purse. She quickened her steps.

Emma approached the house, her gaze drifting to the truck next door. So that's what Adam drove now. What would take her an hour round trip would take him maybe fifteen minutes at most. But that was Adam. Always taking the easy way out.

She walked up the driveway and spied someone heading for her barn. A man wearing a sweatshirt and jeans. She ran toward him. "Stop!"

He turned around, and her heart gave a lurch. "Adam."

"Emma." Adam walked toward her with that confident half slouch he'd always had. He opened his mouth. Shook his head and said nothing.

"What are you doing in *mei* barn?"

"Checking on Dill."

"Dill's fine."

"Not according to Leona."

Emma lifted her chin. "I'm handling it."

"I'm sure you are." He slid his hands into the pockets of his jeans. "Still, I wouldn't mind checking on Dill for you." A light breeze ruffled the edges of his newly cut hair.

She turned away. He looked much better with an Amish cut. More like the Adam she remembered.

He stepped toward her. "She's having trouble walking?"

After a long pause, Emma looked up, meeting his hazel eyes. She inched away from him, wishing he would leave. *"Ya."* She had spent two years trying to forget about him. He was back two minutes, and everything inside her was mixed up again.

"I know you're upset with me," Adam said. "But think about Dill. If she's in pain, maybe I can help her."

His words reached through her resentment. "All right." She shoved past him and went inside the barn. Two of the dogs, Archie and Rodney, came up to her, their long tails wagging. Archie rubbed his black muzzle against Emma's leg.

"New dogs?" Adam opened Dill's stall.

"Archie was a stray. Rodney was hit by a car last year." She knelt down and rubbed both dogs' backs, and got several slobbery licks as a reward. "He's fine now. I never did find out who he belonged to."

"What about Molly?"

Emma was surprised he remembered her other dog, a bluetick hound. "She's getting old. Her favorite place is underneath the porch."

Adam didn't respond. He had already gone into Dill's stall. Emma didn't want to keep talking to him anyway. She added a bit more food to the dog dishes and listened as he spoke to the horse in soft tones.

Adam could sense when horses weren't well, and he usually knew what to do to make them better. Despite being upset with him, she hoped he could find out what was wrong with her horse.

The stall door hinges squeaked, and Adam came out. He didn't look at her. Instead his gaze flicked over his shoulder, back at Dill.

She knew that look, and it wasn't good.

Chapter Nine

❧

"What's wrong with *mei* horse?"

He rubbed his beard, wishing he didn't have to break the news to her. But he didn't want her to hear it from anyone else either. "I've seen it before, in a couple of my father's horses. It's a type of arthritis. Navicular disease."

"She'll get better. Right?"

He paused. "It's incurable."

She backed away. "*Nee*. She can't die." A desperate whisper.

He took a step toward her. "Emma, she's not going to die. She'll probably live several more years." For a minute he thought she might lean against him.

She straightened. "When will she feel better?"

Archie rubbed against Adam's leg. He reached down and patted the mutt on the head. His gaze remained on Emma. "Rest will help with the pain."

"How much rest? A week? Two?"

"Emma." He said her name as gently as possible. "Dill can't pull the buggy anymore. Or do any other hard labor. It's time for her to retire."

She walked over to the stall and stood on tiptoe, looking in at the horse. Adam moved next to her.

"But she's going to live, right?"

He lifted his hand to put it on her shoulder. A gesture he would have done before. But not now. Too much had changed. He let his arm fall to his side. *"Ya.* She will. And she's still a *gut* horse."

"I know that." Emma pressed her lips together and faced Adam. "I have to *geh* to the store." She walked past him. He followed her.

"Emma, do they still have the horse auctions in Bloomfield?"

"Ya."

"Then I can take you to get a new horse."

She faced him. *"Nee."*

"I've got a truck. I can hitch up a trailer—"

She shook her head, turned, and hurried to the house.

Adam heard the back door slam. Was she that angry at him that she wouldn't even consider his offer to help her get the new horse she needed?

Ya, he thought. *She is.*

* * *

Emma leaned against the kitchen door and shut her eyes. Dill wouldn't die. But she couldn't work either. Her eyes grew hot. She couldn't afford a new horse. She couldn't even afford to keep Dill fed, not if she wasn't working. A horse was an expensive pet. Yet Emma couldn't part with her.

She banged the back of her fist against the door. She could sell Dill; the money would help pay for a new horse. But the thought tore her heart to pieces. It would be like selling a member of the family. And who would buy her anyway?

She could go to Adam's father. As the deacon, he could secure funds through the church community to purchase her a new horse. But then Adam would get involved.

Or she could give in to Clara about the fabric shop.

Sorrow and frustration combined in her stomach, a lump heavy as lead. What was she going to do? Sell Dill? Accept charity? Ask for Adam's help? Cave in to Clara?

No good choices, as far as she could see.

After Emma left, Adam had looked for his father in the barn, then in the pasture. Adam couldn't find him anywhere. His mother was busy baking. At loose ends, he had to do something. Replenishing the woodpile seemed as good a task as any.

He dropped a piece of wood on the woodpile and leaned against the handle of the heavy maul. Despite the fall chill, perspiration rolled down his back. The physical labor strained his unused muscles, but he felt energized. He picked up another chunk of wood and split it neatly.

If only he could deal so easily with Emma. He tried to get her empty expression out of his mind. He had expected more emotion from her: Doubt about Adam's diagnosis of Dill. A plan of action, at the very least. But she left without a word, an invisible cloud of defeat hanging over her.

That wasn't the Emma he knew. She never refused a challenge. He'd once spent six weeks in a cast because he dared her to jump over his uncle's pond using the rope hanging from the tree. She made it. He missed. She didn't accept circumstances, not without trying to change them. How hard had she tried to change his mind about leaving?

His gaze drifted to the Shetler house. It needed a lot of work. Four black shingles lay on the ground in the backyard. White paint peeled and flaked off the house. The two poles holding the clothesline tilted inward. Anyone passing by would see a house desperately in need of repair.

Adam remembered what the place used to look

like. Emma's father had kept it in pristine condition. Now it looked sad and broken. Not just the house. Emma too.

He was tempted to go over there and offer to help. But why bother? She'd refuse him anyway.

She would not, however, refuse his father.

Adam finished splitting the wood just as he saw his father pull the buggy into the driveway. He set the maul against the woodpile and hesitated. They had barely spoken since he arrived, only those few words over breakfast. Anything they said to one another was likely to dissolve into an argument. Still, he had to try. For Emma's sake.

He walked toward the buggy as his father pulled to a halt. "Put Samson away," he said.

Thirteen years disappeared with one statement. Adam was ten years old again, following his father's terse orders. He gritted his teeth and took Samson's head. His father got out and went inside the barn.

Adam unhitched Samson and led the horse inside the barn. His father picked up a bucket and filled it with water from the hydraulic pump in the back corner of the barn. He and Adam both reached the stall at the same time.

"*Geh* ahead." His father nodded.

"*Nee*, you," Adam said at the same time.

The men looked at each other, not speaking.

His father went inside the stall. Then Adam. Norman poured water into the trough while Adam settled the horse. The men walked out. Adam closed the latch.

His father headed for the barn door.

"Daed."

He stopped, then turned. "What?"

"I took a look at Emma's horse today. Dill."

"I know the horse's name. She's got a sore foot."

"It's worse than that."

"How do you know?"

Adam grimaced at the doubting tone. "I've seen it before. Navicular disease."

"You're wrong. I'll call the vet in the morning."

"Daed, I'm not wrong." He went to his father. "Remember Casey? And *Onkel* John's horse? They both had it."

"I'll call the vet." Norman turned around.

"You should have caught it."

His dad halted. His fists closed and opened. He faced his son. "And you should shut your mouth." He walked out of the barn.

Stung, Adam stormed over to the wall and slammed his fist. Pain exploded through his knuckles and shot up into his wrist. *Dummkopf.* He couldn't control his emotions, like his father and so many other Amish. Another reason he didn't belong here.

But at least something would be done about Dill and getting the Shetlers a new horse. Emma might refuse his help, but she wouldn't refuse a deacon of the church.

"I'm glad you wanted to take a buggy ride this evening." Peter smiled at Clara. "It's been a long time since we've done this. Just the two of us."

Clara gave him a tight smile. She turned and looked out the window as they traveled the road.

"Although we could have stayed home." His words held a mischievous tone. "Julia would have taken the *kinner* next door, and Mark said he wanted to walk around the area and do some exploring. Knowing him, he wouldn't be back for at least a couple hours."

She turned and looked at his profile. "Doesn't that sound odd to you?"

"Not if you knew Mark. When we were *kinner* he could never sit still. Was always doing something. Coming up with crazy plans. I reckon after he's spent some time in New York he'll move on to somewhere else."

"How come I never met him before?"

"He was living in Tennessee at the time."

"And now he's going to New York."

Peter looked at her. "That's Mark."

Clara settled back against the seat. Two cars sped past them, but Peter kept the buggy moving at a leisurely pace. Suddenly he reached for her hand. She pulled away.

He didn't say anything.

After a long silence, Clara spoke. "Peter, we need to talk."

"I figured that." He said the words through gritted teeth. "What about?"

"I think you already know."

Peter sighed. "I'm not sure I know anything anymore, Clara. So why don't you tell me what's on your mind."

"I'm thinking we should move."

"Move?" Peter looked at her. "We've already had this conversation. What's changed?"

"You invited not only *mei schwester* and *grossmammi* to live with us, but now also Mark. Our *haus* is too small."

"Emma doesn't want to live with us. She's already said as much. And Mark will be here only temporarily. And as you keep saying, we don't have any money. So how could we afford to move?"

"I've been thinking about it. It just makes sense. We could move into *Grossmammi's haus*. Let them move in here."

Peter turned into the Middlefield Cheese

parking lot. He brought the buggy to a stop and angled his body toward Clara. *"Nee."*

"But, Peter—"

"I said *nee*." His eyes narrowed in the dusky light. "I invited them to move in with us because it was the right thing to do. But Emma has made her feelings clear. And I understand why. Your *grossmammi* has lived in that house for, what, fifty years? I'll not deprive her of her home and memories. The matter is settled; we're not even going to ask."

He stared out into the night. "You wanted to move back here from Kentucky. I agreed to it. I spent every dime I had saved to build our *haus*."

Clara crossed her arms. "To make me feel guilty."

"Because I love you." He moved closer to her. "Clara, I would do anything for you. Except move again, especially since we don't have to. I didn't build our *haus* alone. You helped. Remember the kitchen?"

"Ya." Her arms relaxed slightly.

"We painted the cabinets together. White. I can still see that glob of paint on your nose."

"The one you put there." She put her hands in her lap and looked down. She wasn't going to let him get her off track. "If you won't move—"

"I won't."

"Then I had another idea." She told him about

converting *grossvadder's* workshop into a fabric and yarn store. When she was finished she held her breath and gripped the edge of the seat, bracing for his negative answer.

"What does Leona think about it?"

"I haven't told her. I've only talked to Emma."

"And she agrees?"

Clara hesitated. If she told Peter the truth, her husband would probably side with Emma. He seemed to be on everyone's side but hers lately. "She's considering it."

"Really? I would figure she'd say *nee* right away."

"Because she's so stubborn?"

"Or because now isn't a *gut* time for her to be making any big decisions. Especially about something so permanent."

"So you don't think it's a *gut* idea."

"I didn't say that." He moved closer to her. "I think it's a great idea. And if Leona and Emma agree to it, I'll help in any way I can."

"You will?"

He nodded and smiled. "This is the happiest I've seen you for a long time, Clara."

Her smile grew. On impulse she leaned over and kissed him. Once they had the business up and running, there would be no more worries about money. They wouldn't have to go to any of the deacons or the bishop and ask for help. They could afford to build an addition on the house.

For the first time in ages, they would have a little breathing room.

They would have hope.

Chapter Ten

Typical Amish country.

Mark King strolled down Bundysburg Road. He took in the white Amish houses and barns. The square plots of land bordered by woods. A buggy passed by, two men inside. He waved. Even grinned. They didn't give him a second look. Yes, he could stay here unnoticed. Blend in with the rest of the community. No one would think of looking for him here.

Exactly the way he wanted it.

He continued down the road as dusk descended. There was nothing special about Middlefield. Plain. Just like Kentucky. Tennessee. A hundred other Amish settlements. Unremarkable. Like Amish life itself.

A life he hated.

Peter was plain and boring too. Not very smart either. Growing up, he had been content working in his father's shop. Going to school and church. Getting up on Monday and doing it all over again. All he wanted was a wife, children, and an Amish life.

His cousin was so shortsighted. Such a fool.

But Peter's wife—now, she was different. Thin, not too pretty, but decent looking. She had an edge to her, one he didn't see in too many Amish women. A sense of desperation. She didn't think much of her husband, that much he could tell. She thought she was smarter than Peter. Maybe even better.

That attitude came from somewhere. It wouldn't take him long to find out where.

He had a plan, and somehow Clara would be a part of it. He continued to walk, nodding at a young Amish girl playing with a tiny kitten in the front yard of her house. He smiled at her. Such innocence.

But that child wasn't innocent. No one was.

After a while he turned and headed back toward Peter's dreary little house. His dull-witted cousin wouldn't suspect anything. He had already opened his home to Mark, just as any proper Amish family would. Offered him food and shelter without asking for anything in return. And Cousin Peter could barely afford to feed his own children, if the contents of his pantry and the worn-out furniture were any indication.

As for his cousin's wife, well…

Mark grinned, his first true smile since arriving in Middlefield. Clara would give him everything he needed. And she wouldn't even realize she was doing it.

Leona peered through the smudged window in her bedroom. Her gaze swept the Ottos' property. She wiped away a fingerprint and saw Emma walking up the driveway, lugging four bags of groceries from Nature's Nook. Leona moved to get her cane, but stopped. By the time she managed her way downstairs, Emma would have most of the food put away. Instead she remained at the window and watched Emma's cat, Tommy, chase a gray squirrel across the yard.

Maybe Adam was outside. Maybe he would notice Emma struggling with the groceries and offer to help. Something he should have been doing for the past two years. As Emma's husband.

Leona sighed and moved to Ephraim's old hickory rocker on the opposite side of the room. Her arthritic fingers caressed the smooth wood handles as she remembered how her husband's thick, roughened hands would curl over them as he rocked back and forth in the chair. Even twenty years after his death, she could still feel the texture of his skin. Hands that had built a house big enough for their six children, created a wood shop, raised a barn. Those hands, that could repair any machine, build any structure, till any land, had also caressed her with love. Cradled and comforted their babies. Buried three of their children.

"Ephraim, what are we going to do?" she asked. "We had many troubles over the years, but plenty of happiness too. Yet our *grossdoch-ders* are suffering. Where is their happiness?"

Silence met her words. She let out a bitter chuckle and shook her head. "I know, I know. You want me to mind my own business. To re-member that the Lord will work this out." She squeezed the wood crafted by her beloved's hands. "But you know me, *mei lieb*. I can't sit here and do *nix*."

But she would have to. She was too old to do much else. She couldn't force Clara to see the special man God had set apart for her. For some reason Clara had scales over her eyes when it came to her husband—a good provider, a decent man, strong in his faith. What would it take for her to appreciate Peter?

Then there was Emma. For years Leona had been certain that Emma and Adam would marry. Adam Otto was one of the few people who appre-ciated Emma for herself. He didn't seem to care that she liked to spend hours in the woods with her pets, or that she could fish better than he did. She didn't get mad when he beat her at checkers, or when he sometimes forgot he'd promised to help her with something. They understood each other. Accepted each other's faults. Even embraced them. Or so Leona thought.

Then Adam left, surprising them all and breaking Emma's heart. Though Emma would never admit it.

But while Leona prayed that Emma and Adam would find their way back to each other, that wasn't the reason she'd asked Adam to return to Middlefield. Something had happened to Adam's mother. Carol needed her son. And she needed all their prayers.

Leona closed her eyes. Tears squeezed out of the corners and ran down her cheeks. She prayed for those she had lost, and more fervently for those who were lost now.

"Grossmammi?"

Leona opened her eyes. She picked up the white handkerchief in her lap and wiped her cheeks. "Come in."

Her granddaughter stepped inside. A strand of brown hair curved over her forehead, just above her blue eyes. Her face was pink from the chilly air outside. Dirt smudged her cheek, probably from Rodney jumping on her when she got home.

That dog was nearly five feet tall when he stood on his hindquarters.

Leona started to rise. "I was just coming downstairs to help."

"*Nee.* I put the groceries away." She walked over and sat on the edge of the bed. "I didn't have to purchase too many."

She couldn't purchase too many. Everybody tried to protect Leona, but she wasn't ignorant of their finances. She watched as Emma picked at the edge of her sweater.

"What is it?"

Emma looked up, stilling her hands. "Dill can't work anymore."

"Are you sure?"

Emma swallowed, looked away. "*Ya.* Adam looked at her today."

"I see." Leona leaned back in her chair. "And you agree with what he said?"

"I didn't want to, but he knows horses. I told him I'd call a vet." She stood up from the bed and went to the window. "But I won't."

They both knew why. Leona waited for Emma to ask her what she should do. But she should have known better. Emma always had to figure out the answers herself.

"I'm trying not to worry." She wiped underneath her eyes. "I'm trying to be grateful Dill isn't dying. I'm trying to remember the blessings we have." Her voice trembled. "But that doesn't change anything."

Leona's knees creaked as she rose from the chair. "Of course it does, Emma."

Emma shook her head. "There are still bills to pay. Now we need a new horse. And I won't sell Dill, even though she'll cost us more money." She licked her lips. "If I did, someone would put her down."

"You don't have to carry all this yourself." She put her arm around Emma's shoulders. "I have some money saved."

"But it's not enough. It's never enough." She looked at Leona. "I could try to get a job working out of the *haus*. But Peter has been trying for months and hasn't found anything. Whatever job I could get wouldn't pay for what we need. And I don't want to leave you alone."

Leona bristled. "Emma, I'm capable of taking care of myself. I might move slower than I used to, but that doesn't mean I'm useless."

"That's not what I'm saying." She leaned toward Leona. "I couldn't take it if something happened to you."

"Kinn." Leona cupped Emma's cheek, running her wrinkled thumb over her granddaughter's smooth, fair skin. "Nothing is going to happen to me. I promise."

"You can't promise me that." Emma leaned

into her grandmother's touch. "No one can. You're all I have. I won't leave you here alone."

Leona opened her mouth to say something, but changed her mind and shut it again. She couldn't reason with Emma, not while her grief was so raw. But her heart swelled with love for her granddaughter, for putting an old woman above herself.

"I'm going to talk to Clara tomorrow."

"About…?"

"About opening the fabric shop." Emma looked out the window. "She's right. It's the only thing we can do."

"But it's not what you want to do."

Emma stepped away from Leona. "It doesn't matter what I want, *Grossmammi*." She started to leave.

Leona couldn't take the sadness in Emma's voice. She had given up so much, and still had to give up more. "There's another way."

Emma turned. "Selling jams and jellies? Clara won't agree to that."

"*Nee*. I don't mean that." She shuffled over to Emma and looked up at her, straightening her shoulders as much as she could. "You could get married."

Emma's bitter laugh pierced Leona's ears. "To whom? No one here is interested in me. And unless you have another relative who has a son or nephew who needs a pen pal—"

"That's not what I'm talking about."

"Then who?"

Adam. But Leona couldn't mention him. If the two of them were to be together, God would have to make that happen, and not out of desperation or manipulative matchmaking. The stakes were much too high for that.

Still, Leona didn't think the Lord would mind too much if she planted a little seed in Emma's heart.

"There are *yung menner* here in Middlefield, Emma. Don't be so quick to dismiss them."

"I don't have to dismiss them." She looked at her grandmother. "He—I mean they, dismissed me." Emma walked to the doorway.

"It was a thought."

"*Ya.* It was."

Emma left, and Leona sat back down in the rocker and clasped her hands together.

Leona wasn't giving up. She wasn't against the idea of turning Ephraim's workshop into some kind of business. But she didn't want it to happen at the expense of either of her granddaughters' happiness.

Things were moving too fast. Neither of them

was consulting the Lord, or trusting in Him. And if they didn't do that, anything they attempted would fail.

Chapter Eleven

Emma's hands trembled as she slid the last bobby pin onto her *kapp*. Today was the first Sunday service since *Mammi's* death. She didn't want to go to church. Throughout the week a few people had stopped by the house to visit, mostly to say hello and offer condolences again.

Except for Adam. She hadn't seen him since he'd looked at Dill's foot two days ago. But his absence didn't surprise her. When did Adam Otto ever think of anyone but himself?

Emma's shoulders ached with tension. She looked at her stubby hands—nubs where her nails had been. *Grossmammi* would probably tell her that she took out her worries on her fingernails, rather than taking them to God. But why should she bother, when God had taken so much from her?

"Emma?" Her grandmother's fragile voice

traveled up the stairs. "Are you ready? The Ottos will be here any minute."

Norman and Carol were taking them to church today. Adam wouldn't be coming with them. His haircut might be Amish, but the rest of him belonged to the world. The shiny truck, the beard and mustache, the baggy, too-large clothes all proved that.

"Emma?"

"Coming." She padded down the stairs in her stocking feet and slipped on her shoes. Her grandmother waited by the front door with a warm black shawl wrapped around her reed-thin body. Her cane tapped on the floor as she made her way to Emma. "Such sadness in your eyes, Emma."

"I'm sorry." Emma reached for her bonnet and lightweight coat.

"Don't be. Sunday worship will help, *kinn*. It will be a healing balm on your broken spirit."

"We shouldn't keep the Ottos waiting." Emma knew she sounded curt and impatient, but she was growing weary of her grandmother's incessant platitudes.

Norman met them at the bottom of the front porch step. He guided *Grossmammi* to the buggy, where Carol sat in the back. Emma followed. She heard the sound of a car door slam, saw a figure in the driver's seat of Adam's truck. The engine rumbled to life, and the truck pulled out of the driveway, exhaust pluming behind it as it roared down the road.

Norman didn't look in Adam's direction or say a word. He waited for Emma to climb in the back, then helped her grandmother in on the other side.

Emma knew what nobody was saying: Adam would leave again. Maybe he was on his way back to Michigan right now. If he left without saying good-bye, she wouldn't really be surprised. She still didn't know why he had come back to Middlefield in the first place.

She didn't want to know. Didn't want to care. What she wanted was for the pain and worry to cease. Instead, this morning she would sit on a hard wooden bench for three hours and pretend God loved her. Wanted the best for her.

Hadn't she been taught that all her life? Didn't she tell Adam the very same things when he took off for the Yankee world? Now she had to wonder which one of them was right. He still had his parents. A truck, a job, money. Probably a girlfriend too. Plenty of women would want Adam.

The buggy lurched forward. Emma gripped the edge of the seat in front of her.

Carol touched Emma's arm. "Are you all right?"

She nodded but couldn't speak. Carol had been

one of her mother's best friends. The reminder freshened Emma's grief.

Emma had lost, or was on the verge of losing, everything. And now she would be expected to be thankful to God because of it.

"Hope you don't mind walking to church this morning," Peter said to Mark. "Tobias and Rachel live about a mile down the road. No sense hitching up the buggy for such a short trip."

"Don't mind at all." Mark smiled, his black felt hat low on his forehead. "Nice day for it."

Clara shifted Magdalena to her other arm. The baby squirmed, wanting down. They should have brought the small pull wagon. That way she could drag Magdalena behind her. But Peter refused, saying the baby would try to crawl out. Knowing he was right didn't ease the ache in Clara's arms as she held on to her wiggly daughter.

Peter shifted Melvin's hand to Mark. "Would you mind?" Mark nodded and took hold of Melvin's hand.

Without a word Peter retrieved Magdalena from Clara. With his long strides he was soon out ahead of her again. Junior hurried to catch up. Mark and Melvin lagged behind.

Clara turned and saw Mark pointing out an owl hooting in a tree nearby. "Usually they come out at night, but some of them are stubborn," he said to Melvin. "They don't like the rules the other owls follow."

"I don't like no rules either." Melvin wiped his nose with the sleeve of his white shirt. Clara couldn't stand it when the boys did that. Now Melvin would run around with crust on his church shirt. But she held her peace. This time.

"There are rules for a reason," Mark said. The black gravel scratched underneath his shoes. "Or so *mei mudder* told me."

"Your *mudder* was right." Clara gave Melvin a sharp look. Before she could stop herself, her gaze drifted to Mark. He smiled. Nodded slightly. Then walked faster to catch up with Peter.

Clara crossed her arms over her body. For the two days Mark had stayed with them, he'd been the perfect guest. He had assisted Peter with chores, played games with the children, picked up after himself. He even helped her wash the supper dishes last night. She couldn't remember the last time Peter had done that.

As she washed and he dried, Mark joked about Peter's childhood and made comments about the quaintness of Middlefield. She had almost forgotten how good it felt to smile and laugh. His voice was soft, even gentle, as he told her good night.

Then the door shut behind them as she and Peter went into their bedroom. And last night, as they had so many times recently, she and her husband slept far apart in their bed.

Clara shook her head. Thinking about Mark while walking to church of all things! He was her husband's cousin. She had no business enjoying Mark's company over Peter's.

Even if she did.

Clara tried to clear her head as they reached the Bylers' house. Buggies lined up in the yard next to the white barn where the service would be held. A slight chill hung in the air, but not enough to move the service indoors. Clara took Magdalena from Peter and motioned for her sons to follow her. Soon she caught sight of Emma and her *grossmammi* standing near Carol Otto. Emma looked a million miles away, deep in sadness and grief.

Everyone filed into the barn, the men on one side, women on the other. Clara sat next to Emma. Magdalena stretched out her plump arms. Emma took her, settling the chubby baby in her lap and kissing the top of her light blue bonnet.

The service seemed twice as long today. Clara tried to focus on the hymns, on the sermon, on remembering her blessings instead of counting her worries. But she couldn't keep from looking across the aisle toward the men. Mark sat next to Peter, on the end of the bench. His attention faced forward, never straying. She could tell that Mark, like Peter, was strong in his faith. An admirable quality.

An unsettled feeling twisted in her stomach. She took Magdalena from Emma and drew her daughter close. She had to focus on her family. On the plan she had devised. It was the one thing she and Peter could agree on. She couldn't think about anything else.

Or anyone else.

After the service, Emma waited outside the barn. She hoped the Ottos wouldn't stay for the fellowship meal that followed worship. If they did, she would walk home. It was only a couple of miles. She would have walked to the service this morning, but her grandmother couldn't have made the journey.

Men gathered outside the barn, a sea of black hats, jackets, and trousers. White shirts peeked out, some men wearing suspenders, some not. She saw the women head inside Rachel Byler's house to help prepare the meal, a simple fare of sandwiches, pickles, and homemade dessert. She knew she should help them, but her feet wouldn't move.

She stood at the edge of the yard, surrounded by people, yet isolated. She searched the group and saw her grandmother. *Grossmammi* waved a hand in the direction of their home before turning to talk to a small group of her friends. Emma breathed out. Her grandmother understood why she had to leave. She turned to go, only to smack straight into a man's chest.

"*Ach*, I'm sorry!" She took a step back, too embarrassed to look up and see who she'd run into. She moved to brush past him but felt a hand on her shoulder.

"It's all right."

She didn't recognize the voice, and when she looked up at his face, she still didn't know who he was. He was a couple of inches taller than she, with blue eyes. Eyes that suddenly looked a bit familiar. His square chin was clean shaven. He smiled, revealing a chipped front tooth.

Her face reddened. "I'm sorry."

"You already said that." His smile widened. "And it's okay." He opened his arm, gesturing to his slim body. "No harm done."

Emma averted her gaze. "I'm glad." She started to leave when he spoke.

"You don't have to run off." He held out his hand. "Name's Mark King. Yours?"

"Emma." Her face warmed. She wasn't used to men she didn't know talking to her. He was quite bold.

"Nice first name. Do you have a last one?"

Her gaze met his. She pulled at the hem of her jacket, hesitating.

His smile faded. "That probably sounded rude. I didn't mean to be. It's just I noticed you sitting next to Clara King and thought maybe you were related. I'm Peter's cousin."

Her eyebrows lifted. "Clara is my sister."

"Then we're cousins. Very distant ones, by marriage." His smile returned. "Peter is my third cousin."

"Are you from Kentucky too?"

"Ya."

They stood there, and as the seconds ticked away, Emma's face heated more. But Mark seemed perfectly comfortable with the silence, still looking at her, still smiling. Maybe he was waiting for her to say something.

"Have you been in Middlefield long?"

"A few days. Not long enough to get to know my way around. Or to meet many people."

"Clara and Peter know just about everyone."

"I can see that." He poked his thumb over his shoulder. "I left Peter talking with the *mann* who owns this place."

"Tobias Byler."

"Ya. And your *schwester* took the *kinner* and went inside. Guess they kind of forgot about me."

She knew what that felt like. "I'm sure they'll introduce you to everyone once lunch starts."

"Oh, it's fine if they don't. I get along all right on my own. I met you, didn't I?"

She released the hem of her jacket. Mark King had an easy manner, a confidence about him. She could see some resemblance between him and Peter. "*Ya*. I guess you did."

"I should probably remind my cousin I'm still here. Are you coming inside for lunch?"

"*Nee*. I'm on my way home."

He frowned, but his eyes were still bright. "All right then. Maybe we'll see each other soon. Being as we're *familye* and all."

"Maybe."

"I would like that. Very much."

Mark headed toward the house, his stride as comfortable as his bearing. Just as she started to turn away, she saw him look over his shoulder. He grinned. Then he did something she'd never seen a man do, at least toward her. He put his hand over his heart, pointed at her, and walked away.

Clara frowned as she watched Mark approach the men huddled outside the barn. Her gaze went to the end of the driveway, where Emma stood frozen in place. Even from the front porch of Rachel's house, Clara noticed her sister's red cheeks. And they weren't rosy from the October air either.

Clara had seen the gesture Mark made at Emma.

Melvin tugged at Clara's skirt, but she ignored him. She stared at Emma, then at Mark. He had joined Peter and Tobias and a few other men, as comfortable among them as if he'd grown up in Middlefield.

When she looked at Emma again, her sister had started down the road in the direction of home. Clara felt another tug at her skirt. She looked down. "What do you want?"

"I'm *hungerich*."

"You always are." She sighed, brushing his brown bangs back from his forehead. "We'll eat in a few minutes, *ya*? Can you wait that long?"

He nodded and scampered down the porch steps to join a few other boys his age as they ran around the front yard. But she quickly lost interest in the children and looked toward Mark again.

Surely she couldn't be jealous. Of Mark? Of *Emma*? Yet his message to her had been clear. It was a romantic gesture, one that even made Clara's stomach flutter the tiniest bit. He was interested. And he wasn't afraid to let anyone see it.

But why? Clara loved her sister, but Emma was plain, even among their plain people. She had always been round, and over the past year Clara noticed Emma had put on more weight, especially in her hips. Clara had remarked about it a few times, only to be met with a glare and an order to mind her own business.

There were several other single girls in their church district. Unless Mark flirted with every woman he saw, why would he choose Emma over anyone else? Especially since he just met her.

During the rest of the afternoon, Clara watched, waiting to see if Mark paid attention to any of the other girls. He talked to several single young women, all of whom were quite pretty. But she couldn't tell if he'd made a connection with any of them.

Later that afternoon they walked home. Peter lagged behind with a sleeping Magdalena pressed against his strong shoulder. The boys ran a few feet ahead. It amazed her that they still had energy left after spending the afternoon playing and dashing around. Melvin whapped Junior on the back with his hat. Peter admonished them, and Melvin stopped. Soon they started kicking at pebbles on the road.

Mark moved up to walk beside her. "I met your *schwester* today," he said. "Nice *maedel*."

"There are lots of nice *maed* in our district." She stepped over a tiny puddle on the side of the road.

"*Ya*. I talked to a few." He didn't say anything for a moment. "Is Emma married?"

Clara paused. "*Nee*. She's not." She glanced at Mark. "Why do you ask?"

"Just curious. I'd like to get to know a few people around here. Especially *familye*. Living in Tennessee, I spent a long time being without relatives close by. Got kind of lonely sometimes."

She'd never known family members to make the flirty gesture Mark did with Emma. "My *schwester* lives with *mei grossmammi*. Their *haus* is about a mile farther down from ours."

"I see." He looked at Clara, his expression serious. "Maybe I'll have to visit sometime soon." Before she could respond, he ran to Junior and Melvin. "Race you *buwe* home!" Mark and her sons sprinted, Mark slowing his steps to make it an even competition.

"What were you and Mark talking about?"

Clara hadn't heard Peter come up beside her. She looked at her husband. "He was asking about Emma."

"He was?" The corner of Peter's lip lifted in a half smile. "Now that's interesting."

"I don't see anything interesting about it."

The expression of amusement vanished. Magdalena shifted restlessly in Peter's arms.

"Here, let me take her," Clara said.

"I can carry her the rest of the way home."

"I'll take her."

With a shrug Peter handed his daughter to his

wife. Then he lengthened his strides until he was well ahead of her.

Clara barely noticed.

Chapter Twelve

When Emma arrived home, she saw Adam's truck in his parents' driveway. Apparently he hadn't left yet. But it was only a matter of time.

She tried to put him out of her mind and headed toward the barn to check on Dill. She'd given the horse extra oats before church—as if that would make up for her lame leg. Spurred by guilt, Emma hurried. As she neared, she heard a tapping sound coming from inside the building, from Dill's stall. She looked over the top edge of the door. Adam was inside, pounding nails into Dill's foot.

"What are you doing?"

He looked up at her, two nails stuck between his teeth. Instead of answering, he took one of the nails and hammered it into the metal shoe. He had Dill's foot anchored between his thighs, but instead of wearing the leather apron a farrier would use, he had on his baggy blue jeans. Dust from Dill's feet covered his legs. When he finished putting in the final nail, he gently released her leg. She stepped on it gingerly.

"She needed special shoes." Adam patted Dill's back flank. The horse nickered in response.

"Your *daed* told me he called the vet," Emma said. "He's coming tomorrow."

"I know. I thought I'd save him the trouble and you the bill by picking up the shoes this morning. I also put a pad between the shoe and hoof. It will help even her hoof out a bit. Take a little of the pain away."

Emma forgot her anger with Adam and went inside the stall. She knelt next to Dill. "Was she in a lot of pain?"

"Hard to tell. Dill's a tough horse. A *gut* one too."

"Ya," Emma whispered. "She is." She rose and looked at Adam. "Why did you do this?"

"Because I could. I wasn't about to let Dill suffer because of your stubbornness."

Any gratitude she felt toward him disappeared. "I would never let my horse, or any of my other animals, suffer. You have no right to say that to me."

It was an instantaneous, defensive response. But she knew that on some level, Adam was right. She had let Dill down. The horse was suffering, just as her mother had suffered while she was sick. And it didn't matter how many people told her it wasn't her fault, that she had done the best she could, Emma didn't feel any better.

As tears threatened, Emma left Dill's stall. She didn't want to break down. Not now. Not in front of Adam. She'd humiliated herself in his presence before, and it was not an experience she ever intended to repeat.

Tommy meowed from the back corner of the barn. He did figure eights between her legs, and she poured a few more morsels of food in his dish, even though it had been full before she left for church. She sat down on the square hay bale nearby. Away in the woods she could hear the sharp sound of dogs barking, probably chasing the birds or squirrels. At least some of her pets were happy.

Adam went to her. He paused, then sat down. She angled away from him, her hands pressing the dark green skirt of her Sunday dress against her legs.

He leaned forward and rested his forearms on the knees of his dirty jeans. "Emma, I didn't mean it that way. I know you would never hurt anyone, or anything you care about. Dill's leg isn't your fault. I wanted to do something to help her, that's all."

She pulled at the strings of her *kapp*, hard

enough that she felt a bobby pin loosen. As she breathed in, she smelled the mixture of soap and barn dust on his skin and clothes. Why couldn't he just leave? She didn't want to be beholden to him for anything. But as usual, she never got what she wanted.

"How are you doing?" he asked.

"How do you think I'm doing?" She glared at him, sighed, and looked away. "*Mammi* died. Dill's lame. I'm—"

The rest came unbidden to her mind: *I'm alone and shattered.* She swallowed down the truth and said, "I don't need your pity."

"I didn't come back to Middlefield because of your *mammi*, although I am upset she died. And I am sorry about your horse. But I don't pity you."

She turned toward him but couldn't think of a thing to say.

"You don't need my pity, Emma. You're stronger than that."

She looked down at her shoes. Brown specks of dirt covered the toes. "I don't feel strong," she whispered.

"You are. You're the strongest person I know. Except for maybe your *grossmammi.*"

His words made her smile for just a moment, and that made her resent him even more. She was supposed to be mad at him, not charmed by him.

"The reason I came back was because of *mei*

mudder," Adam said. "Leona wrote and said she thought there was something wrong with her. That I should come back and see for myself. But I don't know what she's talking about. *Mamm* seems fine."

Emma shot up from the hay bale. "And you figured that out in a few days? Maybe if you'd been around longer, you would know more about what's going on."

"Do you know something? If you do, you'd better tell me."

She shook her head. "*Nee.* But if *mei gross-mammi* thinks something is wrong, then I believe her."

She heard movement behind her. Felt the heat of his body as he stopped, inches away. But he didn't touch her.

And after all that had happened between them, she still wanted him to.

"I am sorry, Emma. About everything that's happened."

"So am I. But being sorry doesn't change anything."

"I know. I can't change it either. I can only do what you'll let me. And right now, other than taking care of Dill's foot, that isn't much."

She heard his fancy tennis shoes shuffle across the straw and dirt of the floor. When she thought he had left, she turned around. He was standing in the doorway, looking at her.

"When the time comes, Emma, let me know what I can do. I'm sure you don't believe this, but I miss you. I don't think I realized how much until now."

Creak. Creak. Creak.

Mark pushed the toe of his boot against Peter's back porch. The swing moved back and forth. He stared at the small yard. Grass turning brown. Two rows of dry cornstalks edging a dying garden in the corner. A wooden sandbox, covered. Beyond the warped wire fence, a herd of black-and-white cows grazed on the last stubble of edible grass.

Not Peter's cows, or his pasture. He couldn't afford that much land and livestock. The lowing of the herd interspersed with the twitter of birds, the chirp of crickets, the beat of a horse's hooves on Bundysburg Road.

Creak. Creak. Creak.

Peter was inside. No doubt trying to talk to Clara, who was probably ignoring him. Maybe even arguing. The two of them did that a lot. Mark had noticed Clara watching him during church. At the fellowship gathering after the service. But most of all, he saw the spark of envy and confusion in her eyes when he asked about Emma.

Emma. His prospects were getting better by the day. He'd had no trouble winning over Clara, and it would be even easier with Emma. Single. Homely. Fat.

But Emma's looks didn't matter. Neither did her feelings. All that mattered was what she had to offer. What she could give him. She ought to kiss his feet and thank him for even noticing her.

Creak. Creak. Creak.

The back screen door banged shut. Junior ran out carrying a baseball and two gloves. "Wanna play catch, *Onkel* Mark?"

"Sure." Mark hopped up from the swing and took one of the gloves from Junior. "I can't think of anything I'd like to do more."

Adam walked out of the barn. He didn't want to leave Emma alone, but what else could he do? Dill's problems paled next to Emma's, and Adam figured he didn't know the half of it.

He slapped his hands against the legs of his jeans as he walked toward the house. Barn dust and the smell of horse rose in a cloud from the fabric. His father had taught him the skill of horse shoeing when Adam was very young. It felt good to work with a horse again. He'd missed that while living in Michigan. But it wasn't enough to make him come home. Definitely not enough to make him stay.

Adam went inside the house. He wasn't used to quietness, and the silence nearly overwhelmed him. It hadn't taken long for him to become accustomed to constant sound once he'd moved away. Appliances humming, televisions blaring, cell phones ringing. He thought he was used to it, didn't even register the noise anymore. But his soul welcomed the calm quiet of his parents' empty home.

The back door creaked open. His mother came in alone—his father probably unhitching their horse and settling the animals in for the evening.

Basic care of stock was the only work they could do on Sunday. Adam had broken that rule by driving his truck, buying supplies, shoeing the horse. Would his father be surprised, or angry? Adam shrugged. Like it mattered what his dad thought.

He went upstairs, put on a less dirty pair of jeans and a wrinkled shirt, and tossed his dirty stuff into a corner of the bedroom, just the way he did at his apartment. Then he reprimanded himself. He wasn't a two-year-old. He shouldn't be depending on his mother to pick up after him. And besides, he'd better go ahead and wash them, or he'd have to resort to wearing the Amish clothing hanging in his closet.

He grabbed the dirty clothes and took them downstairs. As he passed by the living room on his way to the basement, he saw his mother sitting on the couch. Heard her sniff. He stuffed the clothes underneath his arm and went to sit down next to her. "Something wrong?"

She shook her head. Wiped her eye with the heel of her hand. "*Nix*, Adam. Just missing Mary."

But his mother didn't look at him when she spoke. Instead her gaze drifted to the left and fixed on the wall. There was nothing to look at; no decorations of any kind in the house, other than a couple of plain white candles that were rarely used. Still she stared at the blankness.

Adam studied her. Her eyes were wet, despite the reassurance that everything was okay. He didn't doubt she missed Emma's mother. The funeral had been less than a week ago. Yet there was something else. He sensed it.

He set his clothes on the floor next to his feet. "You're not telling me everything, are you?"

She rose from the couch, smoothed the skirt of her blue church dress, and looked down at him. "There are some things a *mudder* doesn't share with her *sohn*. Or anyone else." She went upstairs. The door to her bedroom closed.

Leona had been right, and so had Emma. Something was wrong with his *mamm*, and if he'd been here instead of in Michigan, he would know what was going on. Maybe even have stopped it from happening. Instead he had no idea why his mother was upset, or what he could do about it.

When he came back to Middlefield at Leona's urging, he had thought his mother might be sick. But she didn't seem physically ill. It had to be something else. Something deeper.

He had to find out. And the only place to start was with his father.

He found his *daed* leaning against the white fence surrounding the pasture. The fence he and his father had made out of thick, heavy oak and painted with milk paint. Adam could practically feel the sweat dripping down his back and the sides of his face as he recalled weeks on end during that blistering August, digging post holes by hand. All he could think about was how easy and quick it would have been if they could have used a tractor with an auger attachment. They could have done the entire job in less than a week. The Amish way, it took almost a month.

Adam used to look at that fence with contempt, a reminder of time and effort wasted. Now, seven years later, it stood as straight and sturdy as it had the day they had pounded the last nail. And this evening, as the sun streaked the sky with purple, pink, and orange hues of dusk, a sense of pride and accomplishment coursed through him. Something he hadn't felt in a long time.

Adam moved to stand next to his father. "There's something wrong with *Mamm*."

His father didn't say anything. He stared at the pasture, his forearms resting on the edge of the top oak beam, his expression iron-hard.

"Did you hear me? I said something is wrong with *Mamm*."

"I heard you. Your *mudder's* fine."

"If she's fine, then why is she inside the *haus* crying?"

A muscle twitched on his father's cheek, but he didn't look at Adam. "Women cry. It's their nature."

"What if she's sick?"

"She's not sick. You would know that if you still lived here."

Adam clenched his fists. "Sounds like you don't care why she's upset."

His father slowly turned and stared at him. "Never tell me how I should feel about *mei fraa*." His tone was low, flat. "You are a stranger to us. You don't belong here anymore."

Adam had spoken those same words to his parents many times before he left, but hearing them echoed back to him from his father felt like a punch in the gut. "I may not belong here, but it doesn't mean I don't care."

"If you cared, you wouldn't have left."

"I couldn't stay. I couldn't stand it here anymore. You know that."

His father's rough, wrinkled hands curled around the fence. "All I know is that *mei sohn* rejects his *familye*. He rejects his faith."

"*Nee!* That's not what I'm doing. I reject the rules. The limits on what I can and cannot do."

"We are doing just fine without you here, Adam." His *daed* released his hold on the fence. "As I see you are doing just fine without us."

Anger built up in Adam. His father remained cold. Emotionless. Never raised his voice. Never yelled. For once Adam wanted him to show some shred of emotion. Even raw fury would be preferable to talking to a wall.

"That doesn't sound like forgiveness, *Vadder.* Isn't that what you're supposed to do? Forgive me? Try to make me stay?"

"When there is no repentance, there can be no forgiveness."

Adam knew that wasn't true. Scripture taught, and the Amish believed, that forgiveness was to be offered whether a person was repentant or not. Adam would have to repent in front of the church if he ever wanted to rejoin, but that didn't mean his father should withhold mercy. "You never wanted to understand me," Adam said. "You never tried."

"I can say the same for you." His father turned around. "I'm going inside." He walked away with his usual slow, measured steps. As if their conversation had never taken place.

Adam gripped the fence so hard that a splinter of wood dug into his skin and drew blood. Maybe he should leave. No one wanted him here. Not his father. Definitely not Emma. Only his mother seemed happy he'd returned. Maybe Leona too.

Then again, what did he expect?

Chapter Thirteen

"Here you *geh, maedel*." Emma coaxed Dill into eating a carrot from her palm. She stroked the horse's nose. Her appetite seemed off this morning. Emma wasn't sure why. Perhaps because Dill had spent several days in the barn, when she was used to getting exercise and working.

"Is that it? Do you need fresh air?"

She held on to Dill's bridle and opened the door to the stall. She led Dill outside. The horse whinnied and pranced a few steps. Then she settled down and allowed Emma to tether her in the backyard.

Emma whistled for Rodney, Archie, and Molly. One by one, with Molly moving the slowest, they came up to her. She sat down on the ground and pulled a couple of dog treats out of the pocket of her jacket. The dogs gobbled the treats, surrounding Emma as she petted and gave special attention to each one.

The eggs needed collecting, the kitchen cleaning, the porch sweeping. She had a pile of clothes to wash, and today was the day she baked bread for the week. She ticked off the tasks in her mind, but ignored them. All she wanted was the unconditional love of her dogs, and to hear Dill grazing behind her. For the first time in days, her spirit felt lighter.

Emma's balloon deflated with the sound of a buggy coming up the driveway. Probably Clara. Emma had avoided her yesterday. She hadn't wanted to talk about the fabric shop; in fact, she had managed to put it out of her mind completely. Now the thought of it made her stomach turn.

She heard the buggy lurch to a stop, and she got up and brushed the grass off her dress. Archie and Rodney loped off into the woods, while Molly slowly made her way to her spot under the back porch.

Emma checked on Dill one last time, breathed in the fresh morning air as if it would make her stronger, and went to face Clara.

Her sister wasn't in the kitchen. She went into the front room. "Clara?" she called. No response.

Then she heard a noise coming from the wood shop, metal clanging against metal. She ran to the shop and opened the door in time to see Peter drop a hammer into a wooden crate. "What are you doing?"

"Didn't Clara tell you?"

"Tell me what?"

"That I was coming to get your *grossvadder's* tools today."

Emma stalked over and looked down into the crate, which was rapidly filling with her grandfather's tools, then scowled up at Peter. "No, she did not." She snatched the hammer out of the box and hung it back on the Peg-Board.

Her brother-in-law lifted his hat and scratched the top of his head. "I don't understand. She was supposed to tell you yesterday at church."

"I left early." Her frown deepened. "What are you planning to do with them?"

"Sell them, of course. What did you think we were going to do?"

"You can't do that."

He laid his hand on her shoulder. "Calm down, Emma."

"Calm down?" She jerked away from him. "You're stealing *Grossvadder's* tools!"

"I'm not stealing anything." He started to reach out to her again, then stopped. "Listen to me. Clara said you two had discussed this. That you didn't have a problem with me taking the tools to the Middlefield Auction. We could get a *gut* price for them there."

"I don't care what kind of price you could get." Pressure filled her chest. "Clara didn't say anything about selling his tools."

Peter shook his head. "I wouldn't have come over if I knew you weren't ready to do this."

Emma forced an even tone. He didn't deserve her anger. He was only doing what Clara had told him. "It's not your fault, Peter. Please put the tools back."

She would never be ready to sell these tools. Or change this wood shop.

But instead of complying, Peter tugged on his beard. "Let's talk about this for a moment, *ya*? You do know about Clara's idea about transforming your *grossvadder's* shop into a fabric store. Right?"

Emma swallowed. "I do."

"And did you agree to it?"

Her head started to pound. Had she said something to Clara that put that thought in her sister's head? With everything that had happened the past week, she wasn't sure. "I can't remember."

"Emma, I understand how you feel." He looked around the dust-covered shop. Motes danced in the sunbeams coming through the one and only cloudy, smudged window. "If this belonged to *mei grossvadder*, I'd feel the same way. I'd want to keep part of him around me. But Clara's idea about turning it into a shop is a *gut* one. She's worried about how you and Leona will make ends meet. I am too. And we both know the tools aren't being used anymore."

"I see now. Clara sent you over here to convince me to agree to all this."

He shook his head. "*Nee*, that's not what—"

"Get out." She moved toward him, pointing at his chest. "I mean it, Peter, leave."

He paused for a moment. "All right, Emma. I'll *geh*." He headed for the doorway. "Believe me, I didn't mean to make you upset. And I'm not trying to talk you into anything."

"*Ya*, you are. Both you and Clara are."

Peter glanced down, then left.

Emma took in a deep breath. She coughed. Inches of old sawdust and dirt covered almost everything. The tools remained where her grandfather had last touched them. Most of them hung on the Peg-Board, but there were a hammer and screwdriver on the worktable, two mason jars of nails on the windowsill, and chunks of leftover wood stacked in the corner. Time stood still in the small building. It was the one thing in Emma's life that hadn't been changed or taken from her.

She leaned over Peter's crate and pulled out the wood plane. Her hands shook as she placed it back in its spot on the Peg-Board. "This is where you belong," she said out loud, "and this is where you'll stay."

* * *

"Clara! *Clara!*"

Mark heard Peter's booming voice echo throughout the house. He cast a sidelong glance at Clara, drying the dishes at the sink. Mark pushed a few pieces of oat cereal toward Magdalena. She grabbed them off the tray of her wooden high chair and shoved the cereal into her mouth. Drool dripped from her tongue in strings, and tufts of fine baby hair stood all over her head.

It was all Mark could do not to vomit. Children were messy, smelly, useless brats, the lot of them. But he had Peter and Clara convinced he thought their children were blessed gifts from God, to be nurtured and loved and shaped into good Amish people.

"Clara!" Peter stalked into the kitchen, his face red, eyes blazing. His gaze locked on her. "You lied to me!"

She dropped the kitchen towel, her eyes wide with shock. "What are you talking about?"

"Your *grossvadder's* tools? Emma?" Peter hovered over her, seeming not to notice that Mark was there. "You didn't tell her I was coming, did you?"

Mark gave Clara credit for not shrinking back. "She and I had already talked about it."

"Not according to her."

"Emma doesn't know what she wants."

Peter took a step back. He held on to his hat with a death grip, rolling and unrolling the brim in his hands. "Of course she doesn't. She's hurt. She's grieving. She wants to hold on to the memories she has left. Can't you understand that?"

"She has *Grossmammi*." Clara bent down and snatched the towel from the floor. "She has that big drafty *haus* that's going to fall down if it's not repaired."

Magdalena banged on her tray for more cereal. Mark tossed a few pieces in her direction, the way he might pacify a dog with a couple of kibbles. He focused on Clara and Peter's argument. This was getting interesting.

"It's not a pile of splinters yet." Peter tossed his hat on the counter. "You're pushing her before she's ready. I thought you were worried about her."

"I am." Clara twisted the towel in her hand. "But I'm worried about us too." She moved closer to him.

Mark had to strain to hear her voice.

"Think about what the shop could do for our *familye*, Peter. You wouldn't have to worry about finding a job. We would have our own business. The bills would be paid. No more scrimping and saving, hoping we can make it from month to month."

"You mean praying we make it month to month. Right?"

"Right."

Mark smirked at Clara's doubtful tone. She didn't believe that drivel any more than he did.

"What if this isn't God's will?" Peter asked. "What if He has something else planned for us?"

"Like what?" Her voice rose. "This is perfect, Peter. We have the facility. The tools we sell will help us start the business. We should have enough customers on our road alone to make a profit right away."

"And what about Emma? What does she get out of this?"

"A part of the profits. Financial security." She stared at Peter. "A purpose."

"And it's your job to decide your *schwester's* purpose?" He turned around and froze. "Mark." He pressed his lips in a grim line. "I didn't realize you were here."

"I'm sorry." He stood, making sure his expression reflected not only the solemn nature of the conversation but enough contrition to ease his cousin's anger. "I should have left as soon as you came in."

"*Ya.* You should have. This was a private argument."

"That you held in the most public room of our *haus.*" Clara moved to stand by Mark. "Don't apologize," she said to him. "It's no secret Peter doesn't have a job. And it doesn't take a genius to know that when no one's working, no money is coming in."

Peter looked ready to explode. He grabbed his hat off the counter, slammed it on his head, and stormed out of the room.

Clara leaned against the chair. She looked spent. Mark hid a smile. It wouldn't do for her to see him enjoying her suffering. "Are you all right?"

She nodded. "I'm fine."

"He was a little hard on you. Considering everything you do to keep your *familye* together and happy."

"I wish he understood." Her tone was filled with defeat. "He thinks as long as we pray hard and have enough faith, God will provide." She looked up at Mark. "He hasn't provided for nine months. And when a perfect opportunity for God's provision does come up, *mei mann* rejects it." She shook her head. "I don't understand him."

"How about if I talk to Emma?" Mark looked at her. They both ignored Magdalena's yammering in the background. "Maybe I can convince her that this is an opportunity she can't pass up."

Clara paused. A shadow passed over her eyes. "You barely know her."

"But I know you. And you're *schwesters*. You can't be all that different."

"You have *nee* idea." She sighed. "Why would you do this?"

"Because you're right. You and your *kinner* deserve to be taken care of, to not have to worry about money. But most of all, because we're *fami-lye*."

"And that's the only reason you want to see Emma?"

Mark shrugged. "She's single." He gave Clara a crooked little grin. "Maybe if she had some-thing else to occupy her mind and time, she wouldn't be so resistant to what you want to do."

Clara raised an eyebrow at him. "Maybe you're right." Then she frowned. "But, Mark, I don't want you to feel you have to like Emma. Or pre-tend to be interested in her. I'm frustrated with her right now because she's not being reason-able. But I don't want her to get hurt. She's had her heart broken before. I don't think she could take that again."

Mark looked into her eyes. "Clara, I promise you, I won't break Emma's heart."

Adam shoved the last bite of a sausage and egg biscuit into his mouth as he turned onto Bundys-burg Road. He hadn't seen either of his parents since yesterday evening, and this morning his

mother hadn't come downstairs to make breakfast. When Adam looked outside the window, his
father's buggy was already gone. He must have
left before sunrise. Which meant he must have
taken care of the animals a couple of hours before
that.

Adam would have made his own breakfast, but
he didn't want to mess up his mother's pristine
kitchen. A cherry Danish in a bag sat on the seat
next to him, and a Styrofoam mug of coffee in
the truck's cup holder. Cherry was her favorite.
She deserved a treat.

A buggy came toward him in the opposite direction. He slowed his speed, remembering his
aggravation at rude drivers when they whipped
by him in their cars, sometimes honking their
horns. Usually reckless teens did that, trying to
spook the horse. They had no idea how dangerous
that was, not only to the horse and buggy driver,
but to everyone on the road. Still, that didn't keep
some morons from doing it.

He parked the truck in the driveway, grabbed
the coffee and Danish, and got out. It was an odd
juxtaposition, the big black pickup truck and his
Amish clothes. He hadn't been able to wash his
Yankee clothing yesterday. Work on Sunday vi-
olated the Sabbath, and he wouldn't do that to
his mother. He couldn't care less about what his
father thought.

The smell of perked coffee filled the kitchen. He went to hug his mother. "I see you're up."

"I'm sorry I slept in this morning." Her *kapp* was perfectly in place, the pleats of her dress pressed and the skirt without a wrinkle. "I should have had breakfast ready for you."

He noticed she didn't mention his father. "That's all right. I brought a treat for you." He held out the cup of fast-food coffee and the bag with the Danish.

She smiled, yet the emotion didn't reach her eyes. "That was thoughtful of you, Adam." She looked him up and down as she accepted the food. Her expression held a little more hope. "I see you decided to wear your Amish clothes."

He couldn't bring himself to tell her the reason why. It was a good thing he had only gone through the drive-through to get breakfast. He would have gotten more than a few strange looks at his beard and mustache. Maybe he should shave them off after all. It would make things simpler. Make his mother happy.

She set the coffee and Danish on the table but didn't touch them. Instead she went to the sink and turned on the tap. "Fried chicken and mashed potatoes okay for supper, Adam?"

"Whatever you fix is fine." He looked around the kitchen. "Where's *Daed*?"

His mother turned off the tap. It took a second

before she faced him. "I'm not sure." This time her smile was too wide. "He was gone before I got up."

"Probably running some errands in town."

"*Ya*. Probably." She didn't say anything for a moment. Then she held up one finger. "Could you do a favor for me?"

"Anything," Adam said.

"I have a pie plate that belonged to Mary." She opened a lower cabinet and pulled out a glass dish. "Could you take it to Leona? I've had it for years, actually. I should have given it back to Mary sooner."

"Sure." Adam took the plate. "I'll be right back."

"Wait." His mother picked up the coffee and Danish. "I'm not hungry, and I already had my coffee. Maybe Emma might want this?"

He took the bag from her. Emma probably didn't want anything from him. But at least he would offer it to her.

Chapter Fourteen

Adam headed for Emma's house with the pie plate tucked under his arm. Steam rose from the small hole in the coffee lid. Even if Emma rejected breakfast, this gave him a good excuse to check on Dill. He'd been thinking about the horse this morning, hoping the pad on her foot had helped a bit last night.

He tucked the folded edge of the bag between his teeth and knocked on the door. Waited for an answer, then knocked again. He didn't hear any movement from inside the house. His eyes drifted to Emma's grandfather's old workshop. He left the porch and walked to the wood shop door. Emma was sweeping with harsh, sharp strokes. A giant cloud of dust hung in the room.

He sneezed. She looked up. Thin white trails ran from the bottom of each eye through the dust on her cheeks. She'd been crying. He hated to see her cry.

Emma turned from him. "*Geh* away."

He ignored her command and set the coffee, bag, and plate on the dirty counter. "Emma, what's wrong?"

"Nothing's wrong. I'm cleaning up." She sniffed. "Can't you see what a mess this place is? I shouldn't have let it get this way." She brandished the broom, kicking up more dirt.

Adam shook his head. The shop hadn't been touched in years. Why was she blaming herself for its condition now? He took the broom from her hand and was surprised when she let him.

"I brought some coffee. And a Danish, if you want it."

She turned to him and swiped at her cheek with her hand. The attempt only smeared the dirt all over her face. He couldn't help but smile.

"What?"

"Remember the time it rained for three days straight? We were like, what, ten, eleven years old?"

She nodded.

"And there was that huge mud puddle in my backyard. You dared me to jump in it."

"But you were too chicken."

"I was too smart." He grinned wider. "Then I dared you."

"But I was even smarter." Her lips began to twitch. "When I said I would, I pushed you in instead."

"And I grabbed you and yanked you down with me." He laughed.

"What made you think of that?"

"Your face."

All the humor in her eyes vanished. She rubbed her face again. "I must look a mess, then."

"*Nee*, Emma. You don't look a mess. Not to me."

Emma couldn't move. She couldn't pull her gaze from Adam. His words reached through her embarrassment, through her pain, to the tender part inside her. Worst of all, he didn't realize how easily he could do it. A kind look. A friendly touch on the arm. An offhand comment, like the one he just made.

She picked up the cup of coffee and took a long drink. The hot liquid scalded her mouth.

"Whoa, careful." He took the cup from her. "That's fast-food coffee. It'll burn the taste buds right off your tongue."

Her cheeks reddened. She looked away, not daring to eat the Danish. She'd probably choke on it if she tried.

Adam set the coffee back on the counter. "How's Dill?"

"She's doing fine. I tethered her in the backyard a little while ago. She needed the sunshine. A change of scenery too."

"*Gut* idea." He picked up the bag. "You going to eat this?" When she shook her head, he pulled out the Danish. "Do you mind?"

She shrugged. She waited for the usual agitation and resentment she felt when she was around him to surface. It didn't come. Things between them felt almost…normal. Or else she was too tired to feel anything at all.

He took a bite of the pastry. "Stale. I like Leona's better." He dropped it back in the bag. Craned his neck, looking around the shop. "Don't you think cleaning this place could wait? It's kinda nice the way it is right now. Feels like your *grossvadder* is close by. He always left the place a mess, if I'm remembering right."

"You are." Emma couldn't believe it. Finally, someone who understood why she didn't want to change the workshop. Then again, Adam usually was the only one who did understand her. But it didn't matter anymore. "It won't be like this for long," she said, not meaning to voice the thought aloud.

"Why?"

A knock sounded on the door. Emma turned. A man stood in the doorway, his smile revealing his chipped tooth. Mark.

"Hope I'm not intruding." He crossed the threshold, not waiting to be invited, and held out his hand to Adam. "Mark King. Peter's cousin."

Adam returned the greeting. "Adam Otto. Emma's neighbor."

Neighbor. Not friend. Definitely not boyfriend. He wasn't even really her neighbor anymore. She looked from Adam to Mark. "If you're looking for Peter, he's not here."

"I know. That's why I'm here. I came to see how you were doing." Mark moved a step closer to her. "Peter said you were upset."

So now Peter was telling everyone what happened. The betrayal deepened. "I'm fine. We had a misunderstanding."

"Sounded like more than just a misunderstanding." Mark looked around the workshop. "This used to be your *grossvadder's*?"

"*Ya.* You really didn't have to come by. I'm doing okay. I'm sorry Peter was upset—"

"Oh, he wasn't just upset. He was angry."

Emma blanched. "He was?"

Mark nodded. "Said something about how you weren't ready to face reality. And about some tools? That if you would sell them it would help all of you out financially?" He shrugged. "But I didn't hear everything. The conversation wasn't *mei* business."

"*Nee.* It wasn't."

Emma turned at the sound of Adam's voice.

Mark's brow lifted. "Oh. I'm sorry. Is it your business, then?"

Adam didn't respond. But Emma saw his jaw clench—a sure sign that he was upset. What did he have to be mad about? This wasn't Adam's business either. At least Mark was *familye*. Adam was…nothing.

"I'm an old *freind* of Emma's," he finally said. "If she's upset about something, I do consider it my business."

Mark scrutinized Adam's face. "Is that your truck in the driveway next door?"

Adam nodded.

"Nice. I noticed the plate is from Michigan."

"It is."

"And I suppose your *fraa* doesn't mind your deep concern for Emma? Or is she on her way over too? It doesn't look very *gut* for a married *mann* to be alone with a woman who isn't his wife."

"I'm not married," he said through gritted teeth.

"Ah. I just thought with the beard…" Mark rubbed his clean-shaven chin. "Then again, you have a mustache. And a truck. You're not Amish, are you?"

"I don't see what that has to do with any—"

"Seeing that you're not Amish, and not *fami-*

lye..." Mark shrugged and looked at Emma. "We should probably talk about this privately."

Emma's head spun. She couldn't tell if Mark was digging at Adam or just pointing out a fact.

Adam's gaze bored into Mark. "You're Peter's cousin? Funny, I don't remember him mentioning you before."

"From what I understand, you haven't been around here for a while."

Emma frowned. What did Mark know about Adam? Maybe Clara had gossiped about him to Mark. She'd never liked Adam much since he left the community.

Adam closed the distance between them. "What exactly are you doing here?"

Mark stepped back, his eyes wide, innocent. "I told you. I'm checking on Emma."

"As you can see, she's fine."

"Because you're here?"

"Ya." Adam lifted his chin. "Your concern is noted, but not needed."

Mark held up his hands. "No reason to get upset." He looked at Emma. Compassion filled his eyes. "You've been through a lot lately, Emma. I wanted you to know, if you need anything, I'm here." He glanced at Adam. "I'm planning to stay in Middlefield for a while. I won't be going anywhere anytime soon."

* * *

It took everything in Adam's power not to lose his temper. Was Emma really buying this? From the soft look on her face, she was.

"Here." Mark turned from Adam and pulled a handkerchief from his pocket. "You have a little dust on your face." He touched Emma's cheek with the corner of the cloth. "Right here."

Emma's face flushed a bright red. So did Adam's, but not for the same reason. She took the cloth, rubbed it on her face for a second, and started to hand it back.

"*Nee*. Keep it." He smiled.

Adam wanted to wipe that smile right off his face. Anger bubbled inside him. This guy was a fake and a phony. There was a dead emptiness in his eyes that all his charm and false concern couldn't hide. Why didn't Emma see it?

"*Danki,*" Emma said in a soft voice.

For some strange reason, the quality of the tone affected him. Seeing her with Mark. Hearing her voice—low, almost sultry. A tight knot coiled in his gut.

Mark took several steps toward Emma. They were close to each other now.

Too close. Adam couldn't stand it anymore. "I think you should leave."

Fake surprise registered on Mark's face. "Did

I do something wrong?" He looked at Emma. "I didn't offend you, did I?"

She shook her head. "*Nee*. I appreciate the concern." She glanced down at the ground. "It's nice to know someone cares."

Adam did a double take. She didn't think he cared?

"I do," Mark said. "And I meant what I told you. Let me know if you need anything." A ghost of a smirk appeared on his face. "Adam. Nice to meet you." He turned and left without waiting for Adam's response.

Not that Adam would have given him one. "I don't believe that guy."

Emma turned toward Adam. There was a round circle of white on her plump cheek where she had used Mark's handkerchief. "What?" she asked.

He pointed in the direction of the door. "Can't you see what he's doing?"

"*Ya*, I can. He's being nice to me." She held up his handkerchief. "He gave me a handkerchief to wipe the dirt off *mei* face, instead of making fun of me."

"I wasn't making fun. I thought you looked—"

"I don't want to know." She turned her back to him. "Just *geh*, Adam. Please."

He hadn't been able to say anything right around her since he'd come back to Middlefield.

But before Mark showed up, they almost had a normal conversation. "Emma, if I hurt your feelings, I didn't mean to."

"You never do." Her voice sounded stuck in her throat. She picked up the broom and started sweeping again. "I've got work to do."

"Can I at least check on Dill?"

She didn't look at him. *"Ya."*

He moved past her. When he reached the door, she said, "Her appetite was a little off this morning."

"I'll let you know if there's a problem."

She went back to sweeping.

Adam stalked outside, grasping for calm. He saw Mark climbing into the buggy. Good. Emma needed that guy around like Dill needed another lame leg. Adam headed for the backyard to check on the horse.

"Adam."

He stopped at Mark's voice. As tempted as he was to ignore the man, he couldn't stop himself from turning around. "What?"

"Sorry to upset you in there." Mark took a step forward and held out his hand. "No hard feelings?"

Adam looked at him. A straw hat, a light blue shirt with a navy blue jacket over it. A bowl-shaped Amish haircut. Broadfall pants and boots.

Everything about his appearance was Amish.

Yet Adam sensed deceit in him. Deep, like an underground stream of poisoned water. And hidden behind a pious Amish life.

Or maybe Adam had spent too much time watching crime shows in his apartment in Michigan. Still, he didn't like the guy.

Adam shook his hand anyway, resisting the urge to wipe his palm on his pants after touching Mark's clammy skin. *"Nee."* He maintained an even tone. "We're *gut*."

"Then I hope you don't mind if I ask you a question. Kind of a personal one."

Adam crossed his arms. *"Geh* ahead."

"You and Emma…anything going on between you two?"

"What do you mean?"

"You know." Mark glanced away. Kicked at a pebble on the ground. Looked at Adam again. "Are you together?"

Of course the answer was no. But memories from two years ago came flooding back, driving a stake of pain in his heart. He tried not to think about the day he left, how badly it had ended for him and Emma. He thought time would have healed at least part of that wound, but it hadn't. No, he and Emma weren't together. They never would be.

But he didn't want Mark anywhere near her.

"We're close." A partial truth, but more of a lie. He wasn't sorry to tell it.

Mark's gaze narrowed. "How close?"

"Close enough that you don't have to be concerned about her. I'm watching out for her."

The man grinned. He was always grinning. Or smirking. "I understand. Then she's a lucky *maedel*, to have someone care about her that much." He stepped into the buggy and gathered the reins, then poked his head out the window. "One more thing."

Would this guy leave already? "What?"

"You're a liar. And a bad one." Mark's smile widened, like a hunter who knew he had his prey cornered. "I'll see you around. Emma too. You can count on it." He tapped the reins against the horse's flank and drove away.

Chapter Fifteen

"I haven't seen much of you this morning." *Grossmammi* put a plate in front of Emma. "I was waiting for you to bring in the eggs."

"I forgot about the eggs." She had put Dill back in her stall and checked the animals' food and water, but collecting the eggs completely slipped her mind, which was already full of thoughts of Adam, Mark, and the workshop. She pushed away from the table. "I'll *geh* get them right now."

The old woman waved her hand. "Sit. Eat your lunch. The eggs can wait. We have plenty in the cooler anyway." She lowered herself into the chair across from Emma. "Shall we pray?"

They bowed in silent prayer. When Emma looked up, her grandmother wasn't eating. Alarm went through her. "Where's your lunch?"

"I'm not hungry."

"What's wrong?"

"Nix." Grossmammi shook her head. "I had a big breakfast this morning."

Emma doubted that. She'd never seen her grandmother eat a large meal. "You would tell me if something was wrong, *ya?*"

"Of course I would. Now you eat. You have to be hungry after all the work you've been doing."

She picked up the tuna salad sandwich, made with the last slices of bread. She should have baked three loaves this morning. Guilt overwhelmed her. "I haven't been doing that much."

"The dirt on your face says otherwise."

Emma touched her cheek. She thought she'd washed all the grime from her hands and face before lunch. "I was checking on Dill. Giving the dogs some attention." She took a bite of the sandwich, surprised that she was hungry after her discussion with Adam. "Sweeping out the workshop."

"Oh? So you've decided to help Clara with her fabric business?"

She swallowed. "They're not giving me much choice." Irritation rose as she thought of Peter taking the tools off the wall. "Peter came over this morning. He wants to sell *Grossvadder's* tools. I told him *nee.*"

"Because?"

"Because he doesn't have a right to." She

dropped her sandwich. "He and Clara aren't even giving me a chance to think about this. Then Mark stopped by—"

"Wait. Who's Mark?"

"Peter's cousin. From Kentucky. He's staying with them." She told her grandmother what Mark had said about Peter being angry.

"Strange. That doesn't sound like Peter. He wouldn't discuss personal business like this with a stranger."

"Mark's not a stranger."

"He is in this situation. Plus, why would Peter be mad that you didn't want to sell the tools today? What is he in such a hurry for?"

"I don't know." Emma shoved the plate away, her appetite gone. "Maybe you should talk to him and Clara. Convince them not to do anything yet."

"I thought you were going to talk to Clara."

"Why bother?" Emma crossed her arms. "She didn't even tell me Peter was coming over. Plus, I can't change her mind. Mark said something about financial problems."

Grossmammi lifted a graying brow. "With her and Peter?"

"I guess. Or maybe they were talking about us."

"I know Peter's been out of work for a while." Her grandmother's forehead wrinkles deepened.

"So have a lot of men in the community. These are hard times for everyone."

"Not everyone." Adam seemed to be doing just fine.

"When did Mark leave?"

"About an hour ago. Right before Adam."

"Adam was over too?"

"*Ya*. He brought coffee. And a Danish." The sharp pain in Emma's shoulders eased as she thought of the memory they'd talked about. When they both fell in the puddle, they'd been covered in mud from head to toe. She'd even gotten some in her mouth, she'd laughed so much. Both of their mothers were furious with them, and they were grounded from seeing each other for a week. But it had been worth it.

"You're smiling a little bit."

"I am?"

"*Ya*. You two are on better terms now?"

She shook her head, the pleasant memories and emotions they evoked disappearing. "No. That's not possible." She held up her hand. "And I know what you're going to say next. 'With God, everything is possible.' Not this time."

Grossmammi tapped her crooked finger on the table. "Maybe you should let me say what's on my mind before you jump to conclusions."

Emma nodded. Kept quiet.

"I was going to ask if Adam said how long he's staying in Middlefield."

"He didn't. I'm sure it won't be much longer. He can't stand being here."

"That's not completely true. Only during his *rumspringa* did he start thinking about leaving."

Which coincided with escalating arguments with his father. But her grandmother didn't know everything. She didn't know how trapped Adam had felt, not just by his parents and the faith. He'd been trapped by her too. He had said as much the night he left.

She jumped up, picked up her plate, and took it to the counter. "I'll get started on the bread dough."

"All right." *Grossmammi* slowly rose from her chair. "I think I'll *geh* upstairs and take a nap. Maybe do a little praying." She looked at her granddaughter. "From what I'm hearing, sounds like we all need it."

"Did you talk to her? Convince her to let us get started?" Clara pulled out one of the kitchen chairs as Mark walked into the room. He sat down, took off his hat, and laid it on the table.

"Where's Peter? The *kinner*?" he asked.

"Magdalena is napping. Peter took the *buwe* outside after lunch." Instead of looking for a job, he was playing with his kids.

The mean-spirited thought brought with it a stab of guilt. Peter was an excellent parent. She couldn't begrudge him that. He was always teaching the children or showing them something new. All the things a father was supposed to do.

Yet it would ease her mind if he would spend more time finding work and less time playing with the boys. There would be plenty of time for that. They had to get this fabric shop off the ground. Emma stood in the way. And now Peter wasn't helping. Ridiculous.

Mark leaned forward, lowering his voice. "I did talk to Emma. I think she'll come around soon. I'll talk to her again about it tomorrow."

Clara breathed out. She was so thankful to have an ally in Mark. "Did she agree to sell the tools?"

"Not yet. But when I got to the *haus* she was cleaning out the workshop. A *gut* start, *ya*?"

"Maybe. A better start would be to sell the tools. It might be preferable if she stayed away from the workshop for a while. Peter can clean it out."

"I can help as well." His usual smile disappeared. "We may have another problem, though."

"What?"

"Adam Otto."

"He won't get in the way."

"I don't know about that." His voice grew

doubtful. "He warned me to stay away from her. He looked angry. Almost to the point of fighting me."

"Did he now?" Clara stood and put her hands on the waistband of her light green dress. "You don't have to worry about Adam. He's always had a problem with his temper. But I've never known him to act on it. Besides, I'm sure he won't be staying in Middlefield for long."

"Why is he here?" Mark rose and stood near her. Too near for comfort. "Obviously he's not Amish anymore. He seemed to hold…contempt… for our ways."

Clara nodded. "*Ya*, he does. And I don't know why he came back. When he left he burned more than one bridge with his *familye* and *freinds*."

"Does that include Emma?"

She paced the width of the table, then halted and turned to him. "He's the one who broke her heart."

"He was with her when I walked into the workshop." Mark crossed his arms over his chest. "Maybe she's forgiven him."

"She's a fool if she has." Clara faced him. "Don't let Adam keep you from Emma, Mark. She's much better off with someone like you. Someone Amish. Who puts *familye* first. Adam only thinks about Adam. No one else."

Mark went to stare out the window. "I don't

know, Clara. If there is something going on with them, I don't want to interfere. That would only cause Emma more trouble. I wouldn't want to complicate things for her."

Touched by the sincerity in his eyes, Clara nodded. "It's a wonderful thing that you're sensitive to her feelings. Adam never was."

"Then he didn't realize how special your *schwester* really is. I haven't known her long, but I can tell she's a caring, sweet *maedel*. She doesn't deserve to be hurt."

"*Nee*, she doesn't." Clara tapped her fingertip against her lip. "You let me take care of Adam. Focus your attention on Emma. Not just because of the shop. That's important, *ya*, but she needs someone who will appreciate her." She smiled. "I think you're that *mann*, Mark."

Clara made a note to visit her grandmother too. She hadn't had a chance to discuss the idea with her. If she had both *Grossmammi* and Mark on her side, Emma and Peter would have to come around.

"What about Peter?"

"I'll talk to him." Tonight. She would be firm with him. More firm than ever before. Being so insistent with her husband would go against everything she'd been taught about being a proper Amish wife. Her mother had modeled that ideal with Clara's father, knowing when to defer to him, when to support him, when to gently nudge him in a different direction than he might have considered.

But Clara's father wasn't like Peter. Her father worked every day of his life in the workshop with his own *daed*. And when business was slow, he picked up odd farming jobs with the neighbors nearby. Clara couldn't remember a time when either of her parents expressed worry about money. They had never gone without.

Her family shouldn't either. And if she had to push Peter, she would do it. If she had to force Adam to stay away from Emma, she would do that too.

She'd do whatever it took to make sure she was secure. Because one thing was crystal clear—it was up to her. Alone.

Adam went home, still fuming about Mark's last words. Maybe he was right. Maybe Adam was a terrible liar, but that was better than being adept at it. Guess it took a really good liar to sniff out a bad one.

One thing he knew: he had to keep Mark King away from Emma.

He slammed through the front door and flung himself down on the couch. Silence washed over him, a balm to his tormented soul. Once again he was struck by the quietness of the house. It wasn't as unnerving as it had been the past few days. It had started to feel like…home.

He shook his head. He had a home. In Michigan.

Yeah, a dingy one-bedroom apartment with a frosted-over freezer, he said to himself. *And don't forget the stains on that ugly brown carpet from the previous renters.* He shuddered to think what caused those. Especially the ones in the bedroom.

He sat up and surveyed the room. The polished wood floor. The stark, dust-free furniture. Someone had cracked open the living room window, and fresh air wafted in, bringing with it the loamy scent of autumn—earth, fallen leaves, wood smoke.

Adam was getting comfortable here. But that might be because he was a guest, not a prodigal son who had returned to live under his father's heavy thumb.

He thought about the Bible story of the prodigal, a story he'd heard more than once in his life. The wayward younger son came home from his wanderings and was greeted by his father with an elaborate welcome, a feast, and forgiveness. But what about the rest of the story? What happened, Adam wondered, after the celebration was done? Did they go back to the way things were before? Did the wandering son come once more to resent his father's rigid ways? Did they settle into an uneasy truce where the two of them barely talked because it was easier on them both?

And what about the prodigal's mother? Was she even in the picture, working behind the scenes to help heal the breach between the men she loved?

He thought about *Mamm*. Emma. Leona. Mark. Four reasons for him to stay, at least a little while longer.

He fingered his beard and mustache. If he was going to stay, he should shave this thing off. Might as well keep the Amish clothes too. The lighter fabrics were easier to wash in the hand-cranked washer anyway. And they dried faster than his sweatshirts and thick jeans.

He stood and went to the bathroom where he found a razor and a small pair of scissors he could use to trim the hair down first. Funny, he didn't remember his mother keeping these scissors in the bathroom before.

As he haphazardly attacked his chin, he planned his strategy. He'd use the emergency telephone in the barn to call work and ask for a leave of absence. He'd drop a check for next month's rent in the mail so he didn't get kicked out of his apartment. He'd pack up his Yankee clothes, so when he was sure his mother was all right and Mark was out of Emma's life, he could

pick up the suitcase and go. His stay here, while
longer than he'd planned, was still temporary.
He didn't see how anything would change that.

Chapter Sixteen

The next morning, before sunrise, Clara slipped out of bed, being careful not to disturb Peter. But as she crept across the room, she stubbed her toe on the edge of the twin bed that lay perpendicular to their double. She gasped a little but managed not to cry out. The boys stirred, then shifted and went back to sleep.

On a chair in the corner she had laid out her clothes the night before. Without turning on the light, she pulled off her nightgown, slid into her dress and long stockings, and started winding her hair into a bun.

"Clara?" Peter's hoarse, quiet voice reached her ears.

Her hands froze for a moment, gripping the thick coil of hair at the crown. She pushed in a couple of bobby pins to secure it. "I didn't mean to wake you," she whispered. She kept her back to the bed and heard the sheets shift as Peter moved.

"I wish you had. I had no intentions of sleeping in."

"I was just dressing." She turned and almost bumped into him. Clara backed up a step. "I would have awakened you before I went downstairs. I didn't want to disturb the *buwe*."

He didn't answer her. Instead he reached up and cupped her cheek. She flinched. He must have felt it. Sensed it. He withdrew his hand. "So. What are you doing today?"

She turned and put on her *kapp*. "I'm going to *Grossmammi's*. I need to talk to her and Emma."

"How are you getting there?" The mattress springs creaked as Peter sat down.

"Walking." She hesitated. "Mark is accompanying me."

"Mmph." Melvin grunted, turned over on his side, and stuck his feet into Junior's face. Junior, who slept deeper than a bear in winter, didn't move.

"Clara." Peter stood. "Outside."

She followed her husband to the hallway. The bedroom door shut with a soft click. "Why didn't you mention this to me yesterday?" he asked.

Clara straightened the ribbons of her *kapp*. "I assumed you'd be busy."

"Doing what?"

"Looking for a job!" At his warning look, she lowered her voice. They both stepped away from the bedroom. This time she faced him, her gaze matched with his. "I thought you might have some prospects. In town, maybe."

"Actually, I do."

Her brow lifted. *"Ya?"*

"Ya." Clara looked at him. Clad in only a T-shirt and the pants he'd slipped on just before leaving the bedroom, he appeared vulnerable. Weak, almost.

"Doing what?"

"Temporary work. Repairing a roof on a school in Parkman."

Now she knew why he was hesitant. "Parkman. How will you get there?"

"A van will pick me up. The job should last a week."

Clara did some mental calculating. "Are they paying transportation?"

Peter looked away. *"Nee.* Have to get my own."

"So most of the money you'll make will pay for the taxi."

He nodded. "It's the only job available right now. I'll keep—"

"Looking. I know." She turned around and headed for the stairs. "I'll get *mariye-esse* started."

Peter touched her arm. "Clara. Wait."

She paused. Turned around. "What?"

"Why is Mark going with you? You and the *kinner* can walk to Leona's by yourselves."

"Julia's watching the *kinner*." Clara's cheeks heated. But why should she feel guilty? Mark was her cousin. He was interested in her sister. And she and Mark were a team, trying to start a business. She could have been a team with her husband, but he insisted on working against her.

Peter's eyebrows flattened. "Just you and Mark."

She swallowed. "*Ya*. He wants to see Emma."

"So he says."

Clara frowned. "What do you mean by that?"

"I mean, his interest in Emma is kind of sudden, don't you think?"

"Just a few days ago you thought it was a *gut* idea."

"I changed my mind. Mark hasn't said anything to me about Emma. He hasn't talked to me much at all." Peter's gaze narrowed. "Can't say the same for you, though. *Mei* cousin seems more than eager to spend time with *mei fraa*."

"You sound jealous."

"Should I be?"

When she didn't respond right away, he pressed his lips together. "Clara, I know you're upset about me being out of work. You think I

want this? That I want the community to know I can't support *mei familye*?"

For the first time in weeks, Clara felt a pang of sympathy. "*Nee.* I don't." She moved forward, tentatively touched his chest with her hand, and looked into his eyes. "That's why we need to have the business. Then I—both of us, won't have to worry about this."

"We shouldn't be worrying. God has a plan. I'm just not sure opening this fabric shop is it."

"I thought you agreed it was a *gut* plan."

"It is, but not at the expense of Emma and Leona." He rubbed the back of his neck. "We've already talked about this."

"*Ya.* But we haven't settled it."

"Clara, I'm saying it's settled."

She looked at him. Her husband. The man she promised to love forever. The man she had been so sure God had set apart for her. She wanted to shake sense into him. "So you're saying there's no business? That *Grossmammi* and Emma will have to fend for themselves? Or Emma will have to get a job? Oh, wait." She put her hands on her hips. "There are no jobs."

Peter's jaw clenched. Without a word he turned his back on her, returned to the bedroom, and shut the door behind him.

Clara lifted her chin. But her lower lip trembled. Her hands shook. She had pushed Peter. He had pushed back. But they were still at the same place they'd always been. At odds.

Near the bottom of the stairs, Mark stayed out of sight, but not out of hearing range. He grinned in the darkness and flexed his fingers. The plan was working perfectly, as he'd known it would. He had convinced Clara of everything—his interest in Emma, his support in seeing the shop become a reality. He rubbed his palm against the smooth wood of the stair railing. For someone who thought she was so clever, she was quite stupid.

Peter, on the other hand, wasn't as dim as Mark had initially thought. Peter suspected too much. He'd have to be more careful. Offer to help Peter out with the chores again, or do something to show his cousin his appreciation as a houseguest. Clara underestimated her husband. She just didn't know it.

The bedroom door shut. With quiet steps Mark went to the kitchen. He picked up the coffeepot from the stove and took it to the sink. As he rinsed it out, Clara entered the room.

"You don't have to do that." She joined him at the sink.

"I don't mind. I'll make the coffee while you start breakfast."

Clara smiled. "All right."

Mark filled the pot with water, then measured coffee into the percolator's basket. He set it on the stove, making sure he bumped into Clara as she reached up into a nearby cabinet.

"Sorry." He stepped away.

"It's okay." She looked at him, a little longer than she should have. He smiled in return.

"Are we still planning to see Emma today?" he asked.

Clara jerked her gaze away. She picked up an egg and cracked it into the bowl. "*Ya*. Julia will be here in a couple hours to watch the *kinner*."

"Do you think Peter should come with us?"

She shook her head, cracked another egg. "*Nee*. He has business in town."

Mark thought about the lousy job his cousin was applying for. Mark would never take on journeyman work. There were better, easier ways to make money. Much more money. And he wouldn't have to break a sweat to do it.

Peter came into the kitchen, dressed and carrying Magdalena. She snuggled against her father's shoulder. Her eyes were puffy. "She was crying upstairs."

Clara glanced at him. "She's up early."

"You started breakfast late."

Clara beat the whisk back and forth in the bowl of eggs with blazing speed, but said nothing. Peter put the child in her high chair. He went to the pantry, pulled out a box of cereal, and put a few pieces on her tray.

Mark didn't move from his spot next to Clara. The percolator started to bubble. The sizzling sound of eggs hitting the iron skillet filled the room. Peter kissed the top of his daughter's head. He looked at Mark. "Would you mind feeding the horse?"

He nodded. "Not at all." He didn't move.

"Now?" Peter asked.

"Oh. Sure." Mark strode out of the kitchen. Behind him he could hear Clara and Peter start to argue again.

Marriage. He'd genuinely considered it once. His teeth ground together as he thought about that time, years ago. Now he was grateful for what he missed. An endless cycle of bickering. Messy, whiny children. Locked in bondage to one woman for the rest of his life.

He'd never live through that nightmare.

But somehow he had to convince Emma Shetler that was exactly what he wanted.

"Just have time for a piece of toast, *Mamm*," Adam said as he hurried into the kitchen. "Still not used to waking up so early."

"Living on Yankee time." His father scooted

back from the table, his breakfast finished. "Wasteful time."

Adam glanced at his father. But he let the comment slide. He grabbed a piece of buttered toast from the dish in the center of the table and shoved it in his mouth. He turned to tell his mother good-bye, only to pause at the shock on her face. He pulled the toast from his mouth. "What?"

She stared at him. Shook her head. "I just can't get over how different you look. Since you shaved."

He grinned. "More Amish?"

She nodded. *"Ya."*

"It's not what's on the outside that makes a man Amish. Or faithful to his God." The screen door slammed behind his father as he stalked out of the house.

"In a *gut* mood as usual, I see," Adam said.

"Ya." She picked up her husband's empty plate from the table and took it to the sink.

Adam was surprised she didn't defend him. But he didn't have time to contemplate that now. He wanted to get to Emma and Leona's, just in case Mark decided to show up today. Plus, he saw a lot of things he could do to help out. Cleaning the barn was one of them. And since his father didn't seem interested in Adam's assistance, he might as well work for someone who needed him. Even if Emma wouldn't admit it.

He paused at the back door. "I'll be at the Shetlers' if you need me."

His mother turned. "I'm glad you're here to help them."

"Me too." He looked at the straw hat hanging on the peg near the back door. *Might as well*. He grabbed it and put it on.

He breathed in the early morning air. Felt the warm sunshine on his back through the thin fabric of the shirt his mother had sewed for him when he was twenty. He thought about putting on a jacket, but he'd work up a sweat soon enough cleaning the barn. He had just crossed his front yard and entered Emma's when he spied two figures walking down the road. A man and a woman. He squinted. The woman looked like Clara. But the man was shorter than Peter.

Mark.

Adam's gut had been right. The man didn't waste any time.

Well, neither would Adam. He hurried to the front porch. Knocked on it a couple of times and waited. The door soon opened. He smiled. "Hey, Emma."

Her response was cooler, yet he saw a spark of surprise in her eyes. "Adam. What are you doing here?"

"I thought I'd check on Dill—"

"She's fine."

"And then I would clean the barn." Her curtness wouldn't put him off. Not anymore.

She tilted her head. "You don't have to."

"I know."

"I don't want you to."

Same song, second verse. They would be on this verbal merry-go-round for a while, he could tell. Undeterred, he pressed on. "I'll be in the barn if you need me."

"Who is it, Emma?" Leona's reedy voice called from behind Emma's shoulder.

Emma started to shut the door, but Adam put his hand against it. She wasn't shutting him out this time.

"It's me, Leona." He removed his hat and grinned. "*Gut* morning."

"Oh, Adam." Leona's smile, unsteady and aged, still lit up her face. "Glad to see you. Why don't you come in for a cup of coffee?"

"I don't think he has time for that," Emma said. Her gaze pierced Adam's. Then she looked past his shoulder. Her frown deepened. "Clara's here."

Adam turned around. At least she didn't mention Mark. Maybe she wasn't interested in him after all. The thought boosted his spirits a bit.

Clara came up the porch steps, Mark directly behind her. "*Gude mariye,*" she said to Emma.

"Hello, *Grossmammi*." She glanced at Adam and said nothing.

Leona leaned against her cane and wiped her nose with a threadbare handkerchief. "Goodness. It's been a while since we've had this much company at one time. Come in, come in. We have plenty of coffee. Emma baked banana muffins last night." Leona's eyes lit up. "They're wonderful, if I do say so myself."

Emma shook her head. "I don't think—"

"—that's a *gut* idea," Clara finished. "I…" She paused. Looked at Mark. "Actually, we came to talk to you and Emma."

"Is that so?" Leona moved closer to Emma. "Then I don't understand what the problem is."

"The problem is him." Clara turned to Adam. "We want to have a private conversation. Just *familye*."

Emma frowned at Mark. Her expression indicated she had the same thought as Adam: if their talk was private, why invite Mark?

Leona smiled. "Yes. Well, Emma, why don't you go with Clara and Mark into the kitchen?"

They both looked at Adam, Clara with her haughty eyes, Mark with his shifty ones. They stepped over the threshold and followed Emma, who cast her grandmother a confused glance over her shoulder.

Adam let out a breath. At least he was in proximity to Mark. And whatever they had to talk about wasn't his business. He wasn't family. Clara was right about that. He replaced his hat. "Leona, I'll be in the barn if you or Emma need anything." He moved forward and bent down. "I mean *anything*, okay?"

Leona straightened. She put her hand on his arm. He felt her tug on him, urging him to come inside. Once he was past the doorway, she spoke. "Do you take cream and sugar in your coffee?"

Chapter Seventeen

Emma led Mark and Clara to the table. "Does anyone want coffee?" She tried to infuse some enthusiasm into her voice, but failed. She knew why they were there—Clara, at least. To talk about the fabric shop again. She didn't want to deal with this. Not today. Not ever. But Clara would make sure she did.

Clara sat down. Mark stood, looking at Emma. "That would be *gut*." He grinned.

Emma turned away. She pulled two coffee mugs from the cabinet next to the stove and, with a sudden flash of clarity, recalled the time after church Mark had put his hand over his heart. Even now she could see the interest in his eyes. Feel his gaze on her every move.

She tugged the bottom of her sweater, trying to pull it down over her hips. She glanced at Mark.

His smile widened. Emma felt herself flush with discomfort.

Her gaze went to Clara. Her sister was watching Mark, frowning. Why would she be upset? Emma turned away and started to pour the coffee. Clara had been acting strange for the past few months, even before *Mammi's* death. Some days Emma didn't know who her sister was anymore.

By the time she gave Clara and Mark their coffee, *Grossmammi* had returned to the kitchen. Emma looked up to see Adam standing behind her. He wouldn't be there unless her grandmother had invited him.

"What is he doing here?" Clara grimaced. "I said this was a private conversation."

"Anything you have to say to me or Emma, you can say in front of Adam. He has known our *familye* longer than this gentleman." The old woman looked at Mark. "What's your name again?"

"Mark King."

"Right. Peter's cousin."

She turned to Clara. *Grossmammi's* tone wasn't rude. Simply matter-of-fact. "I'd say Adam is more a part of our *familye* than someone you've only known a few days."

"Someone we happen to be related to." Clara gripped her hands around the hot mug, only to snatch them away. She gave Adam a cool look. "You're not going to be around much longer anyway."

Emma's heart lurched at the reminder.

Grossmammi shuffled to the head of the table. She sat down, lowering her frail frame into the chair more slowly than usual. She coughed into her handkerchief. Emma didn't like the rough, raspy sound. "Would you like some tea, *Grossmammi*?"

The old woman shook her head. "*Nee*, Emma. I had some a little while ago. I'll be fine. Just a little tickle in my throat." She turned to Adam. "Don't just stand there, *bu*, sit down." She patted the chair on her left.

Adam removed his hat and hurried to sit.

"Not at this table," Clara said. "He's shunned. He can't sit with us."

"In this *haus*," her grandmother said, "he can do whatever I invite him to do. And if you don't want to sit with us, Clara, feel free to *geh* in the living room. Although it will be hard to have a conversation with you from that far away."

Clara frowned but stayed seated.

"Feel free to speak to the bishop when we're done," *Grossmammi* said. "I would welcome a visit from him."

"You know I'm not going to do that."

"*Ya*. I know." Her grandmother smiled. "But if

it would keep you in clear conscience, I wouldn't blame you."

"My conscience is clear."

But Emma didn't miss the note of doubt in her sister's voice. She tried to focus on getting another mug down from the cabinet, in case Adam wanted a cup of coffee. He'd shaved off his beard and mustache. Wore Amish clothes, even down to the hat. Something familiar tugged at her heart. He looked so much like the Adam she had grown up with. The man she'd fallen in love with.

"Adam said he takes sugar in his coffee," *Grossmammi* said.

"I know how he likes his coffee." Emma reached for the pot.

"You don't have to *geh* to any trouble, Emma."

The soft, husky tone of his voice flowed over her. She started to tremble and steadied the mug with her other hand. Hot liquid splashed over the sides of the mug. She set down the pot on the stove with a bang.

She heard the scrape of chair legs against the floor, felt Adam suddenly behind her. His hand covered hers as he took the mug from her. "*Danki*, Emma."

She didn't dare turn. Or meet his eyes. His presence alone affected her.

"We're wasting time." Clara put her hands

on the table, ignoring her coffee. "Adam, since you're so determined to be here—"

"I invited him," *Grossmammi* reminded her.

Clara paused. "Then sit down so we can get started."

Adam returned to his seat. He picked up his hat from the floor and set it in his lap. There was only one other place to sit at the table—the empty seat next to Adam. Emma sat down, making sure she didn't look at him.

"All right, Clara." *Grossmammi* tapped her cane against the wood floor. "You have our attention."

"Finally." She took in a deep breath and squared her thin shoulders. "We need to talk about the fabric store."

Emma moaned. "Right now?"

"*Ya*. Right now. All this time we're wasting not getting the business started is money we're losing." She looked at her grandmother. "I don't know if Emma told you, but we'd like to convert *Grossvadder's* old workshop into—"

"A fabric shop. I know." Her grandmother cleared her throat.

"Then you also know how resistant Emma is to the idea." Clara directed her gaze at her sister, then back at her grandmother. "I haven't had a chance to discuss the plan with you completely."

Emma turned away as Clara gave their grandmother a brief outline of how they would convert the workshop. How it could easily become profitable. Emma knew her sister's idea made sense. It made her dislike the idea even more.

"So what do you think?" Clara looked at her grandmother.

"It sounds to me like you've put a lot of thought into this." *Grossmammi* placed one gnarled hand on the table. "My question is, what's the hurry?"

"The hurry?" Clara's brow lifted. "The hurry is that you and Emma don't have a source of income. The *haus* is in desperate need of repair."

"I wouldn't say desperate." The old woman leaned forward. "And Emma and I could continue selling the jams and jellies, the way we did before your *mammi* took ill."

Clara let out an exasperated sigh. "You can't survive on that. I know the money *Grossvadder* and *Daed* had saved before they died has run out. I'm sure there are other bills that need to be taken care of."

"They will be," Emma said.

"Not if you don't have any money!" Clara brought her fingertips to her brow. "Why is this so difficult for the two of you to understand?"

"I think they're understanding things just fine."

Emma looked at Adam. His gaze was on Clara, his eyes tinted with challenge.

"I didn't ask your opinion," Clara said.

"But I'd like to hear it." *Grossmammi* angled her body toward Adam. "Tell us what's on your mind, *sohn*."

Adam nodded. "I don't think anyone disagrees with the idea of having a business, Clara. Emma, Leona, and Mary had their small jam business. It's the timing they're concerned about. Your *mammi* just died. That's enough of a change to live through right now."

Emma entwined her fingers together on her lap. Adam had expressed her feelings perfectly. But from the explosive look on Clara's face, her sister wasn't going to accept the explanation from him any more than she'd accepted it from Emma.

"How dare you even bring up *mei mudder*? You have no right to talk about her, or anything else that concerns our *familye*."

"But I grew up here. I know how much this place means to Emma, especially the wood shop. I have *gut* memories of your *grossvadder* too. He's the one who taught me how to sand wood until it was as smooth as glass. So I can see why Emma doesn't want to let *geh* of the place just yet. And what about you, Clara? What does this place mean to you?"

Clara stared at him for a moment. "You made your choice, Adam. Go back to the Yankee world. That's where you've always wanted to be. That's where you belong."

Adam didn't flinch. "I loved your *mammi*. All of your *familye*. Almost as much as my own."

Emma's throat caught. He had never admitted this to her.

Clara leaned back in the chair, crossed her arms over her thin chest. "You don't love anyone but yourself, Adam."

"Mark?" *Grossmammi's* voice broke the silence. "We haven't heard from you yet. I'm assuming you have something to say, since you came with Clara to speak to us."

Mark sat back in his chair, slouching a little. He rubbed his chin and looked at Emma. His lips lifted into a smile, then he looked back at the older woman. "I think sometimes it's better just to sit back and listen."

"I wish Adam would heed that advice," Clara said.

"I see." Her grandmother stared at Mark for a long time. Long enough that the smirking grin vanished from his face. He sat up straighter. His eyes hardened. Finally, he turned his head away.

"This is ridiculous!" Clara bolted from her chair. "I have just as much right to this *haus* as

Emma does. But because she refuses to grow up and see reason, we all have to cater to her wishes."

"Nee." Emma raised her voice. "That's not fair, Clara. Where were you when *Mammi* was sick? When the barn needed cleaning? When jam and jelly needed to be made? The lawn mowed? The laundry done?"

"I think we all know how much you do around here, Emma." Clara's voice held a tinge of contempt. "Especially since you remind us about it all the time."

"Now wait a minute." Adam moved to stand, but *Grossmammi* put her hand on his arm. He stayed put.

Tears welled up in Emma's eyes. Was that how everyone saw her? A martyr? A complainer? A *boppli*?

She lifted her hands in the air. "Fine. Do what you want. It doesn't matter anymore."

Emma pushed away from the table and ran out of the house. She intended to go to the wood shop, to look at it one more time before her sister destroyed it. Instead she ran to the barn. Dill greeted her with a nicker, and Tommy rubbed his face against her shin. But even her animals didn't comfort her. She sat on a bale of hay, put her hands over her face, and let the tears come.

* * *

Mark watched Adam pop up from his chair. "I'll *geh* check on her."

Of course he would. Mark hid a scowl. Adam Otto couldn't lie to someone to save his own skin, at least not convincingly. But the man was a master at lying to himself. For whatever reason, he cared for Emma, far beyond friendship. Yet that wasn't what irritated Mark the most. It was clear that Emma cared for Adam too.

No, not just cared for him. Loved him. That gave him two problems to deal with.

"Nee," Leona said. "Stay here, Adam. She needs a few moments alone."

Make that three problems. Mark looked at the withered old crone, making sure not to meet her eyes. He didn't like old people in general. They were as irritating and at times as disgusting as children. But this woman was different. It wasn't her age he resented. It was her spirit.

A serenity emanated from her. Even as her granddaughters fought around her, she remained at peace, observing everyone without saying anything. And when she turned those eyes on him, she looked right through him, right down to his soul, assuming he had one.

He shuddered. The sooner he got away from her, the better.

"How about if I see after Emma?" He looked

at Clara, lifting one brow, reminding her of his supposed interest in her sister.

Clara nodded. "That's a *gut* idea." She turned to Adam. "You'll only cause her more pain."

Adam sucked in a breath but didn't say anything. He couldn't, Mark thought. It was plain as the sun that Adam believed Clara's words to be true.

"I think the last thing Adam wants is for Emma to be in pain." The old woman coughed into her handkerchief again. She sounded sickly. So much the better. Maybe she would die soon and get out of his way.

"Clara, why don't you *geh* into Ephraim's workshop? You can start cleaning in there. Sorting out the tools for sale."

Clara's eyes widened. "So you're supporting *mei* idea?"

Leona nodded.

"Danki, danki." She circled the table and kissed the old woman's withered cheek. "At least someone's being reasonable around here."

Leona looked up at Clara. *"Geh* on now. Before I change *mei* mind."

"All right. Mark, let's get started."

Leona shook her head. She turned to Mark, and her eyes narrowed. "I think you should *geh* see Emma."

Maybe he'd misread the old woman. It didn't

matter. He'd have time alone with Emma. Time to convince her that Adam would betray her again. To show her that she could only trust one person—him.

Clara turned abruptly to her grandmother. "Are you sure?"

The words shocked him. He'd expected Adam to object, but the coward hadn't said a word. Just sat in his seat with a petulant glare on his face, like a chastised little boy. But for Clara to question Leona's suggestion …

He clenched the back of the chair. She was the one person he hadn't worried about. Now he'd have to keep his guard up around all of them.

The old crone pointed an arthritic finger at them. "Mark, check on Emma. Clara, you *geh* to the workshop."

"And me?" Adam asked.

Mark saw the abiding respect Adam had for Leona. It made him sick.

"Stay here."

Mark followed Clara outside and put his hand on her shoulder. "What was that all about in there?"

"What are you talking about?"

"Your *grossmudder* practically gave me permission to see Emma. Why did you question her?"

Clara looked away for a moment. She licked

her lips. "I just thought…I need some help in the workshop."

"Peter can help you with that. And I'll do what I can. But I've been given a chance with Emma." He fought to keep his cool. He smiled. "I'll talk to your *schwester* for a little while, then I'll come help you."

She looked up at him, her cheeks pink from the cool autumn wind. "Spend as much time with Emma as you want." She turned and headed for the workshop.

Mark nodded. Everything was back on track. For a minute he hadn't been so sure.

"I don't trust him." Adam jumped up from his chair, ready to break out of his skin.

"I don't either." Leona remained seated, as calm as ever. Until she coughed again.

Adam went to the cabinet and pulled out a glass. He filled it with tap water and brought it to her. "Here."

She nodded and took a drink. Set the glass on the table and wiped her mouth with her damp handkerchief.

"Are you all right?" Adam sat down next to her. "I don't like the sound of that cough."

"It's just a fall cold." She smiled. "Both you and Emma. So worried about me. I'm fine."

As his concern for Leona subsided, Adam felt

anger rise within him again. "If you don't trust Mark, how could you let that snake be alone with Emma?"

"An interesting description," Leona whispered.

"What?"

"*Nix*. Adam, I don't trust Mark. I can't put my finger on it. But I do trust Emma. She can hold her own with him."

Adam stood. "I think he wants to court her."

"I know."

He turned from Leona, his stomach churning. "We can't let that happen."

"We?"

He spun and faced her. "*Ya*. You, Clara, Peter—"

"And you?"

Adam let out a long breath. "I don't have much sway with Emma anymore."

"But you did at one time." Leona patted the seat next to her. "Sit. Please. It strains my neck to look up at you."

He complied. To his surprise she took his hand. "Adam, I think Mark is a troubled soul."

"I agree."

"But he isn't the only one." Her soft, fragile skin felt cool against his palm. "You are troubled as well, and not only over Emma. Or what is happening to our *familye*. Not even what's happening with yours."

He withdrew his hand and leaned his elbows against the table. His fingers entwined in his hair. "I don't know what to think anymore, Leona. I've never been so confused in my life."

"About what?"

"Everything." He looked at her. "When I left here, I was so sure it was the right thing to do. There was a whole world available to me that I'd never experienced. I wouldn't have to think about all the rules. I could worship God in my own way, not the way my *daed* said I had to."

"And have you? Worshipped God?"

He looked down at the table. He'd vowed when he left he would still attend church. Probably a Mennonite one. And he did. For maybe two Sundays. It became easier to stay out late on Saturday and sleep in on Sunday, like everybody else he knew. To watch football, go to movies, spend time with new friends. To entertain girlfriends, most recently Ashley, who had never been to church in her life. It had taken him less than a month of living in Michigan to not only forget about his faith, but to forget about God.

"I think you've answered my question." Leona leaned toward him. "Look at me, Adam."

Guilt and shame overwhelmed him. It took him a long time to face her.

"We both have concerns about Mark. And

your mother. And I can see you're worried about Emma too."

He hesitated. "*Ya*. I am."

"But you can't help anyone until you get yourself right with the Lord."

"I've heard that all my life, Leona. But what does it mean? Pray? Ask forgiveness for my sins?" He thought about Ashley, and the shame returned. "It can't be that easy."

"It's not a matter of saying the right words, Adam. You have to make some hard decisions."

"I know, I know. The Amish world or the Yankee world."

"*Nee*."

He stared at her. "What do you mean, *nee*?"

"Amish or Yankee, it doesn't matter. You have to first decide who is in control of your life. You or God?"

Adam slumped against the back of the chair. "I don't know."

"Until you can answer that question, you can't move forward. But I can tell you this: If God is in control of your life, you won't be confused. You'll know your place in this world. If He's not..." She shrugged. "I think you already know what happens when He's not."

Chapter Eighteen

Emma heard the sound of footsteps approaching the barn. She wiped her nose and got up from the hay bale, not wanting Adam to see her acting like the bratty child her sister thought she was. She checked on the animals' food. They had eaten all their breakfast, but it was too soon to give them any more. Especially Archie and Rodney, who often ate more than their fair share.

The smell of manure in the barn might have seemed cloying to anyone else, yet Emma found it comforting. She had never mentioned that to anyone. Not even Adam, although after today, she had a feeling he would understand.

"Emma?"

"Mark." She tried to hide the disappointment in her voice. Why had she expected Adam to come?

Not expected. Wanted.

"Just checking on you. Making sure you're okay."

"I'm all right." Suddenly embarrassed by the filthy state of the barn, she grabbed a push broom from a hook on the wall and started sweeping.

Mark took the broom from her hands, much the way Adam had done when they were in the workshop the other day. But instead of feeling pleasant chills at Mark's closeness, she squirmed in her skin.

"You don't have to do that now." He leaned the broom against the wall, turned her to face him, and placed his hands on her shoulders. The desire to shrug them off was overwhelming. A desperate compulsion.

"I'm here for you, Emma."

"I...I appreciate that." She stepped back. "But really, I am okay. Sometimes Clara still thinks I'm her *boppli schwester*. She forgets I'm grown up."

"That you have opinions of your own. Feelings that shouldn't be dismissed." Mark nodded. "I know what that feels like. To be ignored. To have someone treat you as if you don't matter."

She moved out of his grasp, trying to get away, to put space between them. If he had noticed these things about her in such a short time, what must everyone else think? She averted her gaze, ashamed that people saw her as weak.

"You've been hurt, Emma. Deeply hurt."

"Is that what Clara told you?"

"Clara didn't have to tell me anything. I can see it in your eyes." He lifted her chin. "Beautiful blue eyes."

Heat filtered through her cheeks. Against her will, his compliment soothed her.

"Was it Adam? Was he the *mann* that hurt you?"

Emma looked at the ground, tempted to say nothing. But he had already guessed so much about her. As if he had read her thoughts, seen her heart. *"Ya,"* she whispered, unable to hold back. "He did."

"He doesn't deserve you. Clara doesn't either."

Her gaze snapped to him. "Clara? What do you mean?"

"She's bullying you so she can get her way."

"She's being practical."

"She's being selfish." Mark gazed into her eyes. "She doesn't want that shop to help you and your *grossmudder*. She wants it for herself and Peter."

"It's partly their business. Of course they would have a share of the profits."

He shook his head. "I think she wants it all, Emma."

"That's not true. I know she's being pushy, but she's not that selfish."

Mark shrugged. "I've heard a few whispered conversations between the two. It's hard not to, in a *haus* that small. They've been making plans. I don't think they include you and Leona."

"That doesn't make any sense." She shook her head, refusing to believe him. "What are they going to do, take over the shop, then *Grossmammi's haus*? Why would they want to do that?"

"Why wouldn't they want it? The house is bigger, the land is valuable. With all this property, they could sell it off piecemeal and make a decent profit."

He held up his hands. "I'm just letting you know what I've heard. I could be completely wrong. But it would make sense. Clara waiting until your *mudder* died." He fingered one of her *kapp* strings. "Waiting until you were vulnerable. Making you feel bad about yourself."

"Clara's not doing that. Peter would never do it either." Emma's throat burned. "They wouldn't want to move here, or sell off the land. They love their *haus*."

"I'm sure they do. Just like they love you."

Emma turned away from him. Could this be true? It wasn't out of Clara's character to try to control things. And Peter had asked Emma and her grandmother to move in with them. Maybe moving in wasn't what he had in mind, so much as moving them out of *Grossmammi's* bigger house. Emma could easily imagine Clara being the boss of the shop, gradually pushing her sister out of the picture.

Clara and her family would move into the house. Then it would become her house. Emma and *Grossmammi*, one unmarried woman and one widow, would be at the mercy of her sister and brother-in-law.

She shook her head and tried to clear the unwelcome images from her mind. If they wanted to move in, all they had to do was ask. They would be welcome.

She turned and glared at Mark. "You don't know what you're talking about. You may be a part of our *familye*, but you don't know us."

He moved back a pace. "Emma, I didn't mean to upset you. I just thought you should know."

"I don't believe you."

He nodded. "You're right. I don't know your *familye* well. So I'm sure I misunderstood everything. I'm sorry. I should mind my own business."

The sincere tone of his apology took some of the bite out of her response. "*Ya*. You should have."

"I just don't want to see anyone take advantage of you. Or hurt you. That's all." He moved closer again. "Can we start over? We don't have to talk about any of this. I've been learning my way around Middlefield. I know there are places I haven't seen yet. Maybe you could show me around sometime?"

"I can't."

"I can pick you up," he continued, as if he hadn't heard her. "I'm sure Peter won't mind if I borrow his horse and buggy. Please, Emma. Don't be mad at me. I like you." He leaned toward her. "Give me a second chance."

He'd never really had a first one. Yet she didn't have a reason to say no. And it might be good for her to get away for a little while. She had stayed close to the house and to her grandmother since her mother's death. Other than church and one grocery trip, she hadn't been anywhere else. Maybe a change of scenery would give her some perspective.

"Mark?"

They both turned to see Clara standing in the doorway. "I need to get back to the *kinner*. Julia could only watch them for a couple hours."

"Then I'll catch up with you later," he said.

"*Geh* on back with her," Emma said. "I have things to do here."

"Anything I can help with?"

Clara was tapping her toe, the same impatient gesture she'd had since they were young girls. "Maybe another time."

"What about that buggy ride?"

Emma paused. A short buggy ride. What could it hurt? "Tomorrow evening. But just for a little while."

He grinned. "I'll be here at four."

"So you and Emma have a date?" Clara and Mark walked down the driveway. They turned onto Bundysburg Road and headed toward the house.

"Ya." Mark smiled. "I'm going to take her for a buggy ride tomorrow."

"In whose buggy?"

"I was hoping to use Peter's." Mark glanced at her. "That's all right, isn't it?"

Clara fought against her rising anger and impatience. Mark had promised to come help her in the shop, but he had spent the time with Emma instead. She was having a hard time sorting out all her emotions. Isn't that what she wanted, for Emma to find a husband, to be happy? Hadn't she already given Mark her approval? Then why did something ugly twist inside her at the thought of the two of them together?

"Clara? Do you think Peter will mind if I borrow the buggy?"

"I don't know." She stared straight ahead, the soles of her black shoes scraping against weather-worn asphalt. "He might have some business in town."

"And if he doesn't?"

"I said I don't know, Mark," she repeated through gritted teeth. "You'll have to ask him."

Mark stopped walking. "Clara, I don't understand. I thought you wanted Emma and me to be together."

"I did. I do." She faced him, irritated. "But I don't have to devote every spare moment thinking about it. Now that she and my *grossmammi* have finally agreed to move on with the business, I need to focus on that. Not on how you're going to take *mei schwester* out on a date." She turned and started walking again. He quickly caught up.

"What did you do in the workshop?"

"I made some mental notes. Took inventory of the tools. There wasn't much I could do in such little time without more help."

"Sorry if I let you down."

"You didn't let me down. I could have just used the help."

"Then maybe you should have asked Adam."

Clara didn't respond. Adam had still been inside the house when they left. Why did her grandmother want to talk to him anyway? She had already broken one of the rules of the *bann*—being seated at the same table with an excommunicated member. Yet she had included him like he was part of the family. She had welcomed him more than she had Mark. Which was unusual for her grandmother, who normally treated everyone equally.

Mark kicked at a pebble. "You're quiet all of a sudden." The clopping of a horse's hooves filled the quiet air as a buggy approached from behind. Clara moved an arm's length away from him.

"Just thinking."

"And avoiding my comment."

"I didn't ask Adam because he was talking with *Grossmammi*. I didn't want to interrupt them."

"Seems to me you should have." Mark looked at her. "He's obviously got Leona fooled."

They turned into her driveway. "Fooled about what?"

"About everything. He's trying to make you all think he cares about your *familye* again. I think he's up to something."

"I can't imagine what. There's nothing he can get from us. He turned his back on our way of life a long time ago."

"Then why hasn't he gone back to Michigan by now?"

They stopped in front of the door. Mark let the question hang between them for a moment.

But Clara had no answer.

For the rest of the day Clara tried to focus on what she'd accomplished. Her grandmother approved of her plans for the shop. Emma had stepped out of the way. By the time Peter came home from town later that afternoon, her enthusiasm had returned.

After they had all eaten supper, Mark left, saying he was going out for a walk. For the first time in months, Clara asked her husband to sit with her on the back porch while Junior and Melvin played on the tire swing in the yard. Magdalena sat in her playpen nearby, tugging on the clothes of one of her cloth dolls.

"How was your time in town?" Clara asked.

"Fine. But I didn't take the roofing job."

"Why not?"

"Turns out it wasn't for a school, but for a private home." Peter stared out into the yard. "The pay was less than minimum wage, and we were responsible for our own transportation. At the end of the job, I would have lost money."

Clara let out a breath, thankful Peter had made a wise decision. It made her even more excited to tell him the news. "*Grossmammi* agreed we could start working on the shop."

"What about Emma?"

Clara averted her gaze. "Emma came around too."

"So she agreed just like that?"

"*Nee*, it wasn't quite that simple. But the important thing is that they're going to let us get started on the workshop. I was hoping tomorrow you and I could take the *kinner* and *geh* over there. We could sort through the tools together."

Peter shook his head. "I thought I'd *geh* into town again. Start asking around about jobs." He glanced at her. "Like you've been wanting me to."

"But, Peter, don't you see? This is your job now. Our job. Our business. Together."

"Clara, I don't think selling the tools will provide enough money to get the shop off the ground. Ephraim's collection is nice, but people aren't paying top dollar right now."

"The shop isn't going to be fancy. We just need to clean it up and purchase a little bit of inventory. After we make a few sales and the word gets out, we'll be profitable."

Peter set the porch swing in motion. Junior and Melvin chased each other around the yard. Magdalena started to whimper in her playpen. Clara picked her up, settling the chunky baby on her hip.

Her husband remained silent.

"Peter, I need an answer. Will you help me with this or not?"

He turned to her. "I'll help, Clara. But before I do, I want us to pray about it. Together. The success of the fabric shop, or anything else we do, will not be because of hope or wishful thinking. It will only succeed because it's God's will."

Clara nodded. She would pray with Peter. A familiar, distant fluttering stirred within her, something she hadn't felt for a long time.

Everything was going to be all right. Their business, their marriage...

Their life.

After checking on Dill and settling the rest of the animals for the night, Emma went inside. Exhaustion swept through her. And defeat. Adam had gone home by the time Mark and Clara had left. He didn't see her, didn't say good-bye.

She shouldn't have been surprised. But why couldn't she stop caring about him? If he would just leave, everything would go back to the way it had been. Everything would be simple again.

But that wasn't true either. Nothing would ever be the way it had once been. Everything had changed.

She turned off the gas lamps in the living room and went upstairs. As she passed by her grandmother's bedroom, she heard that low, raspy cough again. She knocked on her grandmother's door. "*Grossmammi?* Are you all right?"

A moment passed before her grandmother responded. "Come in, Emma. I was hoping to talk to you before you went to bed."

Emma entered the room. Her grandmother was sitting up in bed, a plain blue and white quilt folded over her waist. A Bible lay open on the side of the bed where her grandfather used to sleep. The old woman patted the empty space next to her. "Come. Sit."

Emma sat. "Are you sure you're okay? You sound worse than you did this morning."

Grossmammi waved her off. "I just have a cold, Emma. They always get worse before they get better. But I don't want to talk about *mei* cold. I want to discuss the situation with you and your *schwester.*"

"We don't have anything to discuss. I understand that opening the shop is important. I know it will help us. And I know I've been acting childish about it."

"Who said you're acting childish?"

"Clara. Didn't you hear her today?"

"Oh, I heard her, all right. But she is smart, and she is right about one thing. If it's God's will that this shop should succeed, it will. Meanwhile, Clara will work hard at doing God's will."

"So will I. I'll start cleaning it out tomorrow."

"I don't think you should help clean the shop just yet." She sneezed. Wiped her nose.

"Why? There's no reason I shouldn't help Clara and Peter."

"Peter and Clara will have plenty of help. I have a feeling Mark will be around here. More than he probably should."

"You don't like Mark?"

"I don't trust him. Something about him doesn't sit right with me. Adam feels the same way."

Emma got up from the bed and went to the window. It was dark outside. Still, she could make out the shadowy outline of the Ottos' house, with Adam's truck still parked in the driveway. "Adam shouldn't have an opinion about Mark."

"Why not? Adam's your friend."

"Not anymore."

"He won't be if you keep pushing him away."

Emma turned around. "I'm not pushing him away. He's the one who left. He's the one who's leaving again."

"Do you want him to leave?"

She didn't respond.

"Maybe if Adam had a reason to stay, he would."

"He had a reason to stay. He chose to leave." She looked at her grandmother. "I know you don't trust Mark. But at least he came to check on me today. I haven't seen Adam since this morning."

Grossmammi nodded but didn't say anything.

"Mark will be here tomorrow at four. We're going on a buggy ride. I'm going to show him a little bit of Middlefield."

"Is that something you want to do? Or do you feel you have to?"

Emma shrugged. "What I want doesn't matter anymore."

Chapter Nineteen

The next morning Adam woke up late again. Without his cell phone alarm clock, he was having trouble getting up at a decent hour.

When he was a kid, his parents had often reprimanded him for oversleeping; his *daed* had been especially hard on him about that. But now his father and mother never woke him. They didn't even knock on the door of his bedroom, which they had to pass to get downstairs. They probably thought he was old enough to get up on his own.

And they were right. He would have to try harder.

He dressed in Amish clothes again and went downstairs to the kitchen. Breakfast had come and gone, and the kitchen was spotless. Sounds of the hand-cranked washer came up from the basement as his mother washed clothes. He took a loaf of bread and a jar of peanut butter from the pantry, made himself a sandwich, and wolfed it down with a glass of milk.

When he was done, Adam went outside. He'd spent a restless night thinking about the question Leona had asked him. Who was in charge of his life?

As a child and a young teenager, he would've said God. He had been taught all his life that God was in control. Everything you did, from the time you woke in the morning until the time you fell asleep, had to be your best, done for the glory of God. Living humbly, plainly, remaining separate from the world.

As he grew to adulthood, Adam couldn't reconcile that part of his life. How did living with all these rules bring him closer to God? None of it made sense. And so he'd left the community and tried to find a place in the world.

But since he'd been back in Middlefield, he'd begun to think about things differently. What if, despite his father's harsh and rigid outlook on things, making a connection with God wasn't really about the rules at all? What if, instead, it was about the heart?

When he entered the barn, he saw his father putting up hay for the winter. Adam stood and watched for a minute as his *daed* tucked his fingers in the twine around the hay bale and tossed the bale to the loft above. At fifty, he had the strength of a man two decades younger.

Without saying a word Adam joined him. Soon they were both in the rhythm of loading the bales to the upper loft.

"What made you so sure you wanted to stay Amish?"

Adam's father froze, his hand still gripping the twine wrapped around the bale. "I don't understand the question."

"You were once my age. You went through *rumspringa*. How did you decide to stay Amish and not live in the Yankee world?"

His father dropped the hay bale and glanced away. Adam took note of the threads of silver in his brown beard and bushy eyebrows.

Maybe the question was too personal. But Adam wondered what might have happened in his life if he had taken the time to ask it two years ago, instead of waiting until now.

"I just knew." His father turned, grabbed a bale, and threw it into the loft.

That was a lot of help.

Adam waited for his father to elaborate. After a minute he realized he wasn't going to get anything else. But he shouldn't have expected more. His dad was always a man of few words, and those words were often harsh, especially when aimed in the direction of his son.

Adam clenched his fists and felt the familiar bile of resentment rising in him.

Who is in control of your life, Adam? You or God?

He took a breath and tried to relax. He wasn't going to get the answers he needed from his father. He had to take his father's response for what it was, his own personal reasoning. Simple, like the man himself. He didn't have to justify it to anyone, especially Adam.

His father's truth was not his own. Adam would have to find his own answers, his own way.

He and his father worked until all the bales were in the loft. Then they swept the floor and fed the horses. By the time they left the barn, midafternoon sunlight slanted across the pasture.

Adam pulled down the brim of his hat and looked at his dad. His father's mouth was set in its usual serious line. Without a word, his *daed* turned and walked toward the pasture. No invitation for Adam to follow. No thank you for his help.

Adam had seen this behavior all his life, and it invariably left him feeling frustrated, neglected, taken for granted. But somehow this afternoon things were different. The harshness in his dad's eyes had softened.

Adam didn't fully understand why. But he hoped he would. Eventually.

In the meantime, he had to accept that it was just his father's way.

Emma picked up Tommy and walked into the workshop, wanting to look at it one last time before it changed. Despite her doubts, Emma knew her grandfather would rather see the shop put to use, instead of rotting away into a pile of dust.

"Ephraim loved working in here."

Emma whirled around to see her grandmother standing in the doorway, leaning against her cane. "*Grossmammi*. I didn't realize you were here. I thought you were resting inside."

The old woman shook her head. "Too many things on my mind. Thought I'd get out into the fresh air. Clear my head."

"The air's not so fresh in here." The cat wriggled out of her arms and raced out of the shop.

"But it's filled with memories," her grandmother said. She glanced around the building and sighed. "Goodness. I haven't been in here in years." With measured steps, she walked over to the Peg-Board that held her husband's tools. She leaned against her cane and touched the empty space where an awl had hung. "I still miss him," she said softly.

Emma went to her grandmother and put her arm around her shoulders.

The old woman looked up, her eyes damp. "The Lord's seen fit to give me seventy-five years of life, and maybe more if that's His plan. So much has changed. I've buried three babies. I've outlived my husband, my grown *sohn*, and my daughter-in-law. My other two *kinner* have left the Amish and live in other states."

Emma thought about her Uncle Eli and Aunt Lois. Their visits were infrequent, although they did write regularly. Pain filled her grandmother's eyes. "I'm sorry, *Grossmammi*."

"Nothing to be sorry about. We're not guaranteed an easy life. And I've had far more joy than heartbreak. God has healed my pain, Emma." She looked at the tools again. "The memories I hold inside are the happy ones." She let out another shaky breath. "This building is about to change, and that's as it should be. But I want to remember it the way it was for just a while longer."

Nodding, Emma quietly left her grandmother to her memories. She stepped outside into the clear afternoon sunshine. Like her grandmother, she had lost the ones she loved most in her life. Yet her grandmother could thank God in her sorrow, celebrate His mercy in her grief. Emma had done neither of those things. Instead she'd felt sorry for herself. But why? How could her grandmother find healing when it was just out of Emma's grasp?

A few moments later Emma saw her grandmother leave the workshop. She went back inside to savor a few final memories, before they changed forever.

Adam was about to go inside when he saw Emma enter the workshop. He wasn't sure if he should follow her, yet he couldn't stay away. He needed to find out what happened yesterday, especially with Mark. Thinking about the two of them alone, even for only a short time, didn't sit well with Adam.

From her place under the Shetlers' porch, Molly, the bluetick hound, came toward him. The old dog moved slowly, but her tail still wagged with vigor.

Adam crouched down and waited for her to meet him. He stroked her graying muzzle and spoke in soothing tones to her.

She rewarded him with a wet and sloppy kiss. Adam patted her head and scratched under her chin. *"Gut maedel."*

In that moment he realized he'd missed everything about this place, even Molly. How could he not have understood all he'd given up when he moved away?

His Yankee friends always talked about the

"modern" things the Amish lacked—technology, entertainment, labor-saving devices. But now that he was back in Middlefield, his life in Michigan seemed empty and hollow by comparison.

He petted Molly a little longer, then went to the workshop. Emma was at the back of the room, sweeping the floor again, this time with slow, deliberate strokes. Suddenly she stopped sweeping and looked up at an old tilted shelf on the wall.

Adam leaned against the door frame. She still hadn't heard him, and he wanted to keep it that way. He liked watching her.

The thought surprised him. How long had he felt this way? Was this the first time he was aware of it—or merely the first time he had admitted it to himself? Either way, he definitely liked it.

What was she up to? She picked up a hammer lying on the dusty counter. Along the windowsill were glass mason jars filled with nails. Emma peered inside a couple of them, stuck her fingers in one of the openings, and pulled out a short, rusty nail.

When she walked back over to the shelf, he understood what she was planning to do. His first instinct was to stop her, or at least offer help. But she'd refuse it anyway. Better to let her realize her problem herself.

She pushed one end of the crooked shelf up

and leaned back to look at it, presumably checking to see if it was even. It wasn't, but she didn't notice. She started pounding the nail into the bracket beneath the shelf. To her credit, she didn't hit her thumb.

Emma propped her hands on her hips and stood back to check her work. Adam found his gaze drawn to those hips. Out of the blue, he wondered what it would be like to touch them. The unexpected thought jolted him with such force he started to cough.

She whirled around, wielding the hammer like a weapon. "How long have you been standing there?"

"Not long." He cleared his throat and avoided looking anywhere but her face. "I just got here."

"You scared me."

"I didn't mean to." He drew closer and nodded toward the shelf. "What are you doing?"

She glanced over her shoulder. "It was crooked."

Adam worked hard to suppress a smile. "And now it's straight?"

"I did the best I could." She frowned at him.

A creaking sound from the plank of wood warned that the shelf wouldn't be stable for much longer. He took the hammer from her hand. "What kind of nails did you use?"

"Metal ones, of course. What other kind are there?"

He chuckled. "*Nee*. I mean what size?"

"I don't know. A big one? Medium-sized? Does it matter? I just grabbed a nail and started pounding."

"It matters." Adam examined Ephraim's old collection of nails and found one long and thick enough to support the shelf. He turned to Emma. "Do you mind?"

She hesitated, then shook her head. "You know more about this than I do."

With the claw end of the hammer he yanked out the nail. The shelf dangled on the wall. "Would you happen to have a level?"

"A what?"

"Never mind. I'll eyeball it."

He straightened the shelf, examined it for a moment. Placed the nail in the bracket, and with a few whacks of the hammer it was secure against the wall.

He stepped back to check his handiwork, his hip brushing against the long, narrow counter lining the back of the shop. "I think that should stay." He noticed the twitching of her lips. "What?"

"I'd brush your backside off if I were you. There's enough dust on that counter to cover your *daed's* field."

He twisted around. She was right. He batted his hands against his pants and looked back at her. There it was. A twinkle in her eyes. Tiny, barely there, but he saw it. "Better?"

Instead of answering she turned and placed her hands on her curvy hips again. Adam surveyed the dusty, abandoned shop alongside her. Dirt coated everything, from the junk on the floor to the long counter that was nailed to the south wall. Above the counter were two more wooden shelves, which barely clung to the wall. A Peg-Board hung on the back of the building, covered in dark, shadowy shapes where tools must have hung. The place was a mess. Was this building even stable anymore?

"Emma, what are you doing here?"

"Fixing the shelf. Doing a little sweeping." She didn't look at him. "Trying to help get this place ready for the store."

"I thought you didn't want the store."

She moved away from him. Ran her finger through the dust on the counter. "Things change. They have to. It's time I accepted it."

"Are you sure you want to do this?"

"There's only one thing I'm sure of." She faced him, and the expression of misery in her eyes nearly broke his heart. "I'm not in control of what happens in my life. I don't have a choice. This shop is going to happen with or without me."

Adam frowned. "I don't think you believe that."

"About the shop? *Mei grossmudder* already told me. Clara and Peter will be here later today to go through the tools."

"That's not what I'm talking about."

He leaned against the counter again. Dirty pants didn't matter to him right now. Emma did. "Leona asked me an interesting question yesterday."

"She has a tendency to do that."

"She asked me who was in control of my life—me or God?"

"What did you say?"

"I didn't have an answer for her. I haven't figured it out yet."

She turned away from him. "So what's your point, Adam? Do you want me to help you solve your spiritual dilemma?" She glared at him over her shoulder. "I tried that once."

"I know." He came up behind her. "This isn't about me, Emma. It's about you having choices. And about you knowing who is in control of your life."

Emma turned around. Adam Otto, talking of spiritual things? Questioning her the way her grandmother would? She shook her head.

"What?"

"It's just that…" She sighed. "You've changed, Adam."

"I guess so. I hope so. I'm trying to work some things out. Things I avoided for a long time."

As he stared at her with his honey-colored eyes, a warmth kindled within her—empathy coupled with attraction. She glanced away, not wanting to be drawn in. At one time she appreciated his concern and his friendship, yet she'd also wanted more. She still wanted more, and always would.

"Have you prayed about this, Emma?"

She crossed her arms over her chest. She hadn't. And she wasn't going to admit it and get a lecture from this new incarnation of Adam. She picked up a jar of nails to move it from the windowsill to the counter near the front of the shop. Pointless, yet it allowed her to avoid the question. "Clara is right. So is *Grossmammi*. I have to let *geh* of the past if I'm going to move forward."

"Does that mean you're willing to let *geh* of what happened between us?"

The jar slipped out of her hand, crashing to the floor. Sharp nails and shards of glass flew everywhere. She sank down to the ground and blindly grabbed at the mess. Pain shot through her hand. A bright stream of blood flowed from her palm.

Adam appeared at her side. "Emma."

His voice, soft in her ear, sent chills through

her. She tucked her hand inside the cuff of her sweater. "I'm such a klutz."

"*Nee*. You're not." He picked up a few pieces of glass, found an old bucket, and tossed them in. "We'll put the glass in here."

She nodded, trying to ignore the throbbing in her hand. She reached for a chunk of the glass jar and saw a dark spot seeping through the navy blue fabric of her sweater.

"Let me see."

"I'm all right."

Adam put his hands on his hips and stood in front of her. "I'm not budging until you show me."

"Fine." She pulled up the cuff of her sleeve. Blood was smeared all over her hand. "It looks worse than it is."

"I hope so, because that looks pretty bad. We need to *geh* inside and clean it up."

"I can do it myself."

"Okay, then you *geh* inside and take care of it. I'll pick up the rest of the glass and nails." He bent down and carefully lifted a large shard of glass.

"Adam?"

"Can't hear you." He tossed the glass in the bucket. "I can't hear you because you're already inside cleaning up your hand, like you told me you would."

Behind his back she smiled. A little. Then she turned and went into the house.

* * *

"Adam."

Adam turned to see Mark standing in the doorway. He stood up, tossing the last pieces of glass into the bucket. "Mark."

"What are you doing here?"

"I could ask you the same question."

Mark strolled into the workshop and looked around. His face registered disgust as he took in the ramshackle place. "Needs a lot of work."

"*Ya.* It does."

"More than Clara realizes, I believe." He turned to Adam. "You still haven't told me what you're doing here."

"You're right. I haven't."

Mark smirked. He rolled his shoe back and forth across one of the loose nails on the floor. "I suppose you don't think you owe me an explanation."

"Not really."

"And I don't owe you one." He leaned against the counter and crossed his ankles. "When are you leaving?"

"I haven't decided yet." He looked Mark directly in the eye. "In fact, I'm thinking about staying around for a while. A *gut* long while."

"Am I supposed to take that as a threat?"

"You can take it any way you want to." Adam

smiled. "But Amish don't threaten. You should know that."

"Oh, I do." He smiled right back. "But you're not Amish anymore."

Adam's smile faded. Nothing seemed to unnerve Mark King. He stood in this building as if he owned it. *Or wants to.*

"I suppose we should clear the air between us." Mark uncrossed his ankles and walked to Adam. "Since you're planning to stay and all."

Adam picked up a couple of nails and clicked them together in one hand. "Suit yourself."

"I intend to court Emma."

Adam's fist tightened, and one of the nails pierced the skin. He hid a wince. "Uh-huh."

"That's all you have to say?"

The words. The tone. The sarcastic sneer. Clearly Mark was itching for a fight. He wanted to match wits, maybe even match fists with Adam. And considering the anger welling up inside Adam's gut, it would be easy to rise to the bait.

But it was a trap. The Amish were peaceful people, and it would only take one argument for Emma to be upset. She already held a cache of resentment toward Adam. Even if Adam won, he'd lose, simply because he took up the challenge. Mark would be the true victor.

Adam wasn't about to fall for that. "You do what you want. I'm not Emma's keeper."

The smirk on Mark's face slipped a little. "I thought you cared about her."

"I do. But I can't tell her what to do. Who to like or who...not to."

"So you're agreeing you'll stay out of my way? That you'll leave Emma alone?"

Adam was about to leave the workshop. He needed to check on Emma, see how her hand was doing. But he caught the uncertainty in Mark's tone.

He stopped in the doorway. "I'm not agreeing to anything, King," he said. "But I'm not your biggest problem. If you want Emma to be your wife—"

He paused and swallowed down the bile that rose at the thought. "You'll have to convince her that you're worth being her husband. And that, you'll never be able to do."

Chapter Twenty

Clara came into the kitchen to find Emma standing at the sink, washing her hands. Behind Clara, Peter entered the room with Junior and Melvin at his heels and Magdalena cradled in his left arm. They had all walked to the Shetlers', including Mark.

Mark had already disappeared into the wood shop. He was probably hard at work now, sorting tools.

Emma glanced over her shoulder. "I guess you're ready to start work?"

"*Ya*. Peter and I are headed to the shop. Could you watch the *kinner* for us?"

Emma shut off the tap, took a towel from the counter, and patted her hand dry. She smiled at Junior and Melvin, who gave her gap-toothed grins in return. "I'd be happy to. I haven't seen these adorable *buwe* in a long while."

Junior's smile turned upside down. "We're not aboradle."

"We're tough," Melvin added.

"Sorry, tough guy," Emma said. "You'll always be 'aboradle' to me." She patted the tops of their hats with the hand that wasn't covered with the towel. Peter came over and started to hand her the baby. "I'll get her in a minute. I just need to bandage my hand."

"What happened?" Peter asked.

"*Nix.* Just cut my hand. Very minor, nothing to get excited about. I'll be right back." She left the kitchen, presumably for the bathroom where the first aid supplies were.

As soon as Emma left, the back door opened. The boys rushed out and Adam came in. What was he doing here again?

Dust covered his clothes, and Clara had a sinking feeling he'd been in the workshop. Had he run into Mark out there? She hoped not. She was tired of the strife in her family, ready for Adam to leave and go back to Michigan once and for all. If he'd just go home, the last bit of conflict would be out of their lives.

Clara and Peter were sorting things out and had prayed together last night. She had asked God to remove the confusing feelings she had about Mark. This morning when she saw her husband's cousin, she didn't have a single reaction.

Things were turning around. She didn't want Adam messing that up.

"Hi, Adam." Peter extended his hand. "*Gut* to see you back."

Adam returned the handshake, nodding. "I never thought I would say this, but it's *gut* to be back."

Clara frowned. What did Adam mean by that? Maybe he was just being polite. She certainly hoped he didn't intend to stay.

Her husband handed her the baby. "I'll go out in the shop with Mark," he said. "Come out when you're ready, Clara."

Adam stayed. "Where's Emma?"

"Did you have something to do with her injury?"

"*Nee, nee.* At least not directly. We were talking and she dropped a jar of nails."

"What were you doing in *mei grossvadder's* workshop?"

"I just told you. Talking."

"You shouldn't be here." Magdalena tried to pull on Clara's *kapp*. She grabbed her daughter's hand and moved it away.

Adam rolled his eyes. "Clara, you've told me that before. Many, many times. But let me tell you this. Just because I left, because I'm shunned, doesn't mean that I stopped caring about Emma, or your *familye*."

"If you cared so much about Emma, you wouldn't have broken her heart."

Adam looked away. "I never meant to hurt her."

"So you say. But the longer you stay, the more you're hurting her. Can't you see that?"

"So you think Mark is better for her?"

"*Ya*, I do. He's a *gut mann*."

"Just because he's Peter's cousin?"

"Because he's been nothing but helpful to me and Peter. And *ya*, it is because he's part of Peter's *familye*."

"Peter is a *gut mann*, but that doesn't mean everyone he's related to is. I'd think you'd be a little more careful with your sister's feelings, Clara. You haven't known Mark that long."

"I only knew Peter through letters, but even then I knew the kind of *mann* he was. And still is. I never met him, but I fell in love with him."

"That's you and Peter. What does it have to do with Mark and Emma?"

"Sometimes you can get to know somebody, who they really are, in a short period of time. Just because Mark hasn't known Emma for years doesn't mean he hasn't come to care for her."

"Don't you think Emma deserves to choose her own happiness?"

"I believe she will find happiness with Mark. She will not find it with you."

* * *

When Emma returned to the kitchen, she found Adam and Clara glaring at each other. They both looked unhappy.

"I'm heading to the workshop," Clara said. "If you need anything, I'll be there." She handed Magdalena to Emma and left, brushing by Adam but otherwise ignoring him.

What was that all about? Emma wondered.

She cuddled Magdalena close and breathed in her scent—powder, baby sweetness, maybe a little bit of strawberry jelly.

Then Emma felt Adam's eyes on her.

He was staring at her, his honey-colored eyes flitting from Magdalena's face to Emma's and back again.

"What?" Emma asked.

Adam's gaze jerked, and he shook his head. "*Nix*. I'll be outside." He took a step back, stared at her again. "In the barn. Working."

"You don't have to—"

But he was gone before she could finish the sentence. Emma shrugged and looked at Magdalena. "Men are strange, don't you think?" The baby sighed and leaned her head against Emma's shoulder. Emma rubbed her back and closed her eyes. Love welled up inside her, and although it was silly and maybe even delusional, for a moment she imagined she was holding her own baby. Hers and Adam's.

Grossmammi shuffled into the kitchen, leaning heavily on her cane. "Ah. There's *mei grosskinskind.*"

Emma turned. "*Ach*, you sound terrible." She went to her and held the back of her hand against her grandmother's forehead. "You have a fever."

"Just a touch." The old woman sounded like she had swallowed a handful of gravel and a few pieces had lodged in her throat. "I came down for some tea."

"I'll make it. You sit down." Emma looked around for a safe place to put Magdalena. The baby wasn't walking, yet she could zip around on her hands and knees almost faster than Emma could catch her.

Typical of Clara not to bring a high chair or playpen. Emma propped the child on her hip and set about making the tea.

"I heard voices while I was coming downstairs." *Grossmammi* leaned back in the chair and closed her eyes, as if the effort had drained her of strength. She coughed into her handkerchief. "I take it Clara and Peter were here. Where are the *buwe*?"

"Helping in the shop, I guess." Emma placed the kettle on the stovetop and turned on the gas burner. She stared at the blue flame as if it might hold answers to her dilemma. "Adam was here. He went out to the barn."

"I hope to clean it out."

"I didn't ask." She didn't want to be beholden to him. But the barn's manure pile did need to be shoveled out. If Adam wanted to do it, Emma wasn't going to argue with him about it.

She didn't want to argue about anything anymore. Not with Adam, or Clara, or anyone. Not even with herself. She craved peace, and getting upset every moment wouldn't bring her that peace.

The kettle whistled. Emma balanced Magdalena on her hip and carefully poured hot water over the tea leaves in the bottom of the cup. *Grossmammi* liked her medicinal tea loose, not wrapped up in cheesecloth like her other home-made teas.

"You sit down right here by great-grandma." Emma put Magdalena in the chair next to *Grossmammi*, and the old woman held on to the child while Emma brought the tea.

"That's *gut*. *Danki*, Emma."

"I'm worried about you." Emma picked up Magdalena and settled her in her lap. "You're getting worse each day."

The teacup trembled in her grandmother's hands. "I'm just about through the worst of it."

Yet her red cheeks contrasted with her pale lips. "I should feel better in the morning."

"If not, I'm taking you to the doctor." Suddenly she remembered about Dill. She couldn't use their buggy. Maybe she could ask Norman Otto for a ride. Or call a taxi.

Or ask Adam.

Even if she wanted to ask him, he was in the *bann*. She and her grandmother couldn't accept a ride with him in his truck. But she realized that the idea of asking Adam for a favor didn't leave as much of a sour taste in her mouth as it used to.

Had she come to the point where she could forgive him for leaving? She didn't think so. She was supposed to forgive him, she knew. But she wondered if there would always be a deep, dark space in her heart that could never let it go.

After spending most of the morning and afternoon cleaning out the Shetlers' barn, Adam was ready to call it a day. His empty belly growled. He should have stopped for lunch, but getting the barn finished was his top priority, and he had to admit he'd done a pretty good job.

He had shoveled out all the old manure and transported it in a wheelbarrow to a pile behind the barn, near the edge of the woods. That had taken five trips. He laid down fresh hay for Dill, cleaned out the dogs' and cats' food and water bowls, and filled them with fresh kibble and cold water. He spread a thin layer of clean straw on the barn floor and hung all the tools on pegs on the wall, the way Emma's father used to.

Adam stretched his arms in front of him, working out the kinks in his muscles. His body appreciated the hard work. A sense of satisfaction filled him. A job well done. When Dill nickered, he grinned. Maybe it was his imagination, but the animals seemed happier too.

He strolled out of the barn, ready for a shower and some supper. Just as he stepped outside, he saw Mark King enter the Shetlers' house. He frowned. The man didn't need to be alone with Emma and Leona. Whatever he was up to, it couldn't be good.

Adam started toward the house, then stopped and looked down at his clothes. He was filthy with dung and dirt. He reeked. He turned around and dashed home.

"Adam?" His mother called as he zipped past her in the kitchen.

"Shower." He hurtled the stairs two at a time. Stripped down and took what had to be the fastest shower on record. Barely toweled off, he threw on a clean pair of broadfall pants and a short-sleeved yellow shirt, then shoved his arms into a clean jacket. His boots were dirty, so he slipped on his tennis shoes, ran downstairs, and skidded to a stop in front of his mother.

"What is going on?" She set down a wooden spoon on a small dish next to the stove. The fragrant scent of tender roasted chicken, homemade noodles, and thick broth filled the air. Chicken stew.

Adam's stomach rumbled, but he ignored it. "Heading over to the Shetlers'." An errant drip of water slid down his cheek from his still-damp hair.

"Don't you want any chicken stew? It's your favorite."

His mouth watered as he peeked into the stewpot. "I'll be back in a bit. Just, um, going to say hi to Leona."

"Hmmm." His mother turned her attention back to the stew. "And Emma, I suppose?"

"Right. Emma too." He kissed his mother on the cheek. "See you later."

He crossed the yard just as Mark and Emma came out on the front porch. Adam stopped in front of the bottom steps.

"Hey." He winced at his breathless voice and leaned against the banister in what he hoped was a casual pose. "What's going on?"

"I'm taking Emma for a walk." Mark's cold gaze met Adam's, despite the grin glued on his face. "Alone."

Adam wasn't about to let that happen. "Really? Where to?"

"Just down the street." Emma yawned. "I'm kind of tired tonight." She looked at Mark. "I'm sorry. I hope you don't mind a short walk."

Mark grinned, life suddenly entering his dead eyes. "Of course not. I'm happy to spend any time with you."

Adam glanced at Emma to see if she was falling for this syrupy mush. To his relief, she seemed almost bored.

He turned to Mark and smiled, wider than he'd ever smiled before. "Mind if I join you?"

Chapter Twenty-One

Mark watched Emma's eyes light up at the question. "Sure," she said, looking at Adam as if he'd offered her not only a rainbow but the pot of gold at the end of it.

"Great." Adam grinned at Emma. A genuine smile. Another confirmation that Adam Otto was interested in Emma beyond friendship. And any idiot could see that she was in love with him. Mark bit his bottom lip until he tasted blood.

"But only if it's okay with Mark," Emma said. She looked at him, the brightness in her eyes dimming. Her question was obviously an afterthought.

"Actually, I'd hoped you and I could spend what little time we had tonight alone." He faced Emma, summoning every bit of charm he could and forcing it into the tone of his voice. It wasn't easy. He'd never been so unattracted to a woman in his life. But she didn't matter to him. What she could give him did.

Adam held up his hands, his expression filled with innocence. But Mark recognized the false sincerity—he'd played that card any number of times. "I wouldn't want to intrude. I just thought we could walk down the road a bit, like we used to. Remember, Emma?" His eyes locked with hers. "Especially when the weather was warm. We'd spend the evening walking the roads, talking until dark."

Emma turned from Mark, nodding. "I remember," she said softly.

Fury built within Mark. She *wanted* Adam to come with them. If he pushed the issue, he'd risk upsetting her.

Well, he could bide his time. It would take patience, but eventually he would be alone with Emma. Just not tonight.

Mark forced a smile. "Sure. Join us."

"*Danki* for the invitation." Adam nodded at Mark, but his eyes narrowed as he pulled the brim of his hat over his brow.

Mark and Emma descended the steps. But as they headed for the driveway, Adam inserted himself between the two of them. Emma crossed her arms over her thick chest as they walked down the road.

The evening grew cool as the sun began to set.

Mark paid little attention to the muted colors in the sky. He had planned to use this time to worm information out of her. The square footage of the Shetlers' large house. The acreage that accompanied it. The size of the barn. Whether she or her grandmother had money stashed away. He couldn't ask the old hag. He could hardly stand to be in the same room with her.

Instead he had to listen to her and Adam rattle on about memories. Pleasant memories. Clara insisted Adam had broken Emma's heart. Either Clara was wrong, or Emma had recovered. There was clearly a bond between the two of them, one that planted a seed of doubt in Mark that he would be able to win Emma over.

"The sky is *schee* tonight." Emma hugged her arms closer to her body.

"I remember how you used to like watching the sunsets." Adam slipped his jacket off and put it around her shoulders. "Better?"

She nodded, smiling shyly.

Mark couldn't take it anymore. This was a total waste of time. He wouldn't get anywhere with her tonight.

He stopped on the side of the road. "I just remembered I promised Peter I'd help him stack wood tonight." He moved between her and Adam, making sure he blocked Adam's view of her. And even though it was risky, he touched

her fat cheek, the move so quick and slight Adam
couldn't have grabbed him if he tried. "Let's do
this again another time." He leaned closer, lowering his voice. "Alone."

Mark moved away before Adam could react.
He headed down the road toward Peter's house,
smiling at the look of shock on Emma's face. He
would get her alone, and soon. And once he got
rid of Adam, he would have Emma—and more
importantly, her house and land—all to himself.

Emma and Adam continued to walk down the
road. The warmth of his jacket seeped through
her sweater and dress, all the way to her skin.
She breathed in his earthy scent and pressed the
fabric against her. Giving her his coat was a kind
thing to do. A romantic thing to do. But of course
he hadn't put his coat around her shoulders because he was attracted to her. He was just being
nice. And even though Adam could be selfish and
hurtful, more than anything, he was nice.

"Whew. I'm glad he's gone."

She looked at him. He strolled on the road
while she walked on the outer edge of it. Behind
him was a cornfield, picked clean, the dry, brown
spears of dead stalks protruding from the ground.
Above the field the sky stretched endlessly,
awash with Emma's favorite colors—cool lav-

ender, warm peach, delicate pink. "Why are you glad he's gone?"

"I don't trust him." Adam scowled. "He's up to something, Emma. And it's not *gut*."

The peace she'd briefly felt disappeared. "What do you mean?"

"Can't you see he's faking you out?"

Emma stopped. "Excuse me?"

"It's Yankee talk. It means…" Adam rubbed the back of his neck.

"I know what it means."

"He's not being truthful, Emma. He's pretending to like you."

"Because he couldn't possibly *really* like me." She stepped away from him.

Adam shook his head. "*Nee, nee.* I'm not saying that at all. He wants something."

"But not me." She handed Adam back his jacket, but he didn't take it. "I need to get home."

Adam blocked her way. "Emma, that's not what I meant. Don't twist my words."

"I'm not twisting anything."

"*Ya*, you are. I'm trying to protect you—"

Emma laughed bitterly. She looked up at the sky. "You've been here two weeks, and now you need to protect me? From the one *mann* who's shown interest…"

She clamped her mouth shut. How pathetic she

sounded. "I don't need your protection. I don't need anything from you."

Adam moved closer to her. "This is about more than Mark. We both know it."

She stared at him, afraid to speak. Memories from two years ago sharpened, piercing her mind and heart. She turned from him. "It doesn't matter anymore."

He grasped her arm. "*Ya*, Emma. It does."

"You made your choice."

"What if I told you I made the wrong one?"

What did he mean? That he shouldn't have left the Amish? That he shouldn't have rejected her?

She swallowed, her throat suddenly parched. "That depends," she whispered. "Did you?"

He opened his mouth, but no sound came out. Not a single word.

She had her answer.

"*Gut nacht*, Adam." She handed him his coat and hurried back home. Before he could see how he had devastated her all over again.

Adam watched Emma rush toward her house. He stayed put, on the edge of the quiet road, dusk surrounding him. Why hadn't he answered her? Why had he let her believe a lie, yet again?

He shook his head, tempted to throw his hat on the ground. But the only thing that would do is make him look like a fool. Which he was. A fool and a coward. Always running away from everything. Church. His family. Emma.

God.

Adam slogged his way back home. Leona had told him to get things right with God. He'd been thinking about that a lot.

But had he done anything? No. He was living in limbo. No job, mooching off his parents, pretending he was here to help his mother and protect Emma. But he hadn't accomplished a blasted thing. His mother and father were still distant, even with each other. Emma was still...

He sighed. Emma was still Emma. Everything he wanted. At least he could finally admit that to himself.

But she was also everything he didn't deserve.

Darkness had descended by the time he reached the house. He ran his hand along the side of his truck and remembered the pride he felt the day he bought it. The liberation. Life on wheels was so much easier. He could get to work and the grocery store. Go to the movies. Listen to the booming stereo that made the bed of the truck rock.

But did any of that bring him closer to God? Closer to discovering who he was? His purpose in life?

He went inside, expecting to find his parents asleep. Instead he saw light glowing from the basement stairs. He went downstairs and found his mother sitting in an old rocking chair. Alone. A tall gas lamp hissed a few feet next to her, casting the room in pale yellow light.

"Mamm?" He moved toward her. She didn't respond until he called her name a second time.

"Oh. Adam. I didn't realize you were here." She turned and looked at him. Her eyes were glassy, distant. She blinked a couple of times. "Did you want me to heat up the chicken stew for you?"

His hunger had disappeared long ago. He knelt beside her, putting his hand on the arm of the chair. "What are you doing down here?"

"Thinking." She stared straight ahead.

The basement was lined with wooden shelves, filled with canned fruit, vegetables, sauces, even meats, some smoked, some salted. The wringer washer sat in the corner, a small clothesline strung taut from one side of the basement to the other, to hang clothes in the winter. A coal stove in the opposite corner filled the room with warmth.

Adam touched his mother's hand. It was icy. "Thinking about what?"

"Things." She turned to him, slipped her hand from underneath his fingers, and touched his face. "How nice it is that you're back. Even if it's for a short time."

How he longed to tell her he was staying for good. Each day he spent in Middlefield, he leaned more toward that decision. But as with Emma, he couldn't say the words. Not until he was absolutely sure. Not until there was no possibility he'd have to take them back. "Why don't you come upstairs? I'm sure *Daed* is wondering where you are."

She shrugged. "I think I'll stay down here for a little while longer."

Adam rose. His mother stared at her lap, her gaze not moving. An alarm went off inside him. Whatever was troubling her, she wasn't going to tell him. Then again, why would she? He hadn't proved the most trustworthy of sons.

He had always known he'd disappointed his father, yet assumed his mother felt differently about him. Now he wasn't so sure.

Emma intended to go straight to her room, to nurse the wound Adam had reopened. Somehow she had to be free of him. She couldn't keep living like this, pretending not to love him. Not as long as he stayed in Middlefield.

She stopped at the bottom of the stairs and touched her forehead to the banister. Maybe there was only one way to get Adam out of her mind and heart. She'd have to marry someone else. Devote her life to another man.

A man like Mark.

Her stomach churned at the thought. She didn't believe Adam's claim that Mark was up to no good, and yet she felt awkward around him. They had little in common. Her skin didn't tingle and her blood didn't warm when he was near. Not like with Adam.

Emma heard a low moan, followed by a hacking sound, and a chill ran through her. She scrambled upstairs to her grandmother's room. As she entered, the old woman was sitting up in bed, wheezing. She reached out toward Emma.

"Grossmammi?"

Her grandmother didn't answer. Another round of coughing seized her, and it sounded as if her lungs might burst. She pressed a handkerchief to her mouth. When she drew it away, it was stained with—

Blood.

Chapter Twenty-Two

Adam was halfway up the stairs when he heard pounding on the front door. He opened it to find Emma, panting and terrified.

"Grossmammi." Her breathing came in spurts. "Something's…wrong."

"Emma, catch your breath." He pulled her into the house and put his hands on her trembling shoulders to steady her. Adam heard his mother ascending the basement stairs behind him. "Is Leona okay?"

"I don't know," Adam said. He turned to Emma again.

"She's bleeding." Emma's words were nearly a sob. "Coughing up blood. Wheezing. Really hard. I need to use your phone. Have to call an ambulance."

"The phone is in the barn. I'll go." Carol

started for the door. "Adam, run upstairs and wake your father."

"I'll take Leona in my truck. By the time the ambulance gets here, we'll already be at the hospital." He turned to Emma. "Is it all right if she rides with me?"

"We'll both ride with you."

His mother pushed Adam's back. "I'll let your father know. Hurry!"

Adam dashed to his bedroom and grabbed his keys off the dresser. He took the stairs halfway down, then vaulted over the banister, grabbed Emma's hand, and ran with her to the house and up to Leona's room.

"Get anything you think she'll need," Adam said. Emma went to Leona's dresser while Adam rushed to the old woman's bedside. His stomach lurched when he saw the bloodstained handkerchief in her hand. "I'm going to take you to the hospital in my truck, *ya*?"

Her eyes barely opened, but she didn't hesitate. "*Ya*. Hand…me…cane…"

"Nee." He scooped her featherlight body into his arms. "Get the quilt off the bed, Emma. We'll wrap her in it." He rushed downstairs, holding Leona against him, cringing with every wheezing breath she took.

"Mrs. Shetler, we have to admit you." The petite doctor, her straight black hair pulled into a tight bun, wrote something on the chart. "You have severe pneumonia."

"I...just...need...my...tea." Emma's grandmother tilted her head toward the bag of IV fluid to her right. "Not...all...this...stuff."

Emma sat in the chair in the corner of the small examination room. "Stop being so stubborn. Dr. Chang is trying to help you."

"Take...me...home."

Emma shook her head and looked at the doctor. "She must be feeling a little better. She didn't put up a fight when we brought her in here."

"That's because she's getting some fluids and a powerful dose of antibiotic." She looked at a computer screen situated above *Grossmammi's* head. Emma didn't understand what the numbers meant. Or what the white clamp was on her grandmother's finger.

Dr. Chang checked the instruments and frowned. "She's resting. Can I speak to you outside?"

Emma followed the doctor into the emergency room hallway. A nurse passed them and entered the room beside her grandmother's. The beeping sound of all the machines pounded in Emma's brain.

"We need to take your grandmother to Intensive Care," Dr. Chang said. "Pneumonia can be deadly for patients her age."

"Admit her, then."

"I can't, not without her consent."

"I'll talk to her."

Dr. Chang nodded. "Once she's in ICU she'll have excellent care. It's her best chance for survival."

Emma nodded and went back into the examination cubicle. She held her grandmother's hand. *Grossmammi's* eyes opened.

"You have to listen." Emma wiped her eyes with her free hand. "You need to stay here. Just for a few days. Until you get well."

She shook her head. "Want...to...*geh*...home..."

Emma couldn't hold back the tears. "Please, *Grossmammi*. Please listen to the doctors. I want you to come home too. But I can't lose you. Not now." She pressed her forehead against the frail, veined hand. "I don't want to be alone."

"Lieb..."

She lifted her head, gazing into her grandmother's pale eyes.

"You will never...be alone." *Grossmammi* took a breath. It racked her chest. She trembled, yet somehow continued to speak. "You will always have God."

"I know." Emma sniffed, wiping her nose on the back of her hand.

"And you will always…have your…*familye*. Clara. Peter."

"It's not the same." *It's not enough.*

The old woman looked into Emma's eyes. "Don't…cry. I'll stay. For…you." Her grandmother managed a small smile. "God isn't ready for me…yet."

Adam paced the length of the empty emergency waiting room. A slow night. Lucky for Leona. No, not luck. God's hand. Adam was sure of it.

The silver doors opened and Emma came out, her eyes red and puffy. "Is she all right?"

She nodded. "She agreed to stay in ICU. She has pneumonia. The doctor wouldn't tell me what her chances were. Just that she wouldn't survive if she wasn't hospitalized." Emma put her hands over her face.

Adam pulled her close, pressing his hand against her *kapp*, gently nudging her to lean against him. "She'll be okay, Emma."

She pulled away. "They told me *Mammi* would be okay too. That they'd caught the cancer in time." She turned her back to him. "I can't lose someone else I love."

He came up behind her. "You won't."

"You don't know that."

He turned her to face him. "Then let's pray."

Her eyes widened. "Here?"

He reached for her hands. "I can't think of a better place." Closing his eyes, he silently spoke everything on his heart. He felt Emma clasp his hands tighter as she offered up her own silent prayer. A short time later they both opened their eyes.

"Adam?" Emma looked up at him, her eyes filled with wonder.

"Ya?"

She reached up and wiped his cheek with her finger.

He stared at the moisture glistening on her fingertip. Until that moment he hadn't realized he'd been crying.

Emma sat next to Adam in the waiting room. She looked at his long, slender fingers intertwined with her stubby ones. He hadn't let go of her hand since they'd prayed together.

As they waited to hear more news about her grandmother, she had to remind herself that Adam held her hand out of compassion. Friendly support, and nothing else. Still, his touch comforted her in a way she'd never experienced. She wished she never had to let him go.

The outside doors to the emergency room swished open, and Clara and Peter came rushing in. Adam and Emma stood up. Adam dropped her hand and Clara moved toward Emma.

"Where is she?" Clara demanded.

"She's okay," Adam said, holding up his hand. "She's—"

"I wasn't talking to you."

"Clara," Peter said, touching her shoulder.

"It's all right." Adam stepped back.

Emma felt the emptiness of her hand, the lack of warmth at her side as Adam and Peter moved to the other side of the room to talk.

Clara turned to Emma. "What happened?"

Emma explained everything. Including the ride in Adam's truck. That news seemed to disturb Clara more than their grandmother's illness.

"You let him bring *Grossmammi* here? He's in the *bann*."

"It was either that or wait for an ambulance."

"Maybe you should have waited."

"There was *nee* time!" Emma lowered her voice. "You should be thanking Adam instead of being angry with him."

Clara glanced at Adam and Peter, who were still speaking in hushed tones. She focused on Emma again. "How long will she have to stay?"

"They didn't say. Probably several days, maybe more."

"Then we'll have to get the shop open as soon as possible."

"Is that all you can think about? The stupid fabric shop?" Emma shook her head, let out a weary sigh.

"Nee," Clara said, her jaw clenched. "I'm thinking about bills. We can't afford to pay for this." Her lower lip shook.

Normally Clara's fears mirrored her own. But not this time. Emma looked at Adam, who had turned his gaze from Peter. Their eyes met. "God will provide," she whispered, too softly for Clara to hear.

And suddenly Emma realized that she believed the words as deeply as her grandmother did. "God will provide."

"Danki for bringing Leona, Adam," Peter said. "Your *daed* came over and told us that she was at the hospital, but he didn't mention you had brought her here." He glanced at his wife. "Probably a *gut* thing, seeing Clara's reaction."

Adam shrugged. "I know."

"I understand the reasoning behind *meidung.* But in this case you did the right thing. I'm sure the bishop, if he hears about it, will understand as well."

The last thing Adam was worried about at the moment was the bishop's reaction. "Where are the *kinner?"*

"With our neighbor Julia."

"And Mark?" Adam was surprised he hadn't come with Peter and Clara. This would be a prime opportunity for him to show Emma how much he *cared*.

"He wasn't home. Took a walk after supper. He's been doing that a lot lately." Peter glanced at his wife, who was still talking to Emma. "To be honest, I'm glad he left."

"Ya?"

"He seems to get along with the *buwe* well enough..." He rubbed his temple. "Let's just say I'd rather *mei kinner* be with Julia right now."

Peter's words fueled Adam's own suspicions. His own cousin didn't trust Mark with his children. Adam didn't trust the man with Emma. He was positive Leona didn't trust Mark at all.

Clara and Emma approached. Clara stood by Peter and ignored Adam. "There isn't much we can do here tonight. Emma said she'd stay while they get *Grossmammi* admitted."

"Ken is still outside waiting." Adam assumed Peter was talking about the driver who had brought them to the hospital. "I told him not to leave until we knew what was going on."

Clara turned to Emma. "Are you sure you're going to be okay?"

Emma nodded. "I'll be fine."

"I'll stay with her," Adam said. Clara wouldn't approve, but he didn't care. Emma didn't need to be alone right now. To his surprise, Clara nodded. She and Peter left.

"You don't have to stay." Emma sat down on one of the chairs. "I'll be all right here. Dr. Chang will let me know when *Grossmammi* is taken to ICU."

Adam sat next to her and reached out for Emma's hand. He wasn't sure if she would take it. But after a moment or two he felt her cold fingers against his palm.

"I'm not going anywhere," he said.

"Do you want to talk about it, Clara?"

Clara thumbed through the fabric catalogs, ignoring Peter's question. They had returned from the hospital a couple of hours ago, retrieved the children from Julia's, and put them to bed. She nibbled at a cuticle as she tried to figure out how much fabric to order. She had to be careful not to spend too much in the beginning, yet they had to have enough inventory to draw people into the shop.

"Clara?" Peter sat down next to her at the kitchen table. A battery-operated lantern on the counter flooded the area with bright light. He took her hand from her lips and held it. "Talk to me."

"There's nothing to talk about." Clara withdrew her hand from Peter's. "*Grossmammi* is getting *gut* care at the hospital. She'll be home in a few days. By that time we should have the fabric shop ready to stock. I should probably order this fabric tomorrow. Maybe some yarn too. Knitting needles, thread—"

Mark strolled into the kitchen. "Is this a private discussion?" Without waiting for an answer, he went to the pantry and took out a box of crackers. "Thought I'd get a midnight snack."

"As a matter of fact, this *is* a private conversation." Peter stood. "*Mei fraa* and I were talking."

"About Leona? I'm sure she'll be fine."

Clara looked up at him. He spoke the right words, the correct sentiment for the occasion, but there was no warmth in his voice, no compassion. His mouth was twisted in a smirk. His eyes held a strange, triumphant look. He seemed almost… happy.

Quickly he cast down his gaze, pulled out a few crackers, and put the package back in the pantry. "I'll pray for your *grossmammi*, Clara."

She glanced at her husband. Had she imagined that gleeful spark? Peter's hand rested on the table, but his fingers were curled under, as if he were trying not to tighten his fist. Had he seen it too?

"Gut nacht." Mark hurried out of the room.

"Clara, we have to talk," Peter said.

"Not about *Grossmammi*." She fought to hold

back tears. Emma wasn't the only one worried about her. How would they cope if they lost her, especially so soon after their mother died?

"*Nee*, not Leona." A softness entered Peter's eyes when he said her name. "About us."

"Peter, not now."

"Then when? When Leona gets back from the hospital? When the fabric store opens?" His Adam's apple bobbed. "When we start sleeping in separate bedrooms?"

She glanced up at him. "That's not going to happen."

"We're drifting apart, Clara. Why can't you see that? Or maybe you do." His brows furrowed. "Maybe it's what you want."

The catalog page bent in her hand. "*Nee*. That's not what I want."

Peter took her hand. "Then come with me. Come to our bed."

Clara snatched her hand away. "*Mei gross-mammi's* dying and that's all you're thinking about? Your marital rights?"

Sadness entered Peter's eyes. "*Nee, lieb.* I want to hold you. Comfort you. Tell you everything will be all right until you believe it. I want you to fall asleep in *mei* arms, at peace. Not toss and turn like you do every night."

She looked away, touched by his loving words. Yet she resisted him at the same time, and didn't understand why. She needed her husband. But she wanted to be alone.

Clara picked up another catalog, not looking at him. "I'll be upstairs in a little bit. Make sure you don't wake the *buwe* when you get in bed."

Peter waited. Clara kept her gaze on the catalog, the fabric selections swimming in front of her eyes. Finally, he got up and left.

When he was gone, she sat there unable to move, holding her chin in her hand as the tears rolled down her face.

Chapter Twenty-Three

"Now, now. I don't need all this fuss."

Emma laughed as her grandmother slowly, but with more strength than she had shown in the past two weeks, made her way into the house, flanked on each side by Peter and Norman. Adam walked behind them.

"We're not making a fuss," Emma said.

"Ya." Clara stood next to Emma. "I had to stop Emma from making a welcome home banner for you."

"I'm glad you did." *Grossmammi* leaned on her cane. She turned to Norman, then to Peter. "Now shoo, both of you. I can make it to *mei* chair by myself." She shuffled over and lowered herself into the seat. She leaned back, her white *kapp* pressing against the high back of the upholstered chair. "It's *gut* to be home."

"And we're glad you're back." Carol Otto came

in from the kitchen, carrying a tray laden with a teapot and several cups. She set the tray on the coffee table in the middle of the living room. "I knew you'd want tea when you got home."

The old woman nodded and accepted the cup. Her hands were steady. Emma released her breath, relieved. Her grandmother's complexion was vibrant, her voice stronger. The week she'd spent in the hospital, receiving medication, being forced to rest, and gaining back her energy was well worth the huge bills that would arrive soon.

Yet instead of fretting as she did after her *mammi* died, Emma clung to the words she'd spoken in the hospital emergency room. *God will provide.* She didn't know how. It wasn't her place to know. It was her place to grasp on to her faith and accept.

"Glad you're back where you belong, Leona," Adam said.

The two of them looked at each other for a moment. Adam nodded. "I'll be outside if you need me."

Emma watched Adam leave. During the week her grandmother had been gone, he'd spent most of his time at the house, taking care of Dill, feeding the chickens, gathering the eggs, tending to the dogs and cats, keeping the barn clean. He had fixed the loose boards on the front porch, had split and stacked enough wood to last them through winter, had done a dozen other odd jobs around the place.

And all without asking anything in return.

Carol sat on the couch near *Grossmammi's* chair. The two women were deep in conversation; Peter and Norman had already left.

Clara nodded toward Emma. "Let's *geh* outside."

It was nearing the end of October. The cool air brushed across Emma's cheeks. She saw Adam disappear into the barn. He'd been checking on Dill every day, making sure the horse spent time outside eating grass and getting light exercise. He'd taken her to his father's pasture. Norman hadn't objected. Maybe he and Adam were finally making amends.

"I guess Peter went back to the shop." Clara folded her hands in front of her. "It's nearly ready to open. We're just waiting on the last of the inventory. You've spent a lot of time at the hospital, so you haven't seen the progress." She turned to Emma. "Would you like to?"

Emma hesitated. Her grandmother's illness had given her an excuse not to go inside her grandfather's workshop. She already saw the changes on the outside. New wood slab siding, complete with a fresh coat of white paint. New roof shingles. There was a brand-new oak door, stained a honey brown color, with shiny brass hardware. The place looked beautiful. Inviting. And ready for business.

With trepidation Emma headed toward the workshop. She and Clara stopped in front of the door. She turned to her sister. "Peter's done a wonderful job," Emma said.

"Wait until you see the inside."

The transformation amazed Emma. The layers of dust and grime and rust had been scoured away, but the walls still had their natural, rough-hewn look. Against one wall a large wooden square, divided into separate cubbyholes, held different colors of yarn. Next to it was a rack filled with fabric. The plain blue, green, gray, purple, and pale green hues used to make Amish dresses, plus some fancier quilting fabric. There was plenty of space in the shop for more bolts of fabric, but enough to get the store started.

As she walked through the shop, her footsteps echoed against a brand-new floor. The old rough wood had been replaced with new varnished planks. It gave the shop a finished look.

"Norman donated the wood," Clara said. "He and Adam installed the floor."

Emma glanced at her sister. Clara stared straight ahead, but Emma could sense her gratitude.

Her gaze traveled to the back wall, next to the window. She saw a small version of her grandfather's Peg-Board attached to the wall. His four favorite tools—an old hammer, a rusty wood plane, a dull chisel, and a T-square hung on the board.

"That was Peter's idea." Clara folded her arms. "I argued with him at first. Tools don't belong in a fabric shop." She sighed. "But he was right. It's like having a part of *Grossvadder* here with us."

Emma swallowed past the lump in her throat. Even among the fabric and yarn, her grandfather's memory shone through.

"So what do you think?"

She turned around at the male voice. "Mark. I didn't realize you were here." She looked back over the shop. "It's wonderful. Beyond what I ever expected." *Or wanted*. But now she could see her sister's vision. She even shared it. She regretted giving Clara such a hard time.

"Can't take much of the credit." Mark shrugged. "Clara and Peter worked overtime this week to get things ready."

"Thankfully Julia was willing to watch the *kinner*." Clara sighed. "I'll be glad when I can spend more time with them again." She looked at Emma. "I've missed them."

Emma vowed to give her sister a break once the shop opened. She looked at it again, imagining customers streaming in. She would set a rocking chair in the corner for *Grossmammi*. Her grandmother would love to visit with the patrons, both Amish and Yankee.

Mark stepped between Emma and Clara. He spoke in a soft tone and grinned. "Now that your *grossmammi's* feeling better, I'd like to take you out to supper. If that's agreeable to you."

"I don't know, Mark. I've been at the hospital so much this week. I really want to stay home."

His smile slipped. "Another time, then. When you've had some time to spend with your *familye*."

Emma paused. She had to be honest with him. It wasn't fair to let him think they had a chance together.

Then a thought occurred to her. She had never seen Adam's decision to leave from his point of view before. Instead she had wrapped herself in layers of anger, hurt, and resentment. But he had only been trying to be fair to her, the way she needed to be with Mark. Why hadn't she seen it?

"Emma?"

She jerked her head and looked at Mark. "Sorry. I was lost in *mei* thoughts for a moment. Can I talk to you?"

"Right now?"

"*Ya*. In private."

Clara started to move. "I'll leave you two alone, then."

Emma shook her head. "*Nee*. I need to check

on *Grossmammi*." She looked up at Mark. "Why don't you come inside? I'm sure she'd like to see you."

He took a step back from Emma, his eyes widening for a split second. Then he smiled, shaking his head. "I'm sure she's not up for much company. I'll pay her a visit later."

"All right. We can talk on the front porch afterward, then. I'll meet you there in a few minutes."

"Looking forward to it."

As Emma turned to leave, Peter came in. He had his hands behind his back. "How do you like the shop, Emma?"

She grinned. "It's wonderful, Peter. Just wonderful."

He turned to Mark. "I need to talk to Clara for a minute. If you don't mind."

Emma noticed that Peter's expression had turned cold when he spoke to Mark. If his cousin noticed, he didn't say anything. "Sure. Emma, I'll walk you to the house."

But as they left the shop, Emma saw Mark glance over his shoulder at Peter and Clara.

"Emma liked the tools," Clara said.

"I thought she would. I couldn't bear to part with his favorite ones."

Clara looked into the gentle eyes of her hus-

band. Over the past week, as they had worked together to refinish the shop, something between
them had changed. They hadn't said much, but
she didn't feel the tension that had been between
them for the past couple of months. She realized
this morning that for the first time they were
working together toward a goal, instead of working against each other. She went to him and stood
on her tiptoes. Kissed his cheek.

His face turned red. "What was that for?"

"Do I need to have a reason?"

Peter's brow furrowed. "Lately, I think so."
When Clara started to frown, he quickly added,
"But I'll take it." He smiled. "I brought you some-
thing."

"Oh?"

Peter moved his hands from behind his back.
"Here. It wouldn't be a proper shop without a
proper sign."

Clara took the carved wooden sign from Peter's hands. SHETLERS' FABRICS. The words were
chiseled in the soft wood. A thin scrolling surrounded the name. The sign was simple. Plain.
Perfect. She set it on the windowsill and stood
back to admire it. "Where did you get this?"

"I made it. Found some spare wood while I
was cleaning out the shop. Didn't take me long."
He glanced away. "I had the free time to do it."

Clara knew he wasn't just talking about not

having a job. Their distance from each other, both physical and emotional, had taken a toll on them both. Suddenly everything she'd been holding inside—the grief, guilt, worry, resentment, empty faith—all came rushing to the surface. She burst into tears.

"Clara?" Peter put his hands on her shoulders. When she didn't resist, she felt him pull her against him and lean his cheek against the top of her head. "Clara, what is it?"

"I'm sorry." She turned her face into his jacket, breathing in the scent of wood smoke and sawdust. "I've been a horrible *fraa*."

"Nee." He stroked her back, tightening his embrace. "You haven't."

"Don't try to make me feel better."

He pulled back from her and rubbed her damp cheeks with his rough thumbs. "Clara, that's what I'm supposed to do. It's what I want to do." He leaned down and cupped her face. "I've been waiting for you to let *geh* of all this for a long time."

"What do you mean?"

"You're the strongest woman I've ever known. I knew that through your letters. I fell in love with your confidence. Your independence. And when I met you, I saw how beautiful you were, how kind. I knew I was blessed."

He held up a hand to stop her from interrupting. "But you're not perfect. None of us are. It's why we need Jesus. Why we need to lean on the Lord. To let Him help us. You want to fix everything, do everything yourself."

Tears continued to build up, making Clara's chest hurt. "But I can't."

Peter shook his head. "*Nee*. You've never taken time to grieve your *mammi*. You've worried too much about money. About me finding a job." He kissed her cheek. "You've worked on this shop until you're exhausted. And then Leona took ill. It's too much to keep inside, Clara. Give some of your burden to me. Let me help you give all of it to God." He drew her back into his arms. "Allow yourself peace, *lieb*."

Mark tapped his fingers against the hickory rocker on the Shetlers' front porch. Emma had kept him waiting here for over an hour. Dusk had already descended, and a short while ago he saw Peter and Clara head for home. He frowned, disturbed at the image of his cousin and his wife. They were holding hands. At one point she rested her head against his arm. Something had happened in the workshop after he left.

He rose and started to pace. It hadn't been this difficult with Laura. And he'd been attracted to her, at least physically. But that didn't stop him from taking what he wanted. She had made it so easy.

Unlike Emma.

He fought the urge to pound his fist against the porch railing. They were all getting under his skin. His dullard cousin, along with his controlling wife. Their noisy kids. Dumpy Emma. That idiot Adam. But most of all, the old woman.

Even being out here on her porch made his soul curdle. He'd never had such a reaction to anyone before. He searched hard to define it. Last night it came to him, unsettling him even more.

Fear.

He was afraid of her. And he had no idea why.

He stepped off the porch and looked around. Was there anything here worth going through with this? While Emma had been at the hospital and Clara and Peter had been working on the shop, he'd taken time to search the land, the barn, the house. No cash assets to speak of, but if he could marry Emma and sell everything out from under her, he'd make out pretty well. Once he left her and Middlefield behind, of course, she wouldn't be able to divorce him and marry someone else; it wasn't the Amish way. But he didn't care. He'd have what he came here for.

During his time spent in town, he had looked into property values. Assuming he could find a buyer, he stood to pocket a tidy sum. But only if he and Emma married. And he didn't see that happening. At least not as long as Adam Otto was in the way.

He ought to just leave Middlefield, cut his losses and get out. But pride wouldn't let him concede, not quite yet. He wasn't about to let these *dummkopfs* get the best of him.

He looked over at the shiny black pickup truck parked in the Ottos' driveway. Adam hadn't parted with it; maybe that was a hopeful sign. Maybe Adam would leave again, breaking Emma's heart once more. And Mark would be there to pick up the pieces.

But his patience was running thin. It was time to give the Yankee boy a little push in that direction.

The door opened with a squeak. Finally Emma had arrived. Mark turned back to the porch.

But it wasn't Emma. It was Leona.

"Sit down, *yung mann*. I want a word with you." Leona leaned on her cane and pointed to her late son's hickory rocker. She wasn't surprised to see Mark recoil for an instant; she knew quite well how he responded to her. It took a moment for him to recover, to resume his casual stance.

"I'm waiting for Emma," he said.

"She's making supper right now." Leona lifted her chin. "Apparently she forgot about you."

"Or someone told her I left." Mark's grin never faltered, although fire reached his eyes. "Since she's busy, I should be on my way. Remind her of our visit. I'll come by again tomorrow."

"Not before you and I have had a talk. Sit."

He didn't say anything, but he didn't sit either. Leona sensed evil from the boy. She'd prayed mightily before coming out here. The courage of the Lord supported her. Yet she also felt something else. Pity for Mark King. Sorrow for what he had become, the path he had chosen to take. "There's still time, *sohn*."

Mark stepped back. "I'm not your *sohn*."

"*Nee*. But you are God's. And He's calling you back to Him."

He shook his head and moved toward the porch steps. "You don't know anything, old woman."

But Leona could see the change in his eyes. The fear that entered them. "Don't be afraid, Mark. God will forgive you. For whatever you have done."

"I have done nothing!" he hissed. Then he took a deep breath, straightened his shoulders, and gave her his chip-toothed smile. "I'm a faithful member of the Amish church. I attend worship. I follow the *Ordnung*." His smile widened. "I wish to court your granddaughter."

"You've made your intentions plain in that matter." Leona breathed in. The chilly air cut through her thin sweater. "Why do you want to court her?"

Mark's smile dimmed. "What do you mean?"

"You've just met her. You've spent little time together. What is it about *mei* sweet Emma that you love?"

"Her kindness," Mark said quickly. "As you said, she is a sweet *maedel*."

"And that's the only reason?"

"*Nee*. There are more." He averted his gaze for a moment. His eyes met hers again. The fear was gone. "But *mei* reasons for wanting Emma are none of your business."

"Wanting Emma? Not caring for her? Or loving her?" Leona hobbled forward, pointing her cane toward him. "Emma's heart belongs to someone else. You'll not have it."

Mark laughed. The sound rang hollow, humorless. "You're *ab im kopp*, you know that? Whatever drugs they gave you in the hospital addled your mind. If it wasn't already addled before."

Leona leaned on her cane again. "Your insults don't affect me, *sohn*. I'm only here to ask you to leave our *familye* alone."

"Or what?" Mark bent halfway toward her to look her in the eyes. He didn't bother hiding his contempt. "You'll chase after me on those feeble legs of yours?"

"I won't do anything." Leona turned her back on Mark, making herself vulnerable to him. God was her fortress and guard, and she did not fear Mark King. She opened the door and looked over her shoulder.

"I won't have to do anything. God will do what needs to be done."

Chapter Twenty-Four

"Laura, this is a terrible idea."

Laura Stutzman pulled her suitcase out of the backseat of her friend Abby's car. "You promised you wouldn't tell anyone where I was going."

"But what about your parents? They'll worry about you." Abby leaned against the car. Behind them buses spewed exhaust. The grinding of the shifting gears nearly drowned out Abby's voice.

"I left them a note." Laura ignored the stares from passers-by at the Nashville, Tennessee, station. "I'm an adult. If I want to take a vacation, I can."

"This isn't a vacation. And they won't like that I helped you. They barely tolerate our friendship."

"That's not true, Abby." Laura looked at her friend. "They're just very…quiet." Laura searched past Abby's shoulder. "What time is it?"

"Eight thirty. And that's another thing. You're traveling all the way to Ohio at night?" She pushed a strand of long brown hair over her shoulder. "They didn't have any buses going during the day?"

Laura shook her head. It wasn't true, but she needed to get to Middlefield as soon as possible. As it was, she would have to take three transfers, plus hire a taxi from Ashtabula to Middlefield. Between fares and food along the way, it would take nearly everything she had.

But it was her only chance to get back what Mark King had stolen from her and from her family. "I'd better *geh*." She gave her friend a one-armed hug, clutching her suitcase with the other hand. "Thank you for bringing me."

"I'm going to regret it. And I'll worry about you."

"Don't. God will watch over me."

"I hope so." Another bus belched a plume of exhaust. "I pray He will."

Laura hurried to purchase her tickets. She climbed on the bus, relieved when she saw that it wasn't full. She sat in the first row, nearest to the bus driver. God might be watching over her, but anxiety still coiled and writhed in her stomach like some poisonous and evil serpent.

Laura stared out the window and watched

as the bus pulled out of the station. Her parents would be furious with her when they woke up in the morning. Not that they weren't already angry. She had made a mistake trusting Mark. A mistake only she could fix.

Her family's future depended on it.

Clara finished the supper dishes as Peter came into the kitchen. "The *kinner* are in bed. Julia must have exhausted them. Melvin fell asleep right away." He came up behind Clara and put his arms around her waist.

She turned in his embrace and gave him a playful tap on the arm. "Peter. Mark could come in any minute."

Peter's smile turned rueful. He dropped his arms to his sides. "I've been thinking about asking him to leave, Clara."

"Why would you do that? He's *familye*."

"He has given nothing in return for our hospitality."

"We should expect *nix*, Peter. You know that."

"Not in this case." Peter took the dish towel from Clara's hand and set it on the counter. "He knows we're struggling, yet he hasn't offered to pay for a single meal. He hasn't worked a day."

"He's helped with the shop. And with you in the barn."

"Chores Junior and Melvin could handle. I don't know how to explain it, Clara. I don't trust him. I haven't for a while." He suddenly stepped away and walked to the kitchen door. He peered out, as if he expected Mark to be waiting there. He returned to Clara, lowering his voice. "I don't know how to explain it. I feel like we're being used."

"But it's for a *gut* reason. He wants to court Emma."

Peter shook his head. "He doesn't act like a *mann* in love, Clara."

"Maybe he shows it differently."

"Or maybe he isn't in love at all."

Clara held up her hands. "He probably isn't because he doesn't know her well yet. If Adam Otto would stay out of the way—"

"Adam cares for Emma. He's the one who acts like a *mann* in love. Not Mark."

"Why, because he drove her and *Grossmammi* to the hospital? Because he cleaned out the barn?"

Peter dropped his hands to his sides. "Clara, you have to forgive him for what he did to Emma. You know that."

She nodded, looking away. "I can't. Not yet." She gazed into her husband's eyes. "I don't want to fight anymore, Peter. Not about Adam. Or Mark, or anything else."

He pressed his lips against hers. "I don't want

to fight either. But I'm asking Mark to leave in the morning. He will be gone, Clara. I think that's the only way we'll have our lives back."

Mark stood under the stairwell in the darkened living room. He could barely see the outlines of the furniture in front of him, but he could hear every word Peter said. First Leona wanted him gone, now his cousin.

The old woman he could understand. But he had underestimated Peter. The man wasn't as weak as Mark thought he was.

Peter suddenly appeared in the living room. Mark didn't breathe. His cousin passed by the staircase, right in front of Mark. He stopped. Mark's lungs burned as he forced himself not to breathe. Red dots swam in front of his eyes. Finally Peter went up the staircase. When the door to his bedroom shut, Mark exhaled, then took in a huge gulp of air.

He cursed under his breath. Everything was going wrong. It had been so easy to dupe Laura and her family, taken so little time to gain their trust. The people here were just as vulnerable, this family just as battered and bruised. Financial troubles. Illness. Recent death. It should have been so simple to take advantage of them.

Mark knew his time in Middlefield was coming to an end, and soon. Yet he wasn't going

to walk away empty-handed. When he had arrived here, he'd made a vow. And nothing would
keep him from fulfilling it.

The first day of November dawned cloudy and
crisp. Emma went about doing her daily chores,
most of which Adam or his father had done while
Leona was in the hospital. She hummed to herself as she collected eggs and listened to the hens'
soft clucking.

The chickens flew out of their laying boxes
and went outside to peck at the last remnants
of grass in the barnyard. Emma scattered a few
handfuls of feed.

Dogs and cats appeared as if by magic as soon
as their bowls were filled. They all seemed fat,
fluffy, and happy, their coats thickening with the
approach of winter. Dill's foot was still tender,
yet she didn't seem to be in as much pain, thanks
to Adam's diligent care. For once, life seemed
almost normal.

Emma grasped the basket of eggs and walked
outside. Adam was in the backyard, rake in hand.
He'd already collected a decent pile of leaves. He
tossed the rake to one side, knelt down, and lit a
match, tossing it into the pile. A thin stream of
smoke rose from the middle of the limp, dead
leaves.

He stood and stared at the pile, his fists resting

at his narrow waist. She hadn't seen him wear his Yankee clothes in a long time. But the truck was still in the driveway, a constant reminder that he could leave at any moment.

Treasure the days you have. She wasn't sure where the thought had come from. Maybe it was one of her grandmother's phrases. Or her mother's.

An ache opened up in her heart. Emma would have done anything to have more time with *Mammi*. She had felt the same way when Adam left. Now he was here, but instead of taking advantage of the time she had with him, all she could focus on was the possibility of him leaving again.

It was a waste, pure and simple.

Emma strolled over and stood next to him. She set the basket of eggs on the ground, well away from the fire smoldering in the leaves.

"*Gut daag* to burn them." Adam kept his focus on the leaves. "No wind. Damp ground from the rain a couple days ago."

"There are so many to get rid of." Emma looked around at the piles. Even beyond those, a carpet of oak and maple leaves covered her yard, small patches of green grass peeking through. Yet she didn't worry about the fire Adam created. She trusted him.

"I'll do what I can." He turned to Emma. "I won't be able to get them all, but I'll at least make a dent."

He paused, staring at her.

Emma frowned. "What?"

"Just waiting for you to tell me I don't have to do anything. Or to *geh* home so you can finish this." The teasing glint in his eyes disappeared. "Or for you to tell me to leave you alone forever."

She looked at him, and something inside her shattered. She'd nursed the past long enough. Since his return a little more than a month ago, they had danced around what happened the night he left Middlefield. It was time to talk about it. Neither of them would have peace if they didn't.

Before she could say anything, he looked at the leaves again. "Seeing Mark again today?"

"Why would you think that?"

He shrugged. Pushed at the edge of the leaves with the toe of his boot. "Figured he'd be by today. To continue your *date*."

"It wasn't a date. I'm not interested in Mark."

"Then why did you *geh* for a walk with him?"

Was that jealousy she heard in his tone? "He asked me to. I didn't want to be rude."

"You could have said *nee*."

"But I didn't." She glanced at him. "Sounds like that might bother you."

He turned and faced her. "*Ya*. It bothers me. I already told you I don't trust him."

She looked into his eyes. "Is that the only reason?"

Chapter Twenty-Five

Adam couldn't answer her. He also couldn't drag his gaze away from her. She seemed different this morning. The lively spark that once filled her eyes had returned. Behind her the clouds had parted slightly, revealing pale yellow streaks of sunbeams. The light illumined her, but the sunshine wasn't what made her glow. It was something else.

"You haven't answered my question." Emma's lips curved into a soft smile.

He'd forgotten the question completely. But he couldn't admit that. Instead he busied himself with the fire, stirring the leaves with the tines of the rake, just enough to let the fire spread a little, but not get beyond his control.

He wished he could do the same with his emotions.

When he glanced at her, he could see her smile

had faded. The spark dimmed. She reached for the basket of eggs. "Never mind. I need to start breakfast. Leona's been sleeping in since she arrived from the hospital. I'm glad; she needs the rest—"

"Emma." He took the basket from her hand and set it down. "I don't trust Mark."

"You've said that." Her brown eyes dulled. "Several times."

"But that's not the only reason I don't want him coming around." The words he wanted to say next stuck in his throat. The words he should have said that night two years ago. The night she begged him not to leave. The night she kissed him. The night she told him she loved him.

"Adam?" Her tone betrayed her annoyance. She shook her head. "Forget it. I'm going back to the *haus*."

"I'm sorry," he blurted. "I'm sorry I left." He stepped toward her. The rich smoky scent of incinerating leaves surrounded them. "I'm sorry I left the way I did."

Emma held his gaze. "I know. And I resented you for it. For a long time." When he started to speak, she held up her hand. "But I realized I resented myself even more. For being such a fool. For putting you in the position I did. Revealing my feelings that way." Her cheeks reddened. She looked down. "I was…desperate."

He could sense her embarrassment. Wanted to wipe it away. An apology couldn't do that. It couldn't erase the regrets they both clung to. "You were being honest. I admired you for that."

She looked up at him. "You did?"

He nodded. "You were honest when I couldn't be. I should have told you the truth, Emma. The real reason I left. I only told you part of it."

Her lips started to tremble. "Then what was it? Why did you leave?"

"I didn't feel like I belonged here." He looked past her shoulder, at the plain Amish house with the simple, brand-new fabric shop just beyond it. Breathed in the scents of smoke, of straw, of cows and horses. "I couldn't see myself as a farmer. Or being Amish. I didn't want to follow the rules." He looked at her. "*Mei vadder's* rules."

"Adam, I know all that."

He looked at her, his gaze stopping at her mouth. Remembered the tender kiss she'd given him. The first kiss for them both. And after she kissed him, he'd walked away. "You deserve better than that, Emma."

Her thin eyebrows knitted together. "I don't understand."

"You deserve better than me. That's why I left the way I did. You didn't need a messed-up kid who confused God's ways with his *daed's.*" He turned from her. "Emma, you need someone worthy of the woman you are. Someone who would put you first before himself. I'm not that *mann*."

He flinched when she touched his arm. He looked down at her hand. Her lovely hand. He longed to cover it with his own.

"Adam, maybe you weren't that *mann* then." When he turned to her, she met his eyes with her soft brown ones. "But you were the *mann* I wanted. The best friend I fell in love with."

"And now?" He barely formed the question.

She dropped her hand from his arm. "You know the answer to that." Emma picked up the basket of eggs and headed for the house.

Adam didn't stop her. Because they both knew he couldn't give her what she wanted. What she deserved. Not now. Maybe not ever.

Clara hummed as she finished the breakfast dishes. Peter had left a few minutes ago, still determined to check out any new job opportunities. "It can't hurt," he told her. Now that the fabric shop would be opening in a couple of days, Clara didn't see the need. But she realized Peter had been doing this all along. While she had been complaining and worrying about him finding work, he had been searching for jobs every day. She'd simply been too involved in herself to realize it.

Behind her, Magdalena banged on her high chair. Clara turned around and smiled at her daughter. After talking with Peter last night, hope had blossomed inside her. She dried her hands on the kitchen towel and picked up her daughter, hugging her close.

Junior and Melvin were outside, supposedly raking leaves. When Clara peeked out the window, they were throwing handfuls of them at each other instead of forming them into neat piles. She started to reprimand them but changed her mind. So what if the leaves didn't get done right now? Later she would go outside while Magdalena napped and they would rake them together. Maybe Peter would be back by then and they could do the chore as a family.

Except for Mark. She hadn't seen him since last night. He'd left before she and Peter got up this morning. Perhaps he was on another of his long walks. She frowned and kissed Magdalena's tiny clenched fist. She still wasn't sure Peter was right about Mark leaving so soon. Yet her husband had a point. His cousin hadn't done much work since he'd been here, hadn't offered to pay for any food, and his interest in Emma seemed erratic.

Suddenly she had begun to see the man with new eyes. Worry touched her heart. She'd been the one to encourage them to get together. What if she had been wrong about Mark all along?

She turned to leave the kitchen and take Magdalena upstairs to change into her dress and tiny *kapp* when she heard a knock. A tall, thin young woman with nearly transparent blond hair stood on the front porch.

Clara didn't recognize her, or her style of clothing. The hem of her dress reached her ankles instead of midcalf, the way women in Middlefield wore them. More pleats in the skirt, a *kapp* shaped just a bit differently. The girl was plainly Amish, but from some other community, a place more conservative, more in keeping with the Old Order.

"Can I help you?"

"I'm looking for Mark King." The girl seemed to be in her early twenties. She might have initially seemed shy, but she looked Clara directly in the eyes and spoke plainly. "I understand he is staying here."

"He is, but he's not here right now." Magdalena made a little cooing noise. Clara cuddled her closer to her chest. She glanced down and noticed a suitcase beside the woman's feet. "I'm not sure when he'll be back."

"I can wait for him."

Clara's brow lifted. "Why don't you come inside."

The woman picked up her suitcase and followed. As the door closed behind her, she set the case on the floor. "You are sure Mark King is staying here, *ya*?"

"As I said, I don't know where he went this morning, or when he's coming back," Clara repeated. Was the girl addled? She was definitely unusual. "You're welcome to wait if you want. Or if you have someplace else to *geh*, I can let him know you've come to visit him."

"I will wait." She stood near the front door, her thin fingers clasped together in front of her navy blue coat. An apron the same color as the dress peeked out from beneath the hem.

Magdalena's changing would have to wait. "Come into the kitchen and sit down. Would you like some coffee?"

"I would like to sit down, but *nee* coffee." She followed Clara into the kitchen and sat down in one of the chairs at the table.

Clara sat across from her, holding her daughter in her lap. "I'm Clara King."

"Laura Stutzman. From Etheridge, Tennessee."

Clara remembered Mark mentioning he'd spent time in Tennessee. "Is that where you met Mark?"

Her full lips set in an angry line. "*Ya*. But I wish I never had."

Laura's words took Clara aback. Clara herself

had never been one to shy away from expressing her irritation, yet this woman—this stranger— didn't seem to care who knew how angry she was with Mark. "Are you sure you don't want any coffee? I have some leftover pancakes from breakfast."

"I'm not hungry. But I appreciate the hospitality." Dark shadows underscored Laura's light brown eyes. She looked exhausted.

"Maybe you would like to lie down while you're waiting?" Clara suggested.

"*Nee.* I wish to speak to Mark. Hopefully he will return soon."

An uncertain dread filled Clara, and suddenly she wished Peter were here. She cuddled Magdalena in her lap. If Laura could be direct, so could Clara. "Is Mark in trouble?"

Laura locked gazes with Clara, her eyes filled with resentment. "*Ya.* He is in trouble with me."

"May I ask what happened?"

"I'd rather not talk about it." Laura looked away for an instant, then faced Clara again. "Mark King is a despicable human being. He's a liar and a thief. He is not to be trusted."

"You can't say that about a member of *mei familye* without an explanation, Laura."

"I cannot give you an explanation."

She *wouldn't* give Clara an explanation. That much was clear. "How did you find us?"

"Through *freinds* of Mark's family. They suspected he might be spending time with his cousin Peter King in Middlefield."

"How did you get here?"

"By bus. And taxi." She folded her hands in her lap. "That's all I will say until I see Mark."

Dozens of scenarios went through Clara's mind, none of them good. Coupled with Peter's growing suspicions of Mark...

Dread gathered inside Clara.

Junior and Melvin suddenly stormed through the back door. "We're *hungerich*!"

"You just had breakfast." She looked at her boys sternly. "I see throwing leaves at each other has built up your appetites."

"We're growing *buwe*." Junior grinned, using his father's common phrase.

"Have a couple of leftover pancakes. Wash your hands first."

The boys dashed out of the kitchen to the bathroom. Clara looked at Laura. She'd had no reaction to any of the children. That increased her alarm. Whatever Mark did to Laura and her family had devastated her. And this wisp of a girl was no match for him.

When Junior and Melvin burst into the kitchen again, she made a quick decision and rose from her chair. "Junior, Melvin, grab one pancake apiece. We're going to Julia's."

"Not again." Melvin's whiny pitch sounded like rust grinding against rust. "We're always going to Julia's."

"I promise I'll bring you a special treat." Clara had no idea what it would be, but the urgency to get her family and Laura out of the house grew. "Let's *geh*." She touched Laura on the shoulder.

"I will wait on Mark."

Clara lowered her voice. "You're coming with me. I'm dropping *mei kinner* off next door. Then we will *geh* somewhere Mark won't expect you to be."

Laura looked up at her, fire sparking in her eyes. "You can't protect him. I will get what he stole from *mei familye*. Even if I have to call the police."

"Laura." Clara leaned close and whispered, "I'm not protecting him. I'm protecting you."

Chapter Twenty-Six

Adam had just finished raking and burning several piles of leaves. His clothes reeked of smoke. He'd raked the remaining leaves into a big pile and looked in Emma's barn for trash bags. Not finding any, he headed for his barn, knowing where his father kept a good supply.

As he crossed his yard, he saw Clara and another woman walking up the driveway. What did Clara want now? Lately whenever they were in the same place she looked at him like he was a bug squashed on the bottom of her shoe. He didn't think so highly of her either. Not when she was so eager to get Mark and Emma together.

Clara and the young woman stopped at his truck. Adam met them there. "What can I do for you, Clara?" He didn't care for her, but she was Emma's sister, and he'd be polite.

"We need your help."

Those were the last words he expected out of her mouth. "*Mei* help?"

"*Ya.*" She pointed to the woman. "This is Laura Stutzman. She's from Tennessee."

"Nice to meet you." Still confused, he turned to Clara. "What's going on?"

"Laura needs a place to stay."

"*Nee.* What I need is to see Mark."

Adam had to respect the stubborn tilt of Laura's chin. She was a slender thing, and looked like a strong wind would blow her down the road. Still, he got the impression he wouldn't want to get on her bad side.

"Laura," Clara said, with more patience than Adam had ever seen her possess. "As I explained, you'll get a chance to see Mark. As soon as Peter comes home, he and I will bring Mark here. Then you can talk to him."

"I want to talk to him alone."

"That's not a *gut* idea."

"Clara?"

Adam turned at Emma's voice. She walked toward them, the ribbons of her *kapp* streaming down her back. As she neared, he thought about their earlier conversation. Wished it would have gone better. But he hid his emotions, much as she seemed to be hiding hers. She didn't look at him, but at Clara.

Clara repeated what she'd told Adam. Emma

frowned, her brows forming that cute V shape they did when she was confused. "Why can't she stay at your *haus*?" Emma asked.

"I...I don't think it's safe."

"You don't think Mark is safe?" Emma walked toward her. "You're the one who wanted the two of us together."

"You don't want to have anything to do with Mark." Laura stepped between them. "He'll do to you and your *familye* exactly what he did to us."

"Which was?"

Adam held up his hand. It didn't feel right, standing out here in the open. He wasn't sure why, but something prodded him to get the women into his house. "Come on. Let's *geh* inside."

"Leona? Leona, wake up..."

Leona's eyes flew open. Instant fear gripped her as Mark King leaned over her bed. How had he gotten in here?

She could see the fury building in his eyes. He stood, his hands behind his back, his sneer derisive. Leona's soul called out to the Lord. For calm. For wisdom. Above all, for courage.

Leona moved to sit up, but Mark shook his head. "Don't trouble yourself."

"What are you doing here?"

"I thought you'd die in the hospital." He paced

back and forth at the foot of her bed. "Coughing up blood like that. Usually old ladies like you don't survive being that sick." He stopped. "Then again, you're no ordinary old *fraa*."

"I don't think you mean that as a compliment."

"You're right. I don't." He walked over to the corner of the room. Took Ephraim's rocker. Opened the bedroom door and placed it in the hallway.

Leona started to move again. Mark rushed to her, making her freeze. "Did you know Laura was coming?"

"I don't know who Laura is."

"The idiot *maedel* came back for her money. She'll never get it." He shot a look at Leona. "Unlike Emma, Laura has looks, but little brains."

"She managed to find you."

Mark raised an eyebrow. "Not yet. She's only found Clara. But you're right. She's not the *dummkopf* I thought she was."

Leona had never seen such cruelty in a man's eyes. Heard such venom in his voice. She prayed for him, that whatever evil resided in him would flee.

"What about Adam and Emma?" he demanded.

"They're not any business of yours." Leona didn't want Mark anywhere near them. "Although

I'm glad you've finally realized that Emma isn't the *fraa* for you."

"Well, according to *mei vadder*, no woman is." Mark steepled his fingers underneath his chin. "Especially Ella."

He sat down next to Leona, his hip touching her side. "Did you know *mei vadder* is a bishop? Surprising, isn't it? He calls me the devil's seed." Mark laughed. "That means he must be the devil, *ya*?"

His laughter stopped abruptly. "He refused to marry me and Ella. Even barred me from his *haus*. Then he shunned me from his church. Of course he told everyone I wanted to leave. And made Ella spread the word that she didn't love me." He looked at the blank, white wall above Leona's bed. "But she did love me. I know she did."

Despite her fear, even her revulsion at the evil radiating from him, Leona felt pity. "I'm sorry."

Mark jerked his gaze to hers. "Don't feel sorry for me, old woman. *Mei vadder* will pay for what he's done to me. Not directly, that would be too easy. But by tearing apart his family piece by piece, I'll make him feel the pain. And he'll know he's responsible. First his sister's *familye* in Tennessee. Then *mei* cousin in Middlefield. And on and on it will *geh*, until all the Kings have lost what they hold dear. For some that is money and land. For others it's love and family. But for most, it's their own lives."

Suddenly he pulled her out of bed, almost gently. He guided her to the window.

"You have a perfect view of the shop, I see." He grasped her arm, holding her steady.

"Mark, listen to me. You don't have to do this. Your *vadder* was wrong. He hurt you." She looked up at him, the bones in her neck creaking. "You can repent, Mark. You can have the peace you seek."

"I don't seek peace. Or forgiveness. Nor do I give it." He took her hands and placed them on the windowsill. "Don't move, or you'll miss the show." He ran out of the room, slamming the door behind him.

Leona heard the scrape of Ephraim's chair against the floor. The doorknob rattled. She hurried across the room as fast as her weakened legs would take her and tried to open the door.

It wouldn't budge.

"I should *geh* check on *Grossmammi*." Emma looked at Adam. They were all gathered in the kitchen, the worry between Clara and Carol palpable, surpassed only by Laura's irritation. "I don't want to leave her alone."

Adam removed his hat and laid it on the kitchen table. He'd never seen Clara this unnerved before. He wondered if something had happened between her and Mark. Or maybe Laura had given her more information than she'd shared with Adam. Either way, he agreed with Clara—Laura didn't need to face Mark alone. Neither did Emma. But Leona couldn't be left alone either.

"All right. But I'll come with you." He turned to his mother, Clara, and Laura. "Stay here. Lock the doors. When will *Daed* be back?"

"I don't know," his mother said. "He left early. Didn't tell me where he was going."

"Don't let anyone in, all right?"

Clara nodded and looked at Emma. "Be careful. He could be lurking around here."

"We will." She and Adam left and walked to the house. As they crossed his yard, he sensed Emma moving closer to him. Above them a large cloud floated over the sun, blocking its rays.

He saw her shiver. "Cold?"

"Nee." She looked up at him. "Do you get the feeling that something is really wrong here? Clara is suddenly afraid of Mark. Laura shows up, saying what a terrible person he is." She looked around the yard.

On instinct, Adam took her hand. Despite her denial, her skin was chilled and clammy. He was glad when she didn't let go. "Something *seltsam* is going on."

Suddenly Dill whinnied loudly, as if she were in pain. Emma gripped Adam's hand.

"I'll check on her," he said. "You *geh* to Leona."

Emma ran toward the house. Adam watched until she was safely inside, then headed to the barn. He hoped Dill hadn't injured herself somehow. The last thing they needed now was more trouble.

Adam stepped into the barn. But before his eyes could adjust to the dimness, something hard and heavy slammed into the back of his head, and everything went black.

Chapter Twenty-Seven

Laura paced the length of the kitchen while the other two women talked quietly near the stove. This wasn't how she'd expected her visit to go. She thought she'd find Mark, demand her money, and threaten him with the police, and like the coward he was, he'd give it back. He was a horrible person, but these people were acting like he was the devil incarnate. It made her wonder if he had already tried to swindle them.

She went to Clara and Carol. "What has Mark done?"

Clara shook her head. "*Nix*, so far. But Peter was upset with him and was going to ask him to leave today." She sighed. "I believe I misjudged him. I thought he would be a *gut* match for Emma. But she wasn't interested." Clara looked at Carol. "There's only one *mann mei schwester* loves."

Carol nodded. "I know. I think they both know it too." She put her hands on her hips. "I don't know what's going on in Adam's head right now. He's been spending a lot of time alone. In the fields, or working at your *haus* when Leona was in the hospital. I keep hoping he's planning to stay. But I'm not sure. I can't ask him. I won't do that again. It has to be his choice."

Clara put her arm around Carol's shoulders. Laura turned away. She had no idea what they were talking about and she didn't care. All she wanted was to see Mark. And they were making that impossible.

Unless she could sneak out to find him herself.

She faced Carol. "Do you have a bathroom I could use?"

"Of course. It's down the hallway."

Laura found the bathroom easily enough. As she hoped, it had a window. The space wasn't large, but big enough for her to slip out. She stood on the toilet and climbed through, but when she landed, her ankle twisted to one side, and she barely managed to keep from crying out.

Laura stood and tested the ankle. Sprained, probably. But not broken. The pain was tolerable.

She appeared to be at the back of the house. Crouching down in case she passed by the kitchen window, she headed for the driveway. When she reached it, she leaned on the hood of the truck parked there, regaining her balance. Her ankle had started to throb.

"Going somewhere?"

She looked up. *Finally.* "It's about time you showed up. I want *mei* money back, Mark King."

His eyes, that deep blue she remembered so well, darkened nearly to the color of coal. "Oh, you'll get what's coming to you, Laura. I guarantee it."

When Emma saw her grandfather's chair wedged beneath the doorknob of her grandmother's door, panic filled her. She yanked away the chair, shoved open the door, and ran to the window where her grandmother stood.

"I'm all right."

"What happened?"

Grossmammi gripped her shoulders. "It's Mark. You have to get Adam. Peter and Norman too. I don't know what Mark is going to do…" She leaned forward, started coughing.

Emma guided her to the bed. *"Grossmammi?"*

The old woman coughed some more. "I'm all right. Do what I said. *Geh!*"

She stared at her grandmother for a moment, then left the room and dashed down the stairs toward the barn.

When Adam opened his eyes, pain exploded in his head. He reached up. Felt a huge goose egg swelling on this temple. When he pulled his hand away, his fingers were covered with blood.

"Don't move."

Through blurred vision he saw Laura hovering over him. "What happened?"

"Mark," she said through clenched teeth. She ripped fabric off of a nearby bolt, balled it up, and pressed it against his head.

"Ach," he moaned.

"Fine, then you hold it." She stood and stalked away from him.

He sat still for a moment, waiting for his vision to clear. Blood trickled through his hair, and pain continued to pummel his brain.

They were in the workshop. The cloth Laura had ripped was from a brand-new bolt that had come in two days ago. He could only imagine how upset Clara would be.

He tried to get up, but his knees buckled.

"You might as well stay down," Laura said. "The door's locked, and the window's apparently nailed shut from the outside. We can't get out of here."

"But why?" He winced. "How?"

"You were already here when Mark pushed me inside and locked the door." Laura sighed. "You all were right about him. I confronted him, asked him for *mei* money, and before I could do anything, he grabbed me and hauled me out here. I tried to get free, but he was too strong for me."

Adam groaned as he turned his head to look at her. Her *kapp* was pulled back from her pale blond hair. Wisps framed her face. "Where's Emma?"

Laura shrugged. "Still at her *haus*, I guess." She stood up and went to the door, limping a little. Yanked on it. Kicked it. Tried to use her elbow to break the glass. She cried out when her arm bounced back like a volleyball hitting a net.

"It's no use," Adam said. "We replaced the door last week. It's solid oak with a dead bolt—" He paused. "Where did Mark get the key?"

Laura gave him a look that made him feel utterly idiotic. "Stole it from Clara, most likely."

Somehow he had to stand. He had to find Emma. If Mark had her...

The thought gave power to his legs. Ignoring the burst of pressure in his head, he made it to his feet. He stumbled to the door, then collapsed against it.

"I'll try the window again," Laura said.

"There's a hammer...on the Peg-Board," Adam said. His words came out slurred. His head was swimming, and all his strength had gone. He leaned against the door and slid down it to the floor. *Lord, help me!*

Laura retrieved the hammer and went back to

the window. But before she could raise it to break the glass, the window shattered inward.

Her agonized scream made Adam's blood turn to ice.

"Adam! Adam!" Emma ran into the barn. It was a small building; if he was there, she ought to be able to find him. She went into Dill's stall. The horse looked fine. None of her other animals were around.

Then Emma saw it: a rusty shovel thrown carelessly against the wall. She picked it up. Something dark and sticky dripped from one side.

Blood.

With a growing sense of dread, Emma dropped the shovel and ran outside. The sound of shattering glass filled the air.

"Adam!"

Just as she started for his house, she saw Peter's buggy pull into the driveway. At the same moment, the smell of smoke reached her nose.

"Fire!" she yelled. *"Grossmammi's* in there!"

But it wasn't her house on fire. It was the workshop.

Smoke filled the shop. With all his strength Adam crawled toward Laura's cries. When he reached her he smelled gasoline. Saw the small gas can with a flaming rag tied to it rolling on the hardwood floor. A bolt of yellow fabric caught fire, inches from Laura's face.

"Laura, grab my hand." He stretched out to her prone body on the floor.

"I...can't...see." She pushed herself up and tried to stand.

"*Nee*. Don't get up. Stay on the ground."

She lifted her head. Turned her face toward him.

He nearly passed out at the sight.

Clara hadn't realized Laura was missing until she smelled the smoke. She and Carol came off the porch at a run. She saw Emma come toward Peter's buggy. Her husband jumped out, shouted something at Emma, who then turned and dashed to Carol.

"Fire! In the workshop!"

Without hesitation, Carol headed for the barn to call the fire department. Emma heaved, trying to catch her breath.

The workshop is on fire?

"Clara, *nee*!"

Ignoring Emma, Clara ran blindly in the direction of the building. She could see flames licking up the back wall and curling over the roof. All that hard work. All her dreams. Disappearing in smoke.

Peter appeared, carrying two buckets of water from the pump in the barn. He tossed them on the fire, but it had little impact.

Clara sank to her knees. Peter came up beside her and put his arm around her. She wept.

Then she heard something that made her tears vanish.

"Help! Help us!"

"Adam!" Emma ran for the building, but Peter caught her arm and dragged her back.

"You can't *geh* in there!"

"Adam's in there." She looked around. "Where's Laura? Dear Lord, she must be in there too!"

"Carol's calling the fire department right now."

"They won't make it in time." Emma burst into sobs. "They'll die before the firemen get here!"

From her room, Leona watched helplessly as Mark threw the flaming gas can into the shop window and then ran like a coward into the woods. She heard glass breaking, saw the smoke rising and the flames growing. Heard the blood-curdling cries of a girl, the weakened voice of Adam Otto. Watched Peter holding Emma back.

It couldn't end like this. Evil would not triumph. Leona closed her eyes, wept, and prayed harder than she had ever prayed before.

* * *

Clara looked on in horror as her husband ran toward the burning building. Smoke snaked through the spaces between the wood planks and underneath the door. Adam's and Laura's voices went silent.

"Peter! *Nee!*"

Sirens sounded in the distance. Peter kicked at the door. After four futile attempts, he ran and grabbed an axe from the woodpile in the backyard. He hacked at the door until it splintered, then kicked it one more time. It fell open, and Peter disappeared inside the smoke-filled building.

She couldn't lose Peter, not now. *I don't deserve him, Lord. But he doesn't deserve to die. Save him, Jesus. Please, save them all.*

Leona continued to pray as Peter ran into the workshop. She held her breath, waiting for him, and for Adam and Laura to come out. After what seemed like an eternity, Peter came out, carrying Laura. He set her gently on the ground. Clara went to her, and although Leona couldn't see what upset her so much, she couldn't miss the horrified look on her granddaughter's face.

Smoke billowed through the broken front door. The fire truck finally arrived. Two men in full gear jumped out of the truck just as Peter dragged

Adam by his arms from the workshop. Adam didn't move. Peter collapsed beside him.

Leona continued to pray as two of the fire-fighters went immediately to attend to Laura and to Adam. And as she watched, the workshop her husband had built alone by hand, the place where he had worked for nearly fifty years, crashed in upon itself in a blaze of flame.

Chapter Twenty-Eight

Adam fought for breath, but all he inhaled was smoke. His eyes refused to open. He tried to reach for Laura again. Felt nothing but unbearable heat.

Emma appeared in his mind. Beautiful Emma. He had never told her how he felt. Never made amends with his father. Never found out what troubled his mother. His return to Middlefield had been a failure. His life, an even bigger one.

No, he hadn't failed. Not completely. He had made peace with God. These past weeks he'd prayed. Asked for the forgiveness he desperately needed. Put Emma and her family before himself. Tried to protect her, because he loved her.

Now he was going to die. And much to his surprise, he wasn't afraid.

He did, however, have regrets. Wished he had done things differently. Wished he had been braver, wiser, more honest about his feelings. If he could do it all again, there were many things he would change. But he wasn't going to get that chance. God would just have to understand.

He hoped Emma would too.

Suddenly he felt cool air on his hot skin. Maybe he had already died.

"Adam?"

Now he was certain he was dead. It was the voice of an angel. Sounding like Emma, sounding very far away. He tried to open his eyes again. Felt drops of water on his cheek. Did it rain in heaven?

"Adam…"

The voice was softer now. Like a loving whisper in his ear. He took a breath. Suddenly his body shook with spasms as he gulped for air.

"Miss, you'll have to move," a man's voice said.

"I won't leave him. Not until I know he's all right."

"We have to get oxygen to him."

The spasms stopped. Someone tried to put a mask over his face. Adam managed to shove it out of the way. He opened his eyes. Saw his Emma kneeling over him, her eyes filled with tears. And love.

He managed to reach up and touch her soft cheek. "I'm okay, Emma. Everything is okay."

She smiled, and he knew the words were true. Emma disappeared as the paramedics put the mask over his face, and he closed his eyes, finally able to breathe.

"Peter, you shouldn't be doing that." Clara went to her husband and helped him put on his shirt. He'd burned his right forearm, yet refused to go to the hospital. *Grossmammi*, of course, had a salve she said would take care of the burn and had applied it to Peter's arm soon after the fire.

"You had a restless night." Clara gently guided Peter's arm through the sleeve of his shirt and pulled it over his head. She looked at the white bandage on his arm. "Are you still in a lot of pain?"

He shook his head. "Not so much. Just hard not to sleep in *mei* own bed." He looked at Clara. "Our bed."

Her cheeks flushed, and she smiled a little. She and Peter had spent the night in her parents' old bedroom, while Laura and Adam were taken to the hospital. The smile disappeared, however, at the realization of everything she could have lost yesterday.

"Clara?" Peter lifted her chin with his hand. "I know you're upset about the shop. We can rebuild it. Order new fabric, yarn. Whatever you need."

She shook her head. "*Nee*. We can't."

He frowned. "Don't lose faith, *lieb*. I'll make sure your dream will happen."

Clara gazed into her husband's eyes. She lifted a hand to his face and ran her fingers through his beard. He still smelled of smoke and fire. And courage. He was the bravest man she'd ever known. "Remember what you told me when I pushed for the fabric shop? How it would succeed if it was God's will?"

He nodded. "I was thinking more about profits. Not *mei* awful cousin setting it ablaze."

"But that might be His answer. I pushed for this shop. I wanted it. I didn't pray for God's guidance." She looked down at her lap. "I didn't ask for His help. I became angry with everyone who stood in my way. Emma. You."

Peter grabbed her hand and squeezed it. "It doesn't mean it wasn't a *gut* idea."

"Maybe God has a better one." As she looked at him, an ache rose up in her chest, and she gripped his hand hard. "It took almost losing you to make me start listening to Him."

He put his arm around her and kissed the top of her forehead. "This can be a new start for us, Clara. It might be God's will for us to rebuild the shop. Or He might have another plan, like you said." He leaned his forehead against hers. "Whatever happens, we need to stand together, *ya*?"

"Ya," she whispered. "I love you, Peter."

He kissed her cheek, his lips lingering on her skin. Then he pulled away. "We should finish getting dressed. As much as I like Leona and Emma's hospitality, I'll be glad to get home. To our *kinner*. To our life together again."

"And what of Mark?" Fear seized her just thinking about him, about how things could have turned out even worse if Emma had listened to her.

Peter didn't say anything for a long time. "I don't know. They'll have to find him first. The police said they would keep us posted, but he might just disappear."

Clara leaned her head against her husband's shoulder. "I don't understand why he did this."

"I don't either," Peter said. "Some things we may never understand."

Mark King bent down and tied the laces of his tennis shoes. He stood and glanced around the bus station in Ashtabula. Pulled a Cleveland Indians baseball cap low over his newly shorn hair. Shoved his hands in the pockets of his jeans and slouched into his sweatshirt, like he'd seen so many Yankee men his age do.

He went to the ticket window and purchased a one-way ticket to New York City. The bus wouldn't depart for another fifteen minutes. He put on a pair of sunglasses and tucked himself into the corner of the station. There were several Amish here, but he was confident none of them could recognize him.

Almost confident. He'd learned he couldn't take anything for granted in Middlefield.

Ten minutes dragged by as if it were ten hours. Finally the bus pulled up. Mark threw a duffel bag over his hunched shoulder and climbed on the bus. Through tinted shades he looked for a seat. Then saw the perfect one.

"Mind if I sit here?"

The young Amish woman glanced up at him for a moment. Her gaze dropped to her lap.

Mark smiled. Shy. She wouldn't say yes. But her eyes didn't say no.

"Thanks." He plopped down in the seat and slouched down. Took off his glasses. Unlike Emma Shetler, this girl was pretty. And hopefully unlike Laura Stutzman, she would be as dumb as a post.

"Matt Kingston." He held his hand out to the girl.

Her cheeks reddened. She looked at his hand. Slipped her tiny one tentatively into his. "Naomi Kline."

He grinned, holding her hand longer than a polite Amish boy would, long enough to capture her attention without offending her. Yes, this one would occupy his time until he found some other relative to take him in.

"Nice to meet you, Naomi Kline," he said.

Leona knocked on the hospital room door. When she didn't hear an answer, she wasn't surprised. She hadn't expected one. She slowly opened the door. Her gaze drifted to the young woman lying in the hospital bed. The sheet pulled up to her chest. The bandages wrapped around her hands and face.

Her heart filled with compassion for Laura Stutzman. Of all of them, she had suffered the most. And from Clara's and Emma's accounts, had deserved it the least. The window had shattered directly into her face. Shards of glass had embedded in her forehead, cheeks, and chin. Thank the Lord, only a few slivers had gone into her eyes. She wouldn't lose her eyesight, but she would be in great pain until the lacerations healed.

Leona opened the door wider. Laura didn't move, despite the noisy door hinge. Emma had tried to visit earlier. Laura had refused to acknowledge her. She might refuse Leona as well. But that wouldn't keep Leona from trying.

Her shoes squeaked and her cane tapped against the shiny floor. Laura didn't have a roommate. Leona was grateful. They could have their conversation in private.

"Laura?"

The young woman turned her head away from Leona.

Leona continued to walk toward her. "I won't ask how you feel. I can't imagine the pain you're going through."

No answer.

"The nurse said they contacted your parents in Tennessee. Have you heard from them?"

After a long pause, Laura said, *"Nee."*

Leona moved closer to the chair in the corner, near the end of the bed. "Do you mind if I sit down? Can't stand too long on these old legs of mine."

"Suit yourself."

"I'm sure your parents will be here soon. Then they can take you home."

For the first time Laura turned in Leona's direction. Her eyes were covered and her face was almost entirely bandaged. Although Leona couldn't see the stitches, she knew from Clara how extensive the damage had been. Her granddaughter had described the girl's face as a spiderweb of cuts and burns, like an image in a shattered mirror. The child's trauma wasn't nearly over, not by a long sight.

"I don't think *mei* parents will come." Given

her circumstances, Laura's voice sounded surprisingly strong and stable. "I disobeyed them. I shamed them. I foolishly trusted a *mann* who stole their life savings." She turned away again. "I'm sure they believe I deserve this."

"Nee. Nee!" Leona banged her cane on the floor, so hard it made Laura flinch. "You did not deserve this. You did *nix*. You were taken advantage of by a cruel and merciless *mann*. That's not your fault."

Laura lifted her shoulders. "It doesn't matter." She lifted her chin in Leona's direction. "You're Emma's *grossmammi, ya*? Why are you here?"

"Because I want to be. I've been praying for you."

"Thanks."

Leona ignored the bitter tone. "And to let you know you'll always have a place to stay in Middlefield." She saw Laura bite her bottom lip. "We are not like Mark King."

"I know." Her voice softened, grew thick. "It hurts," she whispered.

Leona stood up and went to her. She brushed her hand over the girl's pale blond hair, much the way her own mother had many, many years ago. "I know, *kinn*. But your injuries will heal."

"Nee. They won't."

Leona didn't answer right away. In a sense, the girl was right. The stitches and burns would leave scars, scars she would carry forever. But far worse were the wounds inside her heart and soul.

"You may not believe this now, Laura. Or even in a few months or years. But God will heal you. Completely."

"You're right," she said. "I don't believe you." Then the girl turned her face to the wall and said no more.

Chapter Twenty-Nine

The next day Adam returned home. The doctors told him he was lucky: he had only one burned hand, ten stitches to the side of his head, and a pretty severe concussion. But Adam knew it wasn't luck. It was a second chance, at everything.

One he planned to take.

His father had picked him up in a taxi. They hadn't said much on the ride home from the hospital. When the driver dropped them off, his father paid him. Both men watched as the black sedan pulled out of the driveway.

"Danki," Adam said. His head hurt, but he had medication prescribed by the doctor that helped keep most of the pain at bay. It also made him sleepy. "I appreciate you bringing me home."

Norman nodded. "Guess you better get inside.

Your *mamm* is waiting for you. Ready to make a fuss, I'm sure."

Adam tried not to react to his father's emotionless tone. He prayed for patience, tried not to be sensitive to the lack of feeling. But he failed. "If I'm a bother, I can leave."

Norman tipped his hat back. His nose reddened in the chilly air. "If that's what you want to do."

It wasn't what Adam wanted. What he wanted was for his father to ask him to stay. To want him to come back. Not just to Middlefield, but to the faith. But he had never said those words to him. Not even the day Adam left. "Do you want me here, *Daed*?"

His father gazed past Adam's shoulder. "Doesn't matter what I want."

"It does to me." Adam met his father's gaze.

"That's a surprise. Last I heard, you didn't care what I thought."

"That was a stupid *bu* talking. I've grown up, *Daed*. I finally know what's important. What's real." He let out a deep breath. "What I've been searching for."

"And what is that?"

"Without *familye*, I'm empty. Without God, I'm nothing." He reached out to his father. "Without love, I can't survive."

His father's beard trembled. He clasped his

forearm over Adam's uninjured arm. Squeezed it tight. "Then you've come home for the right reasons," he said, his voice shaky. He let go of Adam's arm.

Adam swallowed the lump in his throat as his father headed toward the pasture. His sanctuary, beyond Sunday worship.

He hadn't spoken the words, but the sentiment was clear. His father did want him here. That, Adam no longer doubted.

Adam nodded, satisfied. He turned toward the house and saw his truck sitting in the driveway. The last vestige of his non-Amish life. As soon as he was able to drive, he knew exactly what he was going to do with it.

That evening after supper Norman Otto stopped by. Emma opened the door and let him in. He removed his hat and stood twirling it in his hands.

"How is Adam?" Emma had wanted to visit him in the hospital, yet she resisted. Just as she resisted going to see him now. She had been terrified of losing him during the fire. But now that he was okay, she didn't know where they stood.

"He's doing fine. Resting, like the doctor told him to. Probably will be in bed for a few days. Want to make sure the concussion is healed."

Emma's grandmother nodded. "Did you want

some coffee, Norman? Maybe a piece of goose-berry cobbler? Emma made a delicious one to-night for dessert."

He shook his head. "I wondered if I could talk to you two about something. It won't take up much of your time."

"Of course." *Grossmammi* went to sit down, while Emma gestured for Adam's father to sit on the couch. Emma took the chair opposite her grandmother.

Norman twisted the brim of his straw hat some more. He didn't take off his jacket. He perched uneasily at the edge of the couch and said, "I wanted to speak to you about the workshop." He looked at Emma. "And about the hospital bills—both Mary's and yours, Leona. I know you were planning to use the profits from the shop to pay for the bills. And a new horse."

Emma took a deep breath. She didn't say any-thing about Clara and Peter. If they wanted their situation known, they would go to Norman them-selves.

"But now that the shop is gone, the ministers and bishop met with me earlier today." He faced Emma and her grandmother. "We want you to know that whatever money you need for the bills, the church will help pay."

The old woman nodded. "That's a lot of money, Norman."

"The money doesn't matter. You know that, Leona. No one in the district wants to see you and Emma struggle. Your *familye* has been through enough. And if you aim to build that workshop again, we'll help with that too. Instead of a barn raising, we'll have a workshop raising." He flashed a rare smile.

"We'll have to discuss that with Peter and Clara." *Grossmammi* looked at Norman, a sheen in her eyes. "But we're all very grateful for the kind offer."

"Ya." Emma tried to hold back her tears. At one time she would have refused the help. Her pride would have kept her tangled in a bitter struggle. Not anymore. This was how God provided. Through people who loved God and loved her, and who cared about her enough to give of themselves. She would accept the help, and hope that at some point in her life, she would be in the position to offer the same to someone else.

Norman rose. "That's all I came to say. Let me know what you need. And what you decide about the workshop."

Emma stood. "We will." She twisted her fingers together. "Would it be all right if I visited Adam? Just for a little while."

His gaze narrowed slightly. He shook his head. "I don't think that's a *gut* idea, Emma. Not now."

"You should give him time to rest." *Gross-*

mammi leaned on her cane as she stood. She walked over to Norman and put her hand on his arm. "As soon as Adam's ready for company, let us know."

Norman paused. "I will."

After Adam's father left, Emma looked at her grandmother. "Did you think Adam's *daed* acted a little strange when I told him I wanted to visit?"

Leona shook her head quickly. "Not at all." She smiled. "Norman Otto's always been an odd duck anyway. I'm sure he's just making sure his *sohn's* all right after everything that's happened. Like any *vadder* would. Now, I think I'm ready for a piece of that gooseberry cobbler."

"Nice truck." Sawyer Thompson touched the hood of Adam's pickup. "How many miles?"

"About 20,000." Adam watched as Sawyer walked around the truck, examining it. He'd been given the okay to drive today, nearly a week after the fire. His only disappointment was that Emma hadn't stopped by to visit. His father said she was busy, and Adam had no doubt it was true. Emma was always busy. She had too much work to do.

Sawyer opened the hood. Looked over the engine. If anyone could sell his truck, it would be Sawyer. Adopted by an Amish couple, Lukas and Anna Byler, when he was fourteen, Sawyer had yet to join the church. But he also hadn't left the Byler home, even though he was twenty-one. His hair was cut short, but he often wore Amish clothes. He had a high school education yet worked in his adopted father's wood shop with his dad and uncle. No one straddled the Yankee and Amish life the way Sawyer did.

Sawyer shut the hood and wiped his hands on his jeans. "Sure you want to sell it?"

"Don't have any use for it anymore. But I could use the money."

Sawyer eyed him for a moment from beneath the brim of his baseball cap. He rocked back on the heels of his tennis shoes. "You coming back to the church, then?"

Adam nodded. "Have to have a long talk with Bishop Esh first. But yep. I'm back. I wish I'd never left."

"What made you change your mind?" Sawyer held up his hand. "Forget I asked. It's none of my business."

"I didn't find what I was looking for," Adam said.

"And what was that?"

It would take hours to explain it to Sawyer. But Adam tried to make it as simple as possible. "Peace. I wanted to find peace. I couldn't find that out in the world."

Sawyer leaned against the truck. Adam took that as a good sign he was interested in trying to sell it for him. "I know what you mean," Sawyer said. He stuffed his hands in his pockets. "Some days I think I can stay here forever, you know? Become Amish and leave all the fancy stuff behind." He met Adam's eyes. "Other days I don't think I can stand living here another minute. Don't get me wrong. The Bylers, they've been good to me. The whole family has. But it's a big decision."

"*Ya*. And you don't want to make a mistake, like I did."

"They aren't pressuring me or anything, but I know they wish I'd go ahead and join the church. Especially since I'm working at the wood shop full time, now that Stephen's left to work his farm. Since Lukas's dad retired, it's been me, Tobias, and Lukas filling the orders. We've kept plenty busy."

Sawyer moved away from the truck. "But never mind about me. How much are you wanting for the truck?" When Adam stated his price, Sawyer's eyes widened. "That's it?"

Adam nodded. "That's all I want."

"Wow. You know you could get a lot more for it if you took it to a dealership."

"I know. I just want to get rid of it." He didn't care about the money from the sale. Just needed enough to buy one important thing.

"There are a couple guys I went to school with who might be interested. How does it run?"

Adam tossed him the keys. "Find out for yourself."

Sawyer caught them and opened the driver's side door. He climbed inside and started the engine. He pressed the automatic window button and rolled down the window. "Are you coming?"

Adam shook his head. "You *geh* on without me."

"All right. I'll be back in a minute." He put the truck in gear as Adam held up his hand.

"I'm going to take off. Keep the truck and let me know when you sell it. I'll bring you the title."

Sawyer frowned. "You sure about that?"

"I'm sure."

"Okay." Sawyer shrugged. "I'll be in touch."

Adam watched as Sawyer backed out of the driveway. When his friend disappeared, he walked toward the street and began the four-mile trek back to his house, the last weight of his old life lifted from his shoulders.

Chapter Thirty

The following Saturday Leona was resting in the living room. Emma had gone to the barn to clean it and feed the animals. Just as Leona closed her eyes, a knock sounded on the front door. She slowly made her way to open it.

"Hello, Laura."

The young woman held a suitcase in her hand. "You don't seem surprised to see me."

"I'm not. I'd hoped you'd come by before you left for home." Leona stepped aside and smiled. "Come in. Sit for a little while."

Laura walked inside but didn't sit down. Her hands, now free of bandages, were red and streaked with fresh scars. She didn't look directly at Leona.

Leona could see why. The stitches that criss-crossed her face had been removed, leaving angry red welts on her cheeks, forehead, and chin. Permanent scars in the worst place possible. Yet to Leona, they didn't detract from the girl's beauty at all. Just as she sensed the darkness deep inside Mark King, she could also see the sweetness that Laura kept hidden from the world.

"I can get you something to drink, if you'd like," Leona said.

Laura shook her head. She finally looked at Leona. "I came to ask for something else." Her eyes turned bright. "A place to stay."

"Of course. You can stay the night. We'll have a taxi come pick you up to *geh* to the station in the morning."

Her lips rolled inward. She winced. "You don't understand. I need a place to live." Her voice lowered. "I can't *geh* home. Not like this."

Leona wanted to ask why, but she didn't dare. It had taken a lot for Laura to come here. She wouldn't do anything to make her leave.

Instead she put her arms around her and said, "*Willkum* to our *familye*."

Emma sat on a hay bale in the barn, looking at the mess around her. For once, she didn't care. Tommy was in her lap, and Molly had ventured across the yard to the barn and sat by her feet. Dill grazed outside, enjoying the cool air mixed with fall sunshine. Emma didn't feel a sense of urgency to clean the barn. Just the opposite. She leaned back against the barn wall, closed her eyes, and for the first time in endless months, relaxed.

"Hey."

She opened her eyes to see Adam standing in front of her. She didn't move. Instead she smiled. "Hey yourself."

"Is there room on that hay bale for one more?"

"Sure." She scooted over. Adam sat next to her, his hip pressing against hers. Maybe there wasn't exactly enough room for two on the hay bale, but if he wasn't complaining, she certainly wouldn't.

She looked at him. The side of his head was scarred by the cut Mark had inflicted with the shovel. They had shaved his hair to put in the stitches, and now a fine light brown fuzz grew around it.

"I know. It looks strange." Adam put on his hat. "I'll be keeping this on all the time from now on."

"You look *gut* either way."

The compliment came out spontaneously, naturally, without the least measure of self-consciousness. So much had changed between them. She wasn't a scared, hurt little girl anymore. She was a woman who knew her own heart and mind. And even if he would never return the love she would always hold for him, she could live with that.

It had taken her a while to get there, but Emma knew the truth now. If it was in God's plan for her to remain single for the rest of her life, she would accept it. She had seen how the Lord had taken care of her. Her family. Her friends. She didn't doubt Him anymore.

"You sure are quiet." Adam bumped his shoulder gently against hers, the way he used to do when they were kids. "What are you thinking about?"

The cat jumped off her lap and scampered away. "God," she said. "Life." She looked at him. "You."

"Me?" His eyebrows arched nearly to the brim of his hat. His breath came out in small white puffs, dissipating in the chilly air of the barn. "Something *gut* for a change, I hope."

"Ya." She smiled. "I'm glad you're here. And hopefully we can spend some time together before you *geh* back to Michigan."

Adam shook his head. "I'm not going back to Michigan." He angled his body toward her. "I'm not going anywhere."

"You've decided to stay?"

"Ya. To stay in Middlefield. To be Amish again. So you can't get rid of me that easily."

Without thinking she threw her arms around him, her cheek pressing against the short stubble on his chin. Quickly she drew back. "Sorry." She felt a hot flush run up her neck into her cheeks. She was hopeless.

Suddenly he took her face in his hands and kissed her.

"W-what was that for?"

"I have to have a reason?" A teasing glint appeared in his eyes.

"Ya." Her lips were still warm from his kiss. "You don't just kiss a *maedel* without telling her why."

"Really?" He leaned back. "Is that some kissing rule I haven't heard of before?"

All the playfulness and confidence drained out of her. Emma could tell herself every day for the rest of her life that she would be okay without Adam's love. Maybe eventually she would. But not right now. Not after that kiss. She rose and walked away from him.

He came up behind her and turned her to face him. "That wasn't the reaction I was expecting, Emma."

"What reaction did you want? You know how I feel about you, Adam."

He nodded.

"And I don't appreciate you playing around with my emotions."

"I'm not."

"Then why did you kiss me?"

"Because I wanted to. And I still do."

Then he pulled her into his arms and kissed her again.

Adam moved his mouth away from hers, but he didn't let her go. He could hold her soft body in his arms forever. Why had it taken him so long to realize that she was the only woman for him? He had wasted all this time when they could have been dating. Even married.

Then again, it wasn't time wasted. He wasn't the same man he was two years ago. Or even two months ago. He had to grow into the person he was right now to appreciate the woman he loved. The woman he treasured.

Of course she didn't understand. Why should she, when he'd treated her so poorly in the past? When his cowardice had sent him running away from the one person who kept him grounded, the one person who reminded him of what was important.

She stepped out of his arms, making him feel cold and empty. "Maybe you want to kiss me now. But what about later? You have a habit of changing your mind."

"Then let me prove it to you." He stepped toward her. "*Geh* out with me. On a date."

Emma stood there, not saying a word.

"Emma, what's wrong?"

She looked away. "I'm scared."

He took her hand. "Of what?"

She finally looked at him. "Of losing you. I lost you two years ago. Then I thought I would lose you again in the fire. But you're here…" She looked at their entwined hands. "I don't think I can go through losing you again."

Adam let out a sigh and pulled her into his arms. He rested his chin on the top of her *kapp*. "I'm not going anywhere, Emma. I promise." He took her soft face in his hands. "I know I have a lot to prove to you. And I'll do whatever it takes, for as long as it takes, until you believe how much I care for you."

"I—"

The sound of a vehicle pulling into the driveway cut her off. Adam grinned. They were a little bit early. Yet the timing couldn't be more perfect. He grabbed her hand. "Come on. There's something I want to show you."

Emma followed Adam out of the barn. He dropped her hand as soon as the pickup truck approached and hurried ahead of her. Something was attached to the truck. Was that a horse trailer?

The truck pulled to a stop. A man with a plaid shirt and blue jean jacket stepped out of the truck. "Shetler residence?"

Before Emma could say anything, Adam nodded. *"Ya."*

"Well, here he is." The man walked around to the back of the trailer. Adam motioned for Emma to follow. A few moments later he led a beautiful black gelding out of the trailer.

"Thanks for bringing him out," Adam said to the man. He held on to the horse's halter. The horse stamped and snorted a time or two, then settled down.

"Thank you for your business. You've picked a fine horse. He'll be a hard worker for you."

Adam guided the horse to the side as the man got in his truck and backed out of the driveway. Confused, Emma looked at Adam. "You got a new horse?"

"Nee." He took Emma's hand and put it on the lead rope. "This is *your* new horse."

Emma gripped the halter and looked into the horse's beautiful brown eyes. She could already see how gentle he was. Nearly as gentle as Dill. But young and strong enough to pull a buggy. She looked at Adam. "I can't accept him."

"You have to. I already have a horse." He patted the animal's flanks. "You need him. And from the way he's taking to you, I think he needs you too."

"It's too much." Her voice cracked. "How?" She looked beyond his shoulder to the Ottos' driveway. The truck was gone. "You sold your truck?"

"I told you, I won't be needing it anymore." He grinned. "Let's get this fella settled. What are you going to name him?"

They made their way to the barn. "Elijah. He looks like an Elijah to me."

A short time later Elijah was settled in the stall next to Dill's. Adam brought Dill back inside, and the two horses spent a minute or two sizing each other up. Now they were both munching their grain.

Adam and Emma sat next to each other on the hay bale. He put his arm around her shoulders. She leaned against him. "I don't know how to thank you, Adam."

He chuckled and looked at her. A teasing glint entered his eye, and she laughed. "But I'm guessing you'll come up with something, won't you?"

"Absolutely," Adam said. "You know I will."

Two weeks later, the Sunday after he'd spoken to Bishop Esh, Adam slipped on his black vest over his white, long-sleeved shirt and fastened the hooks on the vest. His church clothes fit as well now as they had two years ago. He picked up his black felt hat and brushed off a few specks of dust.

If only he could brush off his nerves so easily.

Anticipation mixed with anxiety as he made his way downstairs. Today would be the first time he'd attended church since he'd left Middlefield. And this morning he would stand in front of the entire district and confess his sins.

Two years ago he had been filled with pride, thinking only of himself and what he wanted instead of God's will. He had to convince the congregation of his sincerity.

His hands shook as he put on his hat. His stomach growled because he'd barely been able to down more than half a cup of coffee at breakfast. Yet there was a feeling of calm inside him.

He was about to take the final step toward his new future.

Emma sat next to Leona and Clara during the service in the barn. The minister preached on faithfulness and forgiveness. In a monotonous but sincere voice he spoke in *Dietsch*, quoting Scripture about God's steadfastness. "God never breaks His promises," the minister said. "He is true to us, and requires that we be true to Him and to one another."

The sermon ended. Adam was called to the front of the church, and Emma moved to the edge of the bench. She clasped her hands together and listened while Adam answered the bishop's questions, confessed that he had broken his vow to

God and the church, and asked everyone for forgiveness.

She blinked back tears as he spoke, his voice steady, loud, and genuine. She remembered over the years how Adam would complain about the long services, the strictness of the rules, second-guessing his decision to become baptized. They had been baptized together, and even then she had known he was hesitant.

This time it was different. There was no doubt in his eyes, no tentativeness in his voice. When he finished his confession, he went upstairs to wait for the congregation to agree to allow him back into the church.

The vote was unanimous.

The service was over. Outside, on the Yoders' lawn, tables loaded with food and drink stood waiting for the celebration to begin.

Adam stood next to Leona's chair, near enough to Emma that his arm touched hers. In clusters of two and three, members of the community came by to shake his hand and welcome him back to the fold. Once or twice he caught Leona's eye and saw her smiling at him. She nodded as if to add her blessing, and he suspected that she'd had a hand—or at least a prayer—in the changes that had come to his life.

Transformation. That's what it was about. Connecting with God and *familye* and community, and finding contentment and love in God's will. Nothing else mattered. In good times and bad, in struggle and joy, the Lord was present, and that presence made all the difference.

He glanced down at Emma. She, too, had changed. She was no longer dependent upon him for her happiness and contentment, but together they could rely on God and work together to build a life.

On the other side of the lawn, his father stood talking with a small group of men. He looked up, caught Adam's eye, and nodded.

That was all. Just a nod. But it was enough.

His mother came up and put her hand on his arm. "Today is a *gut daag, mei sohn.*"

Adam swallowed down the lump in his throat and smiled. For so long he'd been broken, searching for what he thought was missing in his life. And all along it had been here, in the Amish community. Quite literally in his own backyard.

He leaned close to Emma and felt the pressure of her arm against his.

"Ya," he said. "It is a very *gut daag.*"

* * * * *

Acknowledgments

I always thank my editors and agent in every book I write. But they deserve more thanks than I can say for their help, support, and encouragement during the process of writing *Treasuring Emma*. Natalie, Penny, and Tamela, thank you for being there for me as this book took shape. Thank you for the prayers and guidance that kept me going. Thank you for being by my side as I faced the challenges during the writing process. Thank you for being wonderful at your jobs and for being treasured friends.